BOOKS BY MAURICE DRUON

The Curtain Falls
The Film of Memory
Alexander the God

THE ACCURSED KINGS

The Iron King
The Strangled Queen
The Poisoned Crown
The Royal Succession
The She-wolf of France
The Lily and the Lion

FOR CHILDREN

Tistou of the Green Thumbs

The Glass Coffin
and Other Stories

Maurice Druon

THE GLASS COFFIN

AND

OTHER STORIES

Translated from the French by

HUMPHREY HARE

Charles Scribner's Sons, NEW YORK

Contents

❦❦❦

Part One

THE GLASS COFFIN

TO LILIANE DE ROTHSCHILD

❦ ❦ ❦ The château happened to have two wings and the brothers could live completely apart. Identical twins, they were of precisely the same height, stooped in exactly the same way, had the same bald, yellow, wrinkled skulls, the same way of rubbing their thin hands together, and the same native malice. They were, indeed, two pips of the same fruit—monozygotic as the scientists say—from the last twig of the Paluselles's family tree.

The odd thing about them was that they hated each other.

The Count had never been able to forgive the Marquis for assuming a legally more favorable uterine position at the time of their birth. He had never been able to understand why, since he had seen the light of day first and some three hours before his brother, he should have been subjected during all his sixty-seven years to the inferior standing of a younger son.

The Marquis hated the Count for being a Protestant.

The two old bachelors were the offspring of a marriage celebrated behind the altar, between a Catholic and a Huguenot. These marriages were not unusual in Provence but were generally deplored by both families. On consenting reluctantly to marry their daughter to the most eligible young man in the province, the d'Espinans had made certain conditions and had come to an honorable arrangement with the Paluselles. It was agreed that the eldest child should be baptized in ac-

3

cordance with the Roman rite and the second brought up in the Reformed faith.

The twins had not therefore chosen their respective religions; these had been awarded them, like their titles, in conformity with their precedence at birth. It was nevertheless a continuing source of acrimony.

On Sundays the Marquis went to church and the Count to chapel. Nor were their meetings more frequent during the week. Each had his own dining room and his own servants; and the better to ensure their isolation from each other, they had shut up the great reception rooms which formed the main block of the château and kept the inside shutters closed from year's end to year's end.

The château, which had been built in the best period of the eighteenth century, immediately before the Seven Years War, by a Théodore de Paluselles, who had made a fortune in the Louisiana slave-trade, contained many treasures.

The taste of this somewhat parvenu ancestor had run to elaborately carved furniture, complicated marquetry, heavy silk hangings and large portraits bearing the diagonal of the blue riband, indeed to all that was most expensive and modern at the period, and this penchant, transmitted to his descendants, was apparent in a passion for works of art and rare pieces of furniture, which had developed into a positive mania for collecting.

From time to time packing-cases from Montpellier or Paris, even from Germany and Italy, could be observed being carried in to either the east or west wing. But no one, except the recipient himself, was ever allowed to see what they contained. For the twins had also this in common: they never entertained.

When communication between them became unavoidable due to the essential management of their joint fortune— which was to go in its entirety to the survivor—they made it through their servants. But they were continually spying on each other. They both suffered from the same liver complaint, which was why they both looked like dried lemons, and each expected to bury the other.

The younger brother considered that, since he had been frustrated at birth, death owed him in all justice some reparation; and he hoped from day to day to become at last, and legally, the last Marquis de Paluselles. However, a stone of unprecedented size blocking his biliary ducts deprived him of this last pleasure.

At the news of the Count's death, sixty-two cousins of both sexes, and in all parts of France, began happily to indulge in somber calculation.

None of them had ever been to Paluselles. But there was not one whose imagination failed to conjure up the huge château, lying amid olive groves and heathlands, crammed with masterpieces, and inhabited by two crazy old men who had neither sons nor nephews.

One of the crazy old men was dead. They would soon no doubt hear from the other.

It was a Cardaillan cousin, living at Grenoble, who first received a letter from the Marquis.

"My dear cousin," the Marquis wrote, "I would be grateful if you would visit me at Paluselles as soon as it is convenient to you. I have an important decision to make and would like to discuss it with you. Please give my respects to your wife and believe that I am, etc. . . ."

Monsieur de Cardaillan, cold, stiff and fifty, who wore his grey hair brushed carefully back from his forehead, and pointed shoes which had been resoled at least six times, passed his days in calculating the precise value of his portfolio of stocks and shares, adding up the income from his farms, checking the household books, counting the dusters in the linen cupboard and the cloves of garlic in the store. It was not that he suspected dishonesty, but because he had to know exactly how much he owned.

When he received the Marquis's letter, he said to his wife: "I always told you, my dear, that it was the brother who was so impossible. Now that Marc-Antoine is alone, his first thought is to be reconciled to us."

Madame de Cardaillan had not been out of mourning for nearly thirty years. She had been brought to bed, grown middle-aged and then old in black. She was fat, impulsive and domineering. She heaved puffily amid her funereal lace, and ordered her husband to take the next train.

Throughout the journey, Monsieur de Cardaillan dreamed of indulging his propensity for fussiness. The prospects of being able one day to inventory all the pictures, clocks and saucers his cousin's château must contain intoxicated him. And he was already banking on furnishing his daughters' houses without having to empty his own attics.

He found Paluselles looking very abandoned, for not only were the rooms in the central block shut up but the wing in which the dead twin had lived had also been closed.

A silent manservant led Monsieur de Cardaillan up a back stairs, along a passage entirely hung with prints and etchings, and threw open a door.

The room was more crowded than an antique shop on the Left Bank; the light was deadened by tapestries showing Frederick Barbarossa engaged in various exploits, and they were so big that their bottoms had been rolled back against the skirting-boards. A Flemish reredos stood side by side with a "Saint Sebastian" of the Sienese school reposing on a Gothic lectern. On a huge desk, bearing the royal arms of France, were two busts of Roman emperors. The eight sides and hundred facets of a Florentine cabinet of the Medicis period glowed with ebony, mother of pearl, ivory and lapis lazuli. Scattered among these important pieces were quantities of lesser *bibelots*, silver candelabra, Boulle caskets, Compagnie des Indes soup-tureens.

On the supposition that each room in the château contained even a quarter as much, Paluselles housed incalculable wealth; in any case, so precise a man as Monsieur de Cardaillan would find sufficient employment in making an inventory to last him till the end of his days.

Suddenly Monsieur de Cardaillan's attention was attracted to a glass box lying on a Louis XV bed hung with red damask; it gleamed softly in the shadows.

The glass box contained the body of a dead woman. She was pretty and young, some sixteen or eighteen years of age, and entirely naked. Her skin was the color of amber like a Creole's; her hair curled about her rounded forehead, and spread darkly beneath her thin shoulders; there were soft shadows about her lowered lashes; her mouth, though it had assumed the same color as the rest of her body, was still as shapely and sensuous as a fruit; and the embalmer had fixed her exquisitely formed limbs in a pose that had a sort of non-chalant happiness, one arm gently bent across the stomach.

Monsieur de Cardaillan, who was well-read, murmured:

"Dormeuse, amas doré d'ombres et d'abandons . . ."

The toes alone were still curled up, witnesses to a last struggle, an ultimate panic at the moment of annihilation.

Monsieur de Cardaillan was so fascinated by the glass coffin that he failed to hear his host come into the room and started like a naughty child. He had no time to say the polite things he had prepared.

"I'm delighted to see you, my dear cousin," said Marc-Antoine de Paluselles, rubbing his slender hands together so quickly that he might have been trying to produce fire from them. "Unless I am mistaken, you are my nearest relation, and it seems probable that I shall quit this world before you. I have thought of appointing you my residuary legatee."

Monsieur de Cardaillan stared at him in silence; he omitted to say, as is proper in such circumstances: "My dear cousin, you mustn't think of such a thing! You'll bury us all!"

The Marquis went on: "I must, however, warn you that my

will contains a secret clause. It cannot be revealed till after my death, but you must promise now to put it into effect. A written promise, of course. I'm not going to ask for your answer at once. Send it to my solicitor, Maître Torquasson, at Lunel, within the next fortnight. This was why I wanted to see you."

The Marquis neither asked his cousin to sit down, nor offered him so much as a glass of vermouth. He had him shown out by the same back stairs.

Monsieur de Cardaillan returned to Grenoble in great perplexity.

"Never on your life!" cried fat Madame de Cardaillan, when she heard his account of the visit. "It's a trap. How can one tell what wickedness that crazy old man has put in his secret clause? He'll compel us to keep his naked body in the middle of our drawing-room, or he'll insist we separate, or we shall be obliged to found an asylum or something which will cost twice what he'll leave us. Don't accept at any price."

Monsieur de Cardaillan spent a week of painful indecision; then, since he always obeyed his wife, he wrote to the solicitor, refusing.

The second person to be summoned to Paluselles was Canon de Mondez. He came from Marseilles, delighted to have an excuse for a journey. He was a tiny man and almost as old as the Marquis. His skull was downy as that of a chick hatched in winter; and he was hopelessly absent-minded. On this particular day, he had failed to tie his long black sash properly, and the fringe trailed along the ground a yard behind him.

He scarcely listened to what the Marquis had to say, and replied: "But of course; how well I understand! You were so fond of your dear brother; you lived such very united lives!"

He walked ceaselessly up and down, his hands thrust into the pockets of his soutane, flapping its skirts like wings, to the great danger of the porcelain.

"Duccio da Siena, isn't it? Or his school," he said, pointing to the Saint Sebastian. "A beauty!"

Going to the glass coffin, he said, "What a splendid wax-work you've got here, cousin! A very unusual piece! Is it French?"

But, when the Marquis remarked that he was admiring a real body, the Canon cried: "Oh, my God!" and covered his eyes.

The Marquis tried in vain to talk of the secret clause; but the Canon dismissed it with a wave of the hand, and left at once, as if he had ventured by mistake into the devil's bed-chamber.

Maître Torquasson had to write to him at Marseilles to extract a signed refusal.

The next fortnight brought a newly married couple, called Choulets de Longpois. The husband was a young magistrate at Lodève; his wife, a little brunette, had a pretty round face and laughed a good deal.

The taciturn manservant separated them at the bottom of the back stairs. The magistrate alone was shown in to the Marquis. The visit was as short as the preceding ones; but, just as the Choulets de Longpois were about to drive away in the taxi they had hired at the station, the manservant re-appeared and, asking the wife to come with him, showed her in to the Marquis.

The Marquis looked his young cousin up and down with lacklustre eyes and made a few banal remarks; then, taking her by the hand, he led her to the red damask bed and said: "May I ask you to undress?"

She screamed and ran for the stairs, while old Paluselles cried after her: "No, no! You've completely misunderstood me, cousin! I haven't explained . . ."

He was still shouting when she got into the taxi.

"Let's go, let's go at once! I'll tell you later," she said to her husband.

"What's the matter? The glass coffin?"

"Yes. That's it. The coffin . . ."

"That's what I thought. I think I shall refuse," he added. "It's really all rather alarming."

The procession of cousins continued throughout the following month. Country gentlemen, bourgeois, soldiers, diplomats, comfortably off bachelors, and fathers wondering how to find portions for their daughters, all came in turn, nursing expectations, only to depart with a sense of nightmare.

At first, the Marquis had merely laughed quietly to himself when they left. But he now did so no longer. He was becoming impatient and had reduced the time-limit for writing to his solicitor to a week. It was noticed that he made his proposal only to his male relatives, but that he often desired to make the acquaintance of their wives or daughters.

"Do you know what I think? He's a sadist in search of a victim," said an imaginative female cousin at a family dinner party. She had pretensions to a knowledge of psychology. "And a sadist *post mortem*, if I may so express it!" she added. "He's using the bait of his fortune to draw one or another of us into some hideous tragedy which will become apparent only after his death. Whoever accepts must be either completely heedless or utterly brave."

The brave man eventually appeared. He was thirty-ninth on the list of relations, and his name was Hubert Martineau. He had been saved from committing suicide the previous week only by a bout of malaria which had sent him shivering and delirious to bed with a temperature of 105. Now twenty-eight, he had run through a considerable fortune, partly at the tables and partly in disastrous investments in the Far East. He had recently been deserted by two women, whom he loved equally, but who had unfortunately discovered the fact that they were rivals for his heart. He was also something of an opium addict. He had to borrow his journey money from the porter of his hotel.

"What on earth can it matter to me," he said on his return, "if I've signed a pact with the devil, or undertaken—though that's obviously an absurd exaggeration—to die the following year? I've got nothing to lose. Besides, I shall soon be fixed up; the old man's got one foot in the grave."

It took the Marquis de Paluselles some three and a half years to put his other foot in it. And then the Cardaillans, the Choulets de Longpois, the Mombresles, the psychological cousin, and all the rest received from Maître Torquasson a summons to attend the reading of the will a fortnight later. It surprised them. Surely they had made their refusals clear enough? Besides, they had heard that that disgraceful young Hubert Martineau, that gambler and bad lot, "who was bound to come to a bad end one of these days," had accepted. But perhaps there was going to be a general share-out. Cupidity sprang up in their hearts, like couch-grass after mowing.

Maître Torquasson's office had never before been so full of people at one time. All the cousins were there, huddled on little chairs as if at an auction. Despite the venetian blinds, it was very hot indeed. Madame de Cardaillan was melting among her veils. Canon de Mondez had taken the wrong hat on leaving the train and was wondering how to find the passenger whose panama he had filched. Hubert Martineau was late. It really was the limit! From time to time, an impatient foot tapped the floor.

Hubert arrived at last in a long green sports car. His life had recently become totally transformed. As heir presumptive to the Paluselles fortune, he had become an excellent match, and had married the daughter of an important stockbroker. His wife, a singularly charming girl, had influenced him very much for the better, stopped his taking drugs and borne him a child. He had gone back into business, and this time with success. Now that he was doing well in life and was chairman of three boards of directors, he no longer had the same attitude toward taking risks. But this was the pay-off, and his thoughts were running on all sorts of appalling possibilities.

Surprised to find so many people present, Hubert bowed generally to the company and, since there was no chair for him, perched on the window-sill.

"Ladies and gentlemen," began the solicitor, "I must first apologize for having put you to the trouble of this tiring journey. But your late cousin, even though you had refused his offer through me, expressly stipulated in a codicil that he desired you to be present at the reading of his will."

The solicitor paused for a moment and then went on: "Monsieur Hubert Martineau . . ."

Hubert gave a slight start.

"Yes . . ." he said.

"Are you still prepared to accept the Marquis's legacy together with the clause of which you do not yet know the contents?"

There was a moment's silence. The cousins swallowed their saliva as if coming down a mountain railway. "What's this? Can I still refuse?" Hubert thought. He was conscious of all their eyes on him. He felt like a gambler with a huge banco. Should he keep the hand or pass it? It was no doubt simply ridiculous human pride, and also that gambler's instinct, so often disastrous—I'm having a good run; it must come off— which led him to say to the solicitor, with great outward calm: "Yes, of course; I accept."

"Then, Monsieur," said Maître Torquasson, unfolding a single sheet of paper, "here is the document which concerns you: 'This is my last will and testament. I bequeath to my cousin Hubert Martineau all my goods and possessions, both personal and real, on the express condition, in accordance with the engagement he has entered into, that he will take the name of Paluselles and bear it henceforth together with the titles that go with it.' This," said the solicitor, "is the testator's secret clause; he was anxious that the name borne by his ancestors should not lapse with his death."

There was a rather sharp "Oh!" from stout Madame de Cardaillan. The rest of the family managed to maintain their self-control. Monsieur Choulets de Longpois, biting at his silly moustache, stared furiously at his wife, and the unfortunate little woman felt vaguely guilty, though she was not sure why.

"How right I was to say he was a sadist," hissed the psychological cousin through her teeth.

It was certainly enough to create dissension between several married couples, hasten the committing of adultery, inspire children with contempt for their parents, and bring out into the open all these people's real opinions of each other; it undoubtedly meant twenty years of reproaches, arguments, imputing of blame and door-banging behind their houses' respectable façades. "If you hadn't been such a fool as to refuse the Paluselles inheritance! . . . Well, it was on the advice of that clever mother of yours! . . . And to think it's all going to that little bounder, that adventurer who doesn't even belong to our world!" Oh, there was no danger of the Paluselles's name being forgotten!

Hubert Martineau smiled rather foolishly, and shook a few furious hands that would rather have seized him by throat than the fingers.

Canon de Mondez, concealing the panama behind his soutane, asked the solicitor: "Can you explain that indecent corpse the Marquis kept in his drawing-room, Maître?"

"As far as I have been able to determine the facts, Monsieur le Chanoine, I believe the corpse was brought back from Louisianá, by the Marquis Théodore, nearly two centuries ago. She was a woman of those parts with whom he had fallen passionately in love. Even dead, she was able to arouse the most extraordinary emotions!" said the solicitor, leading the Canon a little apart. "The last Marquis and his twin brother, when still children, found the corpse one day when playing in the Châeau attics, to which the glass coffin had been relegated long before and forgotten. They told no one. Then when they succeeded jointly, as you know, to their father, the Marquis was able to take advantage of the fact that the coffin appeared in no inventory to appropriate it to himself. This may well have been the underlying reason for the quarrel that divided the two Paluselles for over forty years. It is a fact that neither of them ever married; and my predecessor here told me that they had never even—how shall I put it?—well, you understand, Monsieur le Chanoine. . . . But the fact was that whenever they met a woman, they became obsessed by the memory of the corpse, and they were never able to find one that resembled it sufficiently."

"Ah, very odd, very odd indeed!" said the Canon, unthinkingly picking the brim of the panama to pieces. "In the circumstances, they should have become priests—at least the one who was a Catholic!"

The solicitor shrugged his shoulders; he felt vaguely out of his depth.

"In any case," he went on, "it's all over and done with now. When the undertakers were carrying the Marquis's bier out, they knocked against the glass coffin and broke it. The corpse you saw practically turned to dust. It seems that's what happens to bodies that have been embalmed for a long time. The remains were placed in a casket and deposited in the vault."

"At all events, I shall say a Mass," replied the Canon.

THE BLACK PRINCE

TO HERVÉ MILLER

❦ ❦ ❦ He was small but splendidly compact, his legs were slender but well muscled, the feet delicate, the chest deep, the eyes of a velvet brown with long, black lashes, the nostrils short but well open, and there were nobility, pride and panache in his carriage. . . . In short, he had quality as a horse that most men lack as men.

She . . . But I'll tell you about her later.

The story opens in Paris in the spring of 1730, on the afternoon of Corpus Christi, in the Gobelins district.

By tradition, the famous tapestry-makers held an exhibition on that day not only of their celebrated collection but of the products of the past years; the walls of the great courtyard were hung from top to bottom with the most sumptuous tapestries in the world. The exhibition was warmly recommended by *The Guide to Paris for Foreign Tourists*, though the author issued a warning: "I advise foreigners to be careful of their pockets, for owing to the great crowd one cannot tell next to whom one may be standing."

Mr. Coke, an English tourist, wearing a large wig and a little round hat, was returning from the exhibition. He was not particularly knowledgeable about tapestries; indeed, he knew a great deal more about racehorses. His arms swinging and his stomach swelling under his waistcoat, Mr. Coke drifted with the crowd down the Rue Croulebarde which, lined with market-gardens, gave into the Faubourg Saint-

Marcel. He gazed with appreciation at the pretty women in their striped dresses, which were still similar to those Monsieur Watteau, who had died only a few years before, used to paint. Neither the noise nor the crowd surprised him; his guide-book had warned him about them.

"One should take proper care in the streets of Paris. Besides the jostling crowd on foot, a great number of coaches and carts fills the streets till late at night and they frequently travel at a great pace. One should look carefully about one. In trying to avoid a foot passenger in front, one may well be jostled by another bearing down on one from behind, for it is impossible to hear anything due to the noise of the traffic."

And, indeed, Mr. Coke was not keeping his eyes sufficiently about him, for he was suddenly sent sprawling in the dust by a violent blow on the shoulder. A crowd immediately gathered round, but he got to his feet without much harm and saw the cart that had knocked him over. It was a heavy water-cart. Its driver, an Auvergnat like most water-sellers, jumped down and helped Mr. Coke dust off his clothes.

"I'm sorry, Monsieur," said the water-seller; "it's this brute of a horse. He gets the bit between his teeth and I can't hold him. One day he'll kill someone and get me jailed."

He pointed to the horse between the shafts of the water-cart; it looked a wretched screw; it was filthily dirty and so thin its bones stood out. It was covered with galls; and the bit was too big and heavy for its mouth and was obviously hurting it.

"I made a bad bargain when I bought this damned brute," said the Auvergnat, raising his whip to relieve his anger.

But Mr. Coke caught him by the arm. He was looking at the horse, and the horse was looking at him.

To a man who knows and loves horses, the look in a

horse's eye can be as expressive and revealing as that in a human's. And horses, too, can recognize a man who understands them. A horse chooses his master just as much as a man chooses his mount. The large dark eye, which looked at Mr. Coke with both pride and fear, was not that of a draught-horse born to a servile condition.

"Let me have a look at that horse," said Mr. Coke. "Where does he come from? How did you buy him?"

The water-seller recognized the tourist's accent and at once began to address him as "my lord."

"You can look at him as much as you like; he was a bad bargain. I bought him because he came from the King's stables, or so I was told. But what use he was to the King, since he can't even pull a water-cart, I'm damned if I know."

"The King's stables?" said the Englishman, who had as much difficulty in understanding the Auvergnat's accent as the Auvergnat had in understanding him. "How very strange! I didn't know the King of France had Arab horses. What's this one called?"

"Sham! And it's no name for a Christian horse."

Mr. Coke bent down and felt the horse's dusty legs. Then, straightening up, he looked at the angle of the shoulder, the depth of the chest and the set of the head.

"Will you sell him to me?"

"Sell him to you? On the spot, my lord!" cried the Auvergnat.

But he quickly had second thoughts. The horse had been a bad buy, of course; but he had paid a high price for him; and corn didn't cost nothing; besides, he'd have to find another, and prices were rising.

In the end, the Auvergnat mentioned a sum that seemed to him huge: seventy-five francs. Mr. Coke agreed to it without argument.

"What fools the English are!" the water-seller thought

that evening as he led Sham to the stables of the Hôtel
d'Entragues, in the Rue de Tournon.

The grooms of this luxury hotel for rich foreigners turned
up their noses at having to curry-comb the thin, black nag
that looked as if it had been sleeping on a manure heap for
months.

The next day, Mr. Coke set about discovering Sham's history. The horse had already passed through several hands.
Going from one owner to another, all small people who
had used Sham in harness and had accidents with him, Mr.
Coke eventually reached a groom at Versailles.

The Auvergnat had told the truth; Sham had indeed come
from the royal stables. He had been part of a lot of eight
Arab stallions sent as a present to Louis XV by the Bey of
Tunis, on the occasion of the signing of a commercial treaty
two years before.

These small, strong horses, so difficult to ride if you did
not know them, whose fine delicacy, far from being to the
taste of the period, was considered a disadvantage, merely
made the King shrug his shoulders. As it happened, he had
never been able to find a horse to his liking; during the
course of his life he had tried over two thousand of which
none had apparently ever suited him.

Since the King had merely shrugged his shoulders, the
Master of the Horse had followed suit, and so had his under-
lings. The Arab stallions had been relegated to a corner of
the stables and eventually given as presents to members of
the Court, who had in turn disposed of them.

And so Sham, that desert prince, the descendant of an
ancestor known as "Wings of the Wind," a present from a
Mohammedan sovereign to King Louis, had ended up between the shafts of a water-cart in the Rue Croulebarde.

At this time he was six years old. Though he had begun
life in so high a position, had suffered so many vicissitudes

and fallen so low, his true destiny was in fact only just beginning.

He had crossed the Mediterranean in a Barbary galley but
he was to cross the Channel in a good round ship; he had
known the sands of Africa and the cobbles of Paris but he
was to tread the soft turf of England.

In London, Mr. Coke frequented St. James's Street Coffee
House, which was the fashionable resort of gamblers and
racing men. Its proprietor, Mr. Roger Williams, owned racehorses himself."

Mr. Coke was rather embarrassed by his purchase. He
had yielded to sudden impulse, to curiosity and also perhaps
to a desire to astonish. He had a good story to tell, but no
idea what to do with the horse that had knocked him down.
He sold Sham for twenty guineas to Mr. Roger Williams,
who put the young stallion out to grass for some time.

The desert prince began to look like his real self. He
filled out, and once again had a long flowing mane, a magnificent tail that fanned the ground, a big handsome croup,
chiselled muscles and silky coat, which was of such an intense black that it looked almost blue in the sunlight.

Horse-racing had already become very fashionable in England; indeed, had been so for some thirty years. The ideal
horse at that time was still very similar to the medieval war-
horse; tall, heavy, strong enough to carry a great weight of
armor, it made a noise like an avalanche when it galloped.

Mr. Williams of the St. James's Street Coffee House enjoyed a joke.

"I'm going to run 'The Nigger,' " he said, for that was the
name he had given Sham.

But Sham had a sense of humor too. Taken to the race-
course, he refused to start. Pressed a little too roughly with
the spurs, he reared, bucked, threw his jockey and, shaking
his long mane, galloped back to his stable.

Two or three more attempts were made, but in vain. The

horse had no competitive spirit. In training, and when alone, he promised wonderfully well and moved over the grass like a black arrow; but as soon as he was matched against those big competitors he seemed outraged and became a danger to anyone who went near him.

"A bad business," said Mr. Williams, as had said King Louis XV, the Master of the Horse, the Versailles grooms, the water-seller and Mr. Coke before him.

Mr. Williams was delighted to hand Sham over to one of his customers, Lord Godolphin, contenting himself with a small profit. The deal was made for twenty-five guineas.

To Lord Godolphin, formerly Keeper of the Privy Purse and Member of Parliament for Oxford, now a member of the House of Lords and son-in-law to the first Duke of Marlborough whose daughter, Lady Henrietta Churchill, he had married, twenty-five guineas was a mere trifle, as indeed were a hundred or a thousand when it was a question of a horse. This highly civilized man had two passions, chess and racing; the second was to ruin him. He kept a large racing-stable in Cambridgeshire; Sham was merely an exotic fancy.

"I'll send 'The Nigger' to Gog Magog," decided Lord Godolphin for it was on the Gog Magog hills that his stables stood.

It is in the nature of the female to have a taste for the strange and the unusual, to be attracted by the foreign. The arrival of this handsome Oriental created a certain stir among the mares at Gog Magog. Seeing his fillies raise their heads and spread their nostrils wide as Sham went by, Lord Godolphin gave orders that the horse should earn his corn as a teaser.

And for several months the horse, who was already known by the name of the Godolphin Arabian, that is Lord Godolphin's Arab, was employed in this way.

When nuptials had been decided on at Gog Magog, the desert prince was brought to the mare to flirt with her and put her in the mood for love. And when the mare, charmed by the little black horse, seemed sufficiently disposed, the master stallion, the king of the stud, the great Hobgoblin, was brought to her. Complacent, huge, important, strutting a little in his fat, he came forward to do his duty as a sire with the minimum of effort. And the Godolphin Arabian had to retire before this imposing grandee whose pleasure he had prepared for him.

So humiliating a retreat was intolerable to so lively a horse, whose blood was accustomed to conquest, and who had developed so great a sense of his own honor; but a rein, firmly held by Lord Godolphin's stable-lads, forced him away to a respectful distance.

Things went on like this till the day, the most memorable in the whole history of racehorses, when a superb blonde, a golden chestnut, still very young but of opulent build, nervous and anxious at being taken to her first nuptials, appeared before the Godolphin Arabian. Her name was Roxana.

Though she came from the royal stud—Lord Godolphin had paid sixty guineas for her—it did not prevent her from immediately falling in love with the Oriental teaser. More intuitive no doubt than men, she had recognized royal blood in the Godolphin Arabian. And the desert prince from the very first moment showed a compelling and impetuous passion for the fair Roxana—a passion such as he had never shown before.

There began a quivering dance of love between the two horses, an exotic ballet of seduction such as only animals—bees flying through the sunlight to celebrate their union, dragonflies that gambol mirrored in water, birds parading their colors—know how to achieve.

At the very moment Roxana was tremblingly about to yield, the huge Hobgoblin was led up as usual. But the little black horse turned mad with rage and, rearing up, went for his rival, his hooves beating the air. The stable-lads clung vainly to the rein; the Godolphin Arabian broke the leather and the battle began. The frightened lads dared not interfere, for it would have been at the risk of their lives.

The straw flew, the wooden partitions resounded to the drumming hooves, and a cloud of dust half-concealed the fighting stallions. The great Hobgoblin was unaccustomed to such treatment and unprepared for such an attack. He reared up heavily; but he was too slow to meet the furious, whirlwind assault of his slender adversary.

With hooves and teeth the Godolphin Arabian killed the huge Hobgoblin within a few minutes.

The David of horses had destroyed the Goliath and, like David, he demanded the royal princess as his reward. No one dared stand in his way as he broke down the doors and galloped to freedom, taking with him the beautiful Roxana, whose love he had won forever by his victory. Their pounding hooves crashed across the yard as they fled together to the neighboring woods.

They were found that same night, happy and a little tired. They were quiet again now as they nuzzled each other, the fair Roxana's head against her conqueror's black chest.

The stable was far from proud of itself. How was Lord Godolphin to be told that his best stallion was dead and his most promising and valuable filly gone off to honeymoon in the woods with "The Nigger?"

But Lord Godolphin had not only a taste for the eccentric but a sense of honor too. The story of the fight delighted him and, in spite of the damage done, his Arab horse rose in his esteem.

"We shall just wait and see what this produces," he said.

And the product of this romantic mating was a horse called Lath, who was born in 1732 and, from his first appearance on a race-course, carried all before him. Such speed and stamina had never been seen before. His heavy competitors struggled along twenty lengths behind him. The love-child was invincible. And with him that race of horses so oddly called "English thoroughbred" was born.

The Godolphin Arabian was relieved of his role of teaser. Everyone feared he might commit another murder. And Roxana, for her part, refused any other mate; she would belong to the Godolphin Arabian alone.

The two horses seemed unhappy when they were apart; they turned sad and nervous and went off their feed. They had to be put in neighboring boxes and, since Roxana became restive at any other stallion's approach, a second mating was decided on. Roxana was undoubtedly the mate of a single horse.

They had but few children, since the splendid chestnut mare died, alas, ten days after producing her second foal, in 1734. But they had many grandchildren.

Their second son, Cade, was brought up on cows' milk after his mother's death and became the sire of the celebrated Matchem, who won eleven races out of thirteen; and their descendants, crossed with the progeny of two other Arab stallions, the Byerley Turk and the Darley Arabian—called after the names of their respective owners, Captain Byerley and Mr. Darley of Aldby Park—are the ancestors of all the horses who have been racing all over the world since that time.

After Roxana's death, the Godolphin Arabian had still nearly twenty years to live. He was a widower, not inconsolable perhaps, but melancholy. He had several wives, and each time was born a horse famous either because of its own triumphs or because of its line, such as Regulus, such as Siletta, his granddaughter, the dam of Flying Childers, who was unbeaten eighteen times, and of the famous Eclipse, who were the two prodigious horses of the eighteenth century.

The Godolphin Arabian, the Gog Magog stallion, had

become famous throughout England. His master gave him a Moorish groom who had no other duty but to see to him. Nevertheless, the stallion was of a solitary disposition. He seemed to take no pleasure in any companion other than a little tabby cat called Grimalkin, who lived in his box, slept between his legs and, during the day, purred upon his back.

When the Godolphin Arabian began to grow old, he was taken to the course on racing days, splendidly harnessed in the Oriental manner and with his Moorish groom, wearing a turban, on his back, so that he might witness the triumphs of his descendants, though he had never raced himself. The horse that had cost only seventy-five francs had already won, through his descendants, tens of thousands of pounds. The punters saluted him; the children surrounded and acclaimed him. Tossing his fine little head and long mane, he pawed the ground and whisked his tail, pretending to impatience while allowing himself to be admired like an old king.

When he died, at over twenty-nine, an exceptional age for a horse, he was buried in the stables of Gog Magog, in the passage between the boxes, at the very place from which he had fled to the woods with the blond Roxana.

On his tombstone his name was graven and chains were placed round it. Both the Moorish groom and the cat Grimalkin died in the following month.

Two centuries have gone by. There are no longer horses at Gog Magog, which now belongs to the Cambridge Preservation Society. Only an old, white-haired groom, the caretaker of the premises, still remembers the days when the stud farm resounded to the neighing of horses. From time to time he sweeps the Godolphin Arabian's tomb.

The arched doorway is still there by which the two frenzied lovers fled. I have walked in the wood that was the scene of their love.

A striped ginger cat with gold eyes lives in the stables,

haunts the box in which the Godolphin Arabian lived, and walks delicately over the graven stone.

The Godolphin Arabian has had his biographers, his painters and his legend. George Stubbs, the great animal painter, painted his portrait; Rosa Bonheur, in a picture called *The Duel*, painted his fight with Hobgoblin; Eugéne Sue, socialist, racing man, and one of the founders, with My Lord l'Arsouille, of the Jockey Club in Paris, made him the hero of a novel. And, finally, the supreme honor, a page of the *Encyclopaedia Britannica* is devoted to the little desert prince and his descendants.

On every race-course in the world, amid thronging crowds, run horses that are the objects of both pride and passion, on which thousands of pounds are staked and whose victories are headlined on the front pages of the newspapers; and there is not one horse among them that does not possess in his veins at least a drop of the blood of Godolphin Arabian, of that king's horse who dragged a water-cart, of that humiliated lover who triumphed, and whom fate destined to be born on the shores of Carthage only to die at last on the hills near Cambridge.

THE CLOUD OF FIRE

TO LUCY FAURE

❧ ❧ ❧ "It was on the Tuesday, Monsieur!"

The old lady shook her head sadly and there was an absent look about her eyes.

Yes, it had been on the Tuesday. People who survived the tragedy of St. Pierre in Martinique do not say: "It was in 1902." Nor even: "It was the 8th May." They merely say: "The Tuesday"—just as if no other day had any right to bear that name.

We visited St. Pierre thirty-six years after the disaster. Could this be the old capital of the West Indies? Could there have ever been, where there was now a straggling coastal town, a flourishing city of 30,000 souls, spreading its elegant houses, commercial offices, public buildings, cathedral, theater and gardens across the lower slopes of the mountain?

Half of this city had vanished under the vast flood of grey lava pouring out of the volcano; and the tropical vegetation had swallowed the rest.

Death had visited it and left indelible traces. Even in the heart of the town there were ruins still, even the exuberant tropical vegetation had been unable to conceal them.

Even the rebuilt houses looked like ruins, for the stones with which they were built had the black marks of fire on them.

Everything was a uniform grey; the sand on the beach was

26

grey, where a few old ships' guns were up-ended to form useless bollards; grey too was the tumbledown wooden jetty that allowed St. Pierre to call itself a port; and the ancient paddle-steamer, which in the old days had served the coast, was grey as it rotted at anchor. Even the light under the low sky was the color of lava.

In the middle of the enormous square, where there were no trees to give shade, a high bronze fountain—last vestige of a dead splendor—sported two empty basins. Three naked black children played around. Some elderly Creole women, wearing long, faded print dresses, were gossiping apathetically over a basket of fish.

And the heat lay heavily over this desolation.

It was here that we met the old lady, with her gentle features and her moist eyes, who clearly belonged to the old white community of the island. She wore a white hat on her silver hair and a gold chain round her neck, and she leant on a Malacca cane.

She was clearly delighted to answer our questions, tell us all we wanted to know, and to be able to engage us in conversation. She smiled as she spoke.

"It was the Tuesday. I shall remember it all my life, Monsieur, all my life. We had left St. Pierre the previous day. For, on the Monday, the mountain had had a first eruption; and the whole city was anxious. My mother had besought my father to take us all to our plantation, where we normally went only later in the year. I was very disappointed. It was my twentieth birthday and I was engaged to be married. . . . The ball was cancelled.

"So that I should not be too disappointed, my father invited my fiancé to come and spend the night with us at Planchais.

"Working on the plantation there was a cousin of mine, Pierre, who had asked me to marry him. I had refused him;

when you're twenty, you know, you don't mind hurting other people. Sometimes you even enjoy it.

"Pierre was a secretive and brutal man, whereas my fiancé . . . well, he was my fiancé and I was in love with him.

"After dinner my sister Claire sat down at the piano. Pierre walked gloomily about the house. I teased him by saying: 'Why don't you marry Claire? It's all she's waiting for.'

"And then I went for a short walk in the park with my fiancé. . . . We had a fine park, with a great avenue of royal palms. . . . My cousin Pierre saw us kissing; I had known him since . . ."

The old lady was silent for a moment, leaning on her cane, as if her mind were still walking in the park.

"The next morning I got up just in time to say good-by to my fiancé. My cousin was driving him in the dog-cart. I saw them go off together. And when the dog-cart reached the end of the drive I nearly shouted, 'Come back! Don't go down to the town. . . .' There was an odd feel about the day: it seemed hard to breathe, the dogs were restless and there was fear in their eyes. In the sky we could see flights of birds leaving the mountain. Then we went to the village to hear Mass. And when we reached the square we found crowds of people shouting: 'St. Pierre is in flames! St. Pierre is burning! A rain of fire! The sea is boiling in the harbor!'

"My father wanted to go down to the city; my mother fainted to prevent him going. Her health was delicate and she had weak nerves. Our first thought was always for her.

"About noon, my cousin returned on foot, his clothes in rags. The skin of his face and hands was all red and cracked. He staggered. As soon as I saw him I cried to him: 'Pierre, Pierre, where is Simon?'

"He jerked his head toward the valley, and he told us what had happened.

"Very soon after they had started, the horse had become panic-stricken and Pierre had had great difficulty in stopping

it from running away. As they drew near the city, the air had
begun to smell of sulphur. And then, suddenly, they saw the
trees and the sugar-cane in the fields on their right burst
into flame like tinder. A carriage in front of them became a
flaming torch. A huge cloud of fire came toward them, setting
everything alight. The horse went mad; the dog-cart turned
over. Pierre was thrown to the side of the road and saw the
cloud of fire pass by, while my poor fiancé, caught by his
clothes to the dog-cart, disappeared into the furnace. All this
must have taken no more than thirty seconds. My fiancé's
remains were found near the road next day."

Suddenly the old lady began to talk much more quickly, as
if she were in a hurry to finish, but did not want to leave anything out.

"You know, Monsieur, that one of the strangest things
about that huge cloud of burning gas was that its edges were
quite straight and clear-cut. An ox was found with one flank
burnt away and the other untouched. . . . I fell ill; but, so it
seems, you don't die of sorrow at twenty. We were almost
ruined. Our house in St. Pierre was destroyed, and so were my
father's offices and warehouses. . . . I took a violent dislike to
my cousin. Whenever I saw him I thought: 'Why was it not
he? Why was not he the one who was killed?' . . . All the same
I married him two years later.

"From that moment, my life was like that of any other
white woman in the island: my house, my children . . . I had
nine children. . . . There are some things, you know, that one
would rather not talk about to the people one lives among.
Everyone in the island knows everybody else. And yet, sometimes, one does need to talk. . . . My husband died some years
ago. The priest who confessed him when he was dying made
him tell his story to me as a penance. He had lied to us on the
Tuesday. He told me that on that day he had been in such a
state of furious jealousy that all along the road he could think
of nothing but killing my fiancé and dying himself. It was not

true that the horse had bolted. On the contrary, he had jibbed and refused to go any further. But Pierre, when he saw the cloud of fire coming, had whipped the horse as hard as he could, and jumped out of the dog-cart, leaving my fiancé to perish in the fire. Don't you think it's rather cowardly for a dying man to ask for the forgiveness you cannot deny him?"

The old lady fell silent. She looked at the mountain, and the wrinkles on her face seemed to grow closer together.

The brief and colorless twilight of the tropics fell over the dead city of St. Pierre. Both sky and sea turned grey.

Without saying good-by, without even giving me time to ask her name, the old lady walked away with a firm step, leaning on her cane, and disappeared round the corner of the bronze fountain with its two dry basins.

I went across to the innkeeper who was sitting with his knees spread wide, on the threshold of his wine-shop. Under his grey woolly hair he had the sad face of an aging half-caste.

"What's that lady's name? The one I've just been talking to, who's walking away over there?"

The man looked up at me with sad eyes.

"Her? . . . Oh, that's Mademoiselle Harbelot," he said.

"Mademoiselle?" I repeated in surprise.

"Yes, Mademoiselle Harbelot des Planchais."

"But what's her married name?"

The innkeeper shook his head.

"She never married," he said.

"But she's just told me that she had nine children!"

"No, no. No children. . . . She sometimes tells stories though. Her cousin looks after her, but he can't always prevent her from going out. She's weak in the head, is Mademoiselle Harbelot. It happened on the Tuesday."

SO GREAT A LOVE

TO ANDRÉ BERNHEIM

❧ ❧ ❧ Fame in the theater is apt to be delusive since it tends to go out with the lights that illumined it. Legend does little for the actor, however celebrated he may have been, and his name disappears from living memories as soon as the wind has torn away the last bill that displayed it.

So it was with Elise Lambert, "the divine Lambert" as she was called, incomparable in movement, unequalled, it was said, in rendering the music of verse. Who remembered her, who still mentioned her name? And yet for twenty years she had held audiences enthralled by her laughter, her tears, her silences. Princes were her friends, queens her rivals. She aroused many more passions than she was prepared to satisfy; she belonged to a period when scandal had not yet become the necessary adjunct to celebrity; and she played in enough drama on the stage not to want it in her life.

And yet, during the winter after the Universal Exhibition, when people began to see Henri Nauday in Elise Lambert's box practically every night, no one believed, unless they did so themselves, that any happiness could come of it. She was forty-four; he twenty-six. He was at the beginning of a success-ful career; she had almost come to the end of her beauty. She could not act in his plays, for he was already writing noth-ing but vaudevilles and farces; it seemed therefore that she could only hope to be his victim.

Comic writers are nearly always sad men and their humor

an objective way of expressing their bitterness with life. Nauday was a pessimist of this kind. He was tall, silent and exquisitely polite, wore long fair moustaches and stock ties, but he never laughed, had a pitiless sense of other people's absurdities and an instinctive knowledge of the mechanism of hilarity. When attending rehearsals, stop-watch in hand, he would sometimes interrupt the actors to say in a desolate voice: "Here you must stop for fifteen seconds for the laugh. Now go on."

His first two plays had each run for a whole season. He was the fashion, the object of much flattery, and overwhelmed with invitations which gave him an opportunity to note the follies of his fellow-men.

All the women who had nothing to do seemed ready to console him for his happy fate, to devote their idleness to him, and prove to him that a great love was all he needed to enjoy the whole beauty of the world. His were those rare years, which fall to few lives, when physical appearance is in tune with the celebrity which generally comes to men only in their decline, when they can no longer profit by it; and so everything was permitted him.

And this was also true of Elise Lambert, but would be so only for a short time. No one would have attributed her years to her, but she had them. Yet, in spite of them, she had that aura of youth which only luck and success can maintain. Victorious generals conserve an astonishing suppleness of limb and, at seventy, still climb stairs two at a time. Statesmen, even in extreme old age, can sit up all night, provided they are still in the government. So it is with actresses.

Daily applause, flowers, deference, admiration had all preserved in Elise Lambert graces that seemed destined to last forever. She was beautiful; she dressed with studied care, not so much from an innate liking for ostentation, but because she knew that an actress's clothes must make an effect. When she walked down a street, the bakers' boys, basket on head, stopped, gaped and whistled their admiration; and it was this more than any other tribute that assured her she was still "the divine Lambert."

But for how many years more? For how many parts? For how many successful first nights?

Every day that winter, before the performance, she wondered: "Will he come tonight?" And every evening, after the applause of the final curtain, she went to her dressing-room, leaned for a moment against the wall, her arms hanging, her eyes closed, and listened to the beating of her heart as it diminished gradually with the theater noises. The audience went out into the street, the stage-hands deserted the stage, the attendants abandoned the cloakroom, and the great building of plush, stucco and gold was left to the silence and the dusk. And this second life Elise Lambert had been living for the last three hours withdrew from her wave by wave, like the sea ebbing from the shore at night. She opened her eyes. Henri Nauday was there, his long body sitting askew among the furs, the bouquets of roses and tuberoses, the Venetian scent-bottles and the paste tiaras that littered the dressing-room, playing with his eye-glass and slowly swinging the pump that hung from his slender ankle.

While she sat at her dressing-table removing her make-up —she had beautiful shoulders and was not afraid to show them —she would watch the young dramatist's face in the looking-glass, and wonder if she really could accept what life was offering her.

"He was born the year I made my début," she thought. "It's too splendid a present, I've no longer a right to it."

There was a cab waiting at the stage-door. Nauday accompanied her home and there, on her doorstep, there was a moment or two of embarrassed silence, which would have much surprised the people who were whispering about their affair all over Paris. He was awaiting an invitation; she an avowal; but they could neither of them utter the necessary word, for they were both afraid, she of the ravages of passion and he of his love being ridiculed. They hesitated on the brink of their desire as one hesitates to plunge into an enticing but too-high wave, or, when at a ball, to present the same ridiculous spectacle as the dancing couples. And so every night, as they got out of the cab, Henri Nauday held Elise Lambert's hand in his own for a few seconds, while she could bring herself to say no more than a murmured "Thank you."

It was then that Monsieur de Tanthoüet intervened in the rôle of "the friend." It is these "friends" who often designate two people for each other before they have become aware of it themselves, marry people off who have not yet realized that they want to become engaged, and announce separations before the interested parties have even perceived their mutual alienation. In matters of love, we need always to beware of these "friends," for they are not content merely to interpret our feelings; they determine them; and end by making us do the things they have invented for us in spite of ourselves.

Monsieur de Tanthoüet was fifty, had grey eyes and grey hair parted precisely in the middle of his head; he wore grey frock-coats and was a shipbuilder.

For many years past, Elise Lambert had been his life's great luxury, a real luxury because useless to him from every point of view. Authoritarian by nature and extremely bold in business, he devoted to the actress an attachment that could be explained only by the attraction some people feel for that which is contrary to their character and foreign to their understanding. He was the sort of elderly aspirant who has finished by himself forgetting his aspirations and, for want of something better, has come to play the unromantic part of faithful counselor, ever-ready confidant and generous admirer. It gave him a feeling of being admitted into the world, which held a certain glamor for him, of the arts and the theater.

One morning he came to call on the young dramatist in the little house he had leased in the Rue Raynouard.

"My dear Nauday," he said more or less, "we do not know each other well, but you are aware of my long-standing friendship with Elise. It is because of that friendship that I am here. Your interest in our friend is evident to everyone and her interest in you is, alas, no less apparent. You are seduced—indeed, who would not be?—by her grace, and your young career is attracted to that halo of success which shines about her head. Talent calls to talent; she is touched—and how could she not be?—by the gift you offer her of your youth. But you will be committing a crime. You will be her last great passion, and what for you will be merely a pleasure will be a tragedy for her. One cannot escape the universal law of age; you are at the age of conquests, Elise is entering on that of desertions. After a few months, a few weeks perhaps, you will leave her, and I am not at all sure, knowing her as I do, that she will be able to bear the shock with resignation. If you wish to behave well, abandon this game in which the stakes are so unequal."

Henri Nauday, wearing a velvet dressing-gown, puffed silently at his cigar.

He could hardly say: "Monsieur, I was fifteen when I saw Elise Lambert act for the first time. I came away in a state of rapture and enthusiasm such as I shall never know again. I believe it was she who first awakened in me a desire to write for the theater and to become famous. I swore to myself then that I would win her one day. And it is myself I contemplate, the ten years I have lived since then, when I am in her dressing-room and accompany her home at night."

"I can see in your eyes, my dear Nauday," went on the shipbuilder, "that you doubt my disinterestedness. But whatever you may think, I have never had any relations with our dear Elise other than those of the purest friendship, and I never shall. Indeed, in two days' time, I am leaving for America, to which I have transferred my business affairs, and I shall certainly not come back for a very long time, if ever. If it were not for the imminence of my departure, I should scarcely have dared to come to talk to you as I have. I am sure that you have a generous heart and that you have understood. Believe me: don't pursue this; it would be a crime."

Henri Nauday showed his visitor out and wished him a good journey. Once the door was closed, he shrugged his shoulders. "I know all about 'noble fathers' on the stage," he thought, "but this is the first time I have met a 'noble friend.' "

Monsieur de Tanthoüet's visit had the opposite result to that which he had intended and brought about precisely what he had wished to prevent. When he thought of Elise Lambert's age, Nauday realized that he must be quick if he were to exorcise his boyhood's dream before it was too late; he convinced himself of the urgency of his desire and that very night found words with which to express it. It was all Elise Lambert had been waiting for.

Things turned out as they were bound to do; that is to say that to begin with the actress loved the young man prudently, but as time went on with all the anxious pangs of passion. And just as she was beginning to be reassured and to feel that her happiness might last forever, Nauday left her.

At one blow, she lost all her beauty which had been so miraculously prolonged. A summer of weeping deprived her face of that freshness which grease-paint, late nights and foot-lights had never been able to impair. The bakers' boys no longer turned to gape at her in the street. The following autumn she had a failure in a new play, the first in twenty years. The lamp had gone out. Shortly afterward, she retired from the stage.

When he left her, she had sworn never to see Henri Nauday again. She had both sent word to him and had written to him to that effect. Happy at the interdict which relieved his conscience, Nauday saw to it that she kept her oath.

It is a strange fact that, when two people are on the point of falling in love, fate seems casually to arrange for their paths constantly to cross, recross and cross again; and then, when they have parted, this mysterious will, which had caused them to run into each other so frequently, arranges equally mysteriously that they shall meet no more. Not once in twenty years did Elise and Nauday chance to hail the same cab, find themselves side by side in a traffic block, attend the same private view, party or even funeral. Then, suddenly, twenty years later, chance placed them side by side at a banquet in honor of some distinguished theatrical personality. Henri Nauday's career had taken exactly the course that it had promised. He was no longer handsome; work, success and much dining out had caused him to put on weight. His moustache was shorter, his hair retreating, and his cravats quieter. He talked more than he used to do, aware that he was expected to make a witty sally or two between courses.

Elise Lambert had become a white-haired old lady. You could see at a glance that she had been very beautiful; and her eyes and smile had retained their infinite sweetness. She realized that to put Nauday at his ease she must raise at once the subject there was no possibility of avoiding.

"You made me very unhappy, Henri," she said, "and I think I hated you for a long time afterward. But it was more my fault than yours, and it's all wiped out now. I remember only the happy times you gave me. I have been a passionate admirer of all you have done; and I have been delighted by your success. You really have a splendid talent."

Praise, no reproaches, and not even forgiveness. To Nauday, Elise Lambert's voice was like an old and long-forgotten tune instantly recalling some vista of the past. Nauday was now close enough to his declining years to be moved by sudden recollections of his youth. "I am as old now as she was when we loved each other," he thought. And as he listened to the woman he had so gravely injured, his sympathy was not for her but for himself.

"I should like to see you again from time to time," she said with a smile. "You have nothing to fear now. And you must have so much to tell me."

"I should like it too," he said.

"Come and have tea with me one day next week."

"I would love to. Do you still live at the same address?"

"I haven't moved. What about Thursday?"

"Thursday then."

It was pouring with rain on the following Thursday, drowning the town, overflowing the gutters, curtaining the streets. Henri Nauday was drenched when he arrived.

"My poor dear," cried Elise Lambert, "you've actually come out in this appalling weather! And you couldn't even find a cab! It's really too kind, much too kind of you! But your coat's soaked through. You mustn't sit like that or you'll catch your death."

She clapped her hands.

"Mariette, Mariette!" she cried, calling her maid. "Take Monsieur Nauday's coat and dry it. Bring him my long dressing-gown, the blue one. I think he'll manage to get into it. And your shoes, my dear! Mariette, see if you can find some slippers or something!"

She fussed over him like a mother. She had nearly committed suicide because of him; and now she was anxious that he should not catch cold. She was so delighted he had come!

Well wrapped up, Nauday was soon sitting by the fire, in the very place where twenty winters ago he had played with his eye-glass and swung his pump to and fro.

They had hardly begun to talk of the past when there was a ring at the front door. Mariette was busy ironing the wet coat. The old lady went to open the door herself.

Nauday failed to recognize the visitor's voice. He merely heard Elise Lambert say: "Oh, what a surprise! Come in, Pierre, and see who's here. When did you arrive?"

Monsieur de Tanthoüet came in. He had arrived back from America the night before with the intention of ending his days in his native land; and his first visit was to his "dear Elise." As he entered the drawing-room, he saw Nauday sitting by the fire in a dressing-gown, apparently enjoying the most intimate conjugal felicity. He nearly had a stroke. Nauday had not even time to shake his hand, before Monsieur de Tanthoüet cried: "You? Oh, Monsieur, so you're here! When I think of what I might have done! Thank God, you didn't listen to me! I owe you my most humble apologies. I shall never forgive myself. I shall never dare look you in the face again."

He dashed out past the astonished old lady and fled, clutching his head muttering: "So great a love! To think I might have ruined so great a love!"

THE WIFE OF
A SINGLE DAY

TO CHRISTINE DE RIVOYRE

❦ ❦ ❦ Monsieur de Longeville had been born at Longeville, had grown up there, lived there and eventually inherited it on his father's death. He was attached to his estate by such deep roots, was so much at one with the stones of his château, the grass in his fields and the sap rising in the trees of his forests, that he could imagine himself living nowhere else in the world.

He often said: "I'd rather lose my head than Longeville." These were rash words, for he uttered them on the eve of the Revolution he had not foreseen; and he was to be compelled to make the choice.

The Bastille in Paris fell and Monsieur de Longeville, because he had read much history, believed it to be merely one of those unimportant riots such as occurred in every reign. Then there was talk of a constitution, and Monsieur de Longeville, because he was a Voltairean, saw no reason to object to that. Then the King was sent to the scaffold, the Mountain began to mow down the ranks of the Gironde, and aristocrats were being harvested bloodily on every side. It was the Terror. But Monsieur de Longeville remained at Longeville.

He was alone. All his friends and relations had left the province, some to join the Princes' army, some to go to the guillotine. He lived alone in his château, because his old servants were dead and the younger ones had been enrolled in the army of the Republic. Even the maidservants had gone, for fear of being compromised.

Time did not weigh heavily on his hands for, indeed, he had never been so busy. He cooked himself eggs on the hearth in his salon; he had to comb his own wig each night and powder it each morning (he had laid in a good stock of powder); and he spent the day going from room to room with a bunch of keys in his hand, shaking out the spiders that were spinning their webs in the curtains and dusting the portraits of his ancestors. When he went out, it was only to gaze with a sigh at the weed invading the moat, to beat down with his stick the nettles and thistles overrunning the garden, or go to the espaliers in the kitchen-garden to pick a late peach the caterpillars had been kind enough to spare him. Even abandoned and in decay, Longeville seemed to him more beautiful than anything else in the world and well worth his devotion.

In spite of the most sinister stories, he obstinately refused to be frightened: the peasants of Longeville, like the fields they cultivated, seemed to him different from peasants elsewhere. He had been their master in the past and was sure he would become so again thanks to the Count of Artois' army; he was persuaded that he ran less risk by staying among them than he would elsewhere.

One of his farmers, Philippon, had become Mayor and President of the Revolutionary Committee. The Marquis knew Philippon well. He was not a bad man, but he had the gift of the gab, and his passion for the sound of his own voice had got him where he was. Naturally, Philippon no longer paid rent for his farm.

"They won't dare go further, they won't dare touch me," Monsieur de Longeville thought. "But if I leave, they'll burn the château and sack the whole place."

He tried to comfort himself by pretending to believe day

by day that the Republic would be destroyed on the morrow, and that things would be restored to what they had been in the past. He would have saved Longeville.

Love and devotion for a place, such as his for Longeville, are rare in a young man. For I have forgotten to tell you that Monsieur de Longeville was still young and also handsome. He was tall and slender, had a well-turned leg and a high forehead. His face had no outstanding features, except perhaps for his nose, which gave him an air of authority. Dressed in a flowered waistcoat, lace and red heels, he was the very image of a provincial marquis of the period.

From time to time, there are people who are exactly like one's imagined idea of them. Apart from certain odd personal habits, as for instance wiping the snuff off his fingers on his breeches instead of on his shirt frill, Monsieur de Longeville was one of them. You have only to look at a portrait in the museum at Alençon, which is said to be of him, to be persuaded of it.

In the days when the whole province had been gay with balls and picnics, he had had a great success with the ladies. But now he had nothing but memories to keep him company. They did not make him sad, for he considered it better to have memories than nothing at all.

On the evening of his thirty-fifth birthday, which was in September 1793, Monsieur de Longeville decided to give himself a dinner; that is to say, he lit three candles in the candelabra instead of one, brought up one of the last bottles of good wine from the cellar, and had his eggs scrambled instead of boiled. Then, when he had changed into a dressing-gown, he made music for himself, regretting merely that he could not dance at the same time. But since he was playing the harpsichord he could not be everywhere at once. For an hour, he played minuets, gavottes and cavatinas, then he sat down by the hearth and, no doubt partly due to the wine, fell asleep.

He was awakened by someone pulling him by the sleeve

and shouting: "Monsieur le Marquis, you must fly, they're coming to arrest you!"

He opened his eyes to see a young girl. She was breathless and her cheeks were red from running. She was fifteen years old and Philippon's daughter. There was a kerchief over her auburn hair which fell to her shoulders, her skirt was in tatters, her calves were round and her eyelids like rose petals. She was really a very pretty little girl, with the true Norman accent that lingered on the vowels. Monsieur de Longeville knew her well, as he knew all the children in the village.

"What do you want, child?" he asked.

"You must fly, Monsieur le Marquis, you must fly I'm telling you! They're coming. I heard them talking at my father's. You must go at once. They'll certainly send you to Paris."

Monsieur de Longeville got to his feet and went to the window. How beautiful his garden was under the night sky! At this hour, you could not see that the trees needed pruning, and the reflection of the moon lay white across the lake. He suddenly saw a group of men hurrying toward the château, saw them and heard them too, for they were shouting at the tops of their voices: "Death to the aristocrats!" It was almost as if some among them wanted to warn him. The noise they made could be heard clearly within the château walls. Flashes of summer lightning lit them up.

And so it was that Monsieur de Longeville had to decide between his château and his head. It only took him a second to reach the decision he had been deferring for so long.

He allowed himself to be led by the hand through his own house. The girl took him down the back stairs, the only ones she knew, and then out past the offices, across the kitchen-garden and, through a breach in the park wall, into the open fields.

Monsieur de Longeville was surprised to discover how fast he could run in slippers. The skirts of his dressing-gown flapped about his legs and, as he hurried along, he wondered:

"What's her name? Her Christian name, I mean. She's Philippon's daughter, I know that, but what's her Christian name?"

From time to time, he turned round, expecting to see flames rising from the roof of the château, but, since he saw nothing of the sort, he imagined the Revolutionary Committee pillaging his showcases and slitting up his pictures before they set fire to the house.

"Where are you taking me, my girl?" he asked.

"To a place I know of, Monsieur le Marquis, where they won't find you."

Monsieur de Longeville slowed his pace a little to regain his breath. There was not a sound to be heard; no one seemed to be pursuing them. Suddenly, the Marquis remembered: "Marguerite! Of course, her name's Marguerite."

"Why are you doing this, Marguerite?" he asked. "Why do you want to save me? And how will you be able to face your father?"

"I'm not going to tell him."

"You're taking a serious risk, you know!"

"I don't want you to die, Monsieur le Marquis. I won't have it!" she cried. "I don't want them to send you to Paris to have your head cut off."

She rubbed her eyes and, when she took Monsieur de Longeville's hand again, he realized the child's palm was wet. And now, as Marguerite clutched his hand, it was less, it seemed to him, to guide him than as an excuse to lean against him.

And so, hand in hand, they went down into the valley, and then climbed a little way up the opposite hill. They had come at least half a league. And there, masked by a clump of elders, was a low cave with a brick-built entrance, which had for many years been used for growing mushrooms. Later, the mushroom-growing had been abandoned. A barn nearby had fallen into ruins. The ground was very wet; water squelched under their feet; and a horrible smell of manure lay over the whole place.

Marguerite Philippon began moving aside the rotten boards and pea-sticks which blocked the entrance to the cave.

"Is this where you're going to hide me? In this stinking hole?" cried Monsieur de Longeville. "Never!"

"Monsieur le Marquis," replied Marguerite, "if you don't go in, I shall give myself up to the Revolutionary Tribunal and we shall both die together."

She showed great determination for so young a girl, and Monsieur de Longeville was much surprised at it.

"Go in," she said. "With all due respect, don't be so silly. You'll have nothing to fear here. The peasants won't come to get their pea-sticks before the spring."

"The spring?" cried Monsieur de Longeville in horror, seeing himself spending the winter in the cave.

"Go on in, Monsieur le Marquis. I'll bring you food tomorrow."

You can get used to anything if you have to and, even in the worst of circumstances, a man can discover minor pleasures. And this was what happened to Monsieur de Longeville. The heap of manure, which lay at the back of the mushroom cave and was well rotted, gave out a warmth that was not unwelcome during the cool September nights. Monsieur de Longeville's nostrils became accustomed to the smell. From the ruins of the barn, he constructed a sort of pallet which he covered with bracken, also a table of a kind and a chair.

Though the mushrooms were no longer cultivated they still grew; Monsieur de Longeville ate them raw and found them quite pleasant. He also got used to the cold soup Marguerite brought him every day at nightfall in an earthenware pot with a handle; and he was delighted when he found meat in it.

One evening, he asked the girl how she managed to get hold of the food.

"When I go out in the morning to take the cows to the meadow," she explained, "my mother gives me the soup for my midday meal. So I keep it, and bring it to you. I daren't come any earlier, in case someone should see me.

"But what do you eat then?"

"Oh, I eat at night when I get home."

However great a lord one may be, hunger is always moving and Monsieur de Longeville was much moved when he heard this. Here was a young girl starving herself all day in the presence of a full earthenware pot so that he might remain alive.

"If God and Monsieur of Artois so will it, I shall reward you handsomely later on," he said.

"If it were merely for a reward, Monsieur le Marquis, I should not do it," she replied, blushing.

And she left him rather more quickly than usual that night.

Monsieur de Longeville often asked her for news of the château. It had come to no harm. Philippon, who at this time was trying to model himself on Danton, had made a fine speech to the members of the Committee from the château steps.

"Citizens," he had said, "from now on the château belongs to the Republic, and to plunder it would be stealing from the people. So watch over it!"

Upon which, he had put the keys of the château in his pocket, while awaiting orders from a superior authority. Apart from a snuff-box or two looted from the console tables and the wine in the cellar, which had been drunk to the death of all tyrants, nothing had been touched.

The village was convinced that the Marquis's disappearance was due to somebody's treason. They expelled from the Committee a member who they suddenly decided had Girondin tendencies, and they sent a priest, who had been caught saying Mass in a barn, under arrest to Alençon. Eventually, the affair was closed by a terrific speech from Philippon in

which he blasted the conspiracy of the "*ci-devants*," and
asserted that Monsieur de Longeville had joined the Princes'
army.

The Marquis, however, was still rotting in his cave. He no
longer wore his wig since mushrooms had begun to grow on it.
In any case, it no longer fitted him for his hair had grown too
long.

Owing to the fact that Philippon had taken the keys, Marguerite was once able to borrow them secretly and go to the
château to fetch things Monsieur de Longeville wanted: gold
to escape with, and a pair of nail scissors. She had, however,
been unable to manage the mechanism of the lock of the
bureau in which the gold was hidden—at least she said she
had been unable to manage it—and so brought him only the
scissors. She watched attentively while he cut his nails and
trimmed his beard, for every movement he made as he did so
seemed to have a peculiar beauty. She sighed; but it never occurred to him to wonder why she did so.

Monsieur de Longeville had also asked her to bring him
clothes, for his silk breeches had split during their flight that
first night, and his dressing-gown, which was hardly suited to
a bed of bracken, was beginning to fall apart at the seams. But
to Marguerite it seemed that he would be better disguised in
an old pair of cloth trousers and a fustian smock of Philippon's rather than in fine clothes from the château wardrobe.

She also brought the Marquis candles and, so that he might
while away the time, books and broadsheets, which she borrowed from her father's cupboard and later replaced.

Monsieur de Longeville was therefore able to read such
edifying works as *A Republican Family, The Liberation of
the Negroes*, and *The Great Interview in the Tower of the
Temple Between Charles Libre, a Patriot Without Moustaches, and Louis Veto, the Slave and His Family*.

And then one day, a Sunday, she brought a rapier to the
cave.

"I found it by chance in a chest in the attic. Keep it, Monsieur le Marquis. You must have a weapon."

Monsieur de Longeville seemed delighted. He tore off a bit of the fustian smock that had been Philippon's and began polishing it.

Nevertheless, in Philippon's house, Marguerite's parents were somewhat surprised by her appetite at supper. She was growing, they thought, and the young needed feeding up. Yet, when she began dreaming over the food, they began to wonder. And when her father asked her why she was not attending to her supper, she forgot to answer him.

And then a cow disappeared; it was found only after a night-long search with lanterns. Marguerite had to admit she had neglected the herd. However they could get no more out of her than that. Her father concluded she must be in love.

And a few evenings later, when Marguerite had brought Monsieur de Longeville his basin of cold soup, the rotten planking that concealed the entrance of the cave suddenly collapsed under a kick. Philippon walked in, accompanied by two farm-hands.

"I thought so, I thought so!" he cried. "I thought you were seeing a man! And what a man! A tramp, a gipsy!"

Then suddenly, he recognized Monsieur de Longeville behind the long beard and the unkempt hair. The Marquis was standing there, rapier in hand.

"Good God!" cried Philippon, forgetting he had decided to give up swearing in His name since he had become an atheist. "Good God! And so it was you, Monsieur . . ."

He was on the point of saying "Monsieur le Marquis," but just managed to alter it in time to "Monsieur le *Ci-Devant!*"

Philippon found himself in some difficulty. His report on his failure to arrest the Marquis had not been well received in high places. And now, here was his daughter together with the Marquis. If there had only been no witnesses, if he had only not brought the two farm-hands along with him! But in these dangerous times a man in his position could hardly adventure out alone.

And now he was in a spot, all because of his daughter, and even Danton's example could furnish no precedent for this.

All he could say was: "And what's more, you've given him my trousers, and I was looking for them this morning to go and milk the cows!"

Then, his eye fell on a broadsheet that was lying on the ground and he said: "I know now why my cupboard smells of manure! Come on, citizens, hold him!" he added, turning to the two farm-hands, and pointing to Monsieur de Longeville.

"Thank you, Philippon, I can still walk unaided," the Marquis replied.

They went back to the village in silence, each concerned with his own thoughts. The November mist lay close over the bottom of the valley and hung low under the apple trees. Philippon, who was leading the way, appeared merely waist up out of the fog. And then, suddenly, when they were within some hundred yards of the house, he cried: "To think a *ci-devant* should have seduced my daughter! That this should happen to me! They've no respect for the decencies, they think they're still living in the Middle Ages!"

"Philippon," replied Monsieur de Longeville, "it is quite true that your daughter has hidden and fed me, because she's a good-hearted child. But I give you my oath . . ."

Marguerite interrupted him.

"Father," she said, "I love him and I shall never love anyone else."

Then she whispered to Monsieur de Longeville: "I said that merely to save you. You do understand, don't you?"

"Whether you love him or not," replied Philippon, "I shall send him to the Tribunal tomorrow."

"If you dare send him to his death, I shall die too. I'm warning you!"

"Are you telling me you're not a Republican?"

"Of course I'm a Republican, but I won't let him die!"

She was not weeping. She was tense and upright, with her head in the air, her hair hanging down her back, ready to face the whole world. As we have seen, she was a determined girl. Her father knew very well that she was capable of doing what she said she would. He was convinced she was in love with the Marquis. She was Philippon's only daughter and she had always had him pretty much under her thumb.

He could well imagine her admitting all her guilt to a Tribunal, or even committing suicide by throwing herself down a well. The village Tribune adored his child, and when children behave like grown-ups, they nearly always have their own way.

"I'll hide him for a night or two myself, and then he'll have to get out," Philippon thought. But the trouble was that the whole village was bound to know about it. Besides, how could one know she had not been seduced?

People were coming out of their houses to meet them. And, suddenly, he had an inspiration.

"Well, if it's like that, he must marry you, there's nothing else for it," Philippon said. "Citizen, are you prepared to marry my daughter?"

"Say 'yes,' " Marguerite whispered, digging Monsieur de Longeville in the ribs. "Say 'yes,' and you're saved."

Monsieur de Longeville, seeing the guillotine retreating, placed his hand on Marguerite's head and replied that he would be most happy to take her for his wife.

Philippon assembled the Committee in the Mayor's parlor by the light of candles. Heavy-jowled, bull-necked, and large of fist (one tends to model oneself on the people one resembles), Philippon explained to the members the reasons for his decision. The Marquis had taken no part in the conspiracy against the Republic and had preferred to live hidden on his estate. By marrying Marguerite, he was espousing the people's cause.

"And now, citizens," cried Philippon, "would you rather his blood made us new enemies or see him come over to our side? The Republic must have open arms. . . ."

His speech had a smell of the Gironde about it. But no one in the village really had anything much against Monsieur de Longeville. Besides, now that he had no wig, no cane and no waistcoat, that his skin was as white as chicory raised in the dark and his beard was two months grown, he looked more like an out-of-work woodcutter than a *ci-devant*. And not for Philippon alone, but for the other peasants too, there was a certain satisfaction in seeing the former lord of the manor marrying a farmer's daughter. This was also part of winning the Revolution.

All the women of the village were waiting outside the Town Hall. The marriage register was opened and Citizen Longeville took up a pen and signed it.

Clinging to his side, Marguerite whispered in his ear: "It's only a token marriage, you know, Monsieur le Marquis. We can now divorce; but you'll be able to go free."

Monsieur de Longeville kissed her for the first time on both cheeks; and he did it so charmingly that all the mothers present dabbed at their eyes with their handkerchiefs.

That very night he escaped to Paris. He reached it in three days, thanks to the kindness of a number of wagoners who not only gave him lifts but fed him. He was able to hide for a few days with his cousin, Anthénor de Longeville, who, as attached to his town house in the Faubourg Saint-Honoré as the Marquis had been to his château, was living in the porter's lodge.

Monsieur de Longeville realized he had better not delay long, and the tumbrils passing each day beneath the windows emphasized the fate he had so far managed to escape.

He was lucky enough to obtain a false passport and reached England. There he lived the wretched life of the *émigrés*. He gave French lessons for a livelihood; but at that time there were more people in London wanting to teach French than there were people wishing to learn it. Monsieur de Longeville made friends with Monsieur de Chateaubriand and together they felt faint with hunger at the sight of butchers' shops.

This life, which can be recorded in four lines, lasted four years.

Monsieur de Longeville often thought of his château and feared he would never see it again; and he frequently told the story of his escape to prove that all the peasants of France were not the bloodthirsty monsters they were made out to be. He quarrelled with many of his compatriots about this.

When the laws concerning the *émigrés* were repealed, Monsieur de Longeville was among the first to return to France. In Paris, it was the middle of the Directoire. New furniture and new women were in fashion. The blood shed in Thermidor had dried on the cobbles of the Place de la Révolution, and the shoes of the "Merveilleuses" had worn it away.

Anthénor, though he had not yet managed to recover the whole of his house in the Faubourg, was nevertheless living on the first floor where, in the hope of getting himself elected to the Cinq-Cents, he entertained such women as Madame Tallien and Madame de Beauharnais, whom Monsieur de Longeville did not like.

He was doing his best to set his affairs in order, when one day he received a letter from his province which ran as follows:

> Monsieur le Marquis,
>   My father is dead and our farm is to let. My duty is
> to hand it over to you, but I do not know how to do

so. As for the marriage which circumstances obliged you to contract, I am told that, even though it meant nothing, it will be necessary for you to obtain a divorce if you wish to contract another which will make you happier. I am sending this letter to the house of Monsieur le Comte Anthénor, your cousin, in the hope that it will reach you and that you will give your orders to her who signs herself respectfully,

Your wife of a single day,
Marguerite Philippon.

Monsieur de Longeville was surprised by the style of this letter and also by the elegance of the handwriting. The next day, he set off, taking the coach as far as Alençon and there hiring a post-chaise. He felt considerably moved as he approached Longeville and it was only the fear of being laughed at by the coachman that restrained his tears when he saw the roof of his château. Since he had not the keys, he went straight to the farm.

Marguerite turned pale when she saw him.

"Oh, Monsieur le Marquis," she cried, "here you are at last!"

"Did you write that letter yourself?" Monsieur de Longeville asked her.

"Yes, Monsieur le Marquis. I've been educating myself for the last four years. I did not want to disgrace you too much."

She was wearing a grey dress with a white collar. Her golden hair was done in curls and ringlets in the fashion of the time. There was something dignified and collected in her gaze and, indeed, in her whole manner.

Had he met her elsewhere, Monsieur de Longeville might not have recognized her, so much had she altered, grown and gained in beauty.

"How old are you now?" he asked.

"Nineteen, Monsieur le Marquis."

"And you haven't married?"

"You see, already I was married," she replied with a smile.

They went to the château together. The weed had been cleaned out of the moat, the trees in the garden had been pruned, and the salon had been aired regularly and hardly smelled of damp at all.

"I've done my best to look after it," said Marguerite. "It was not sold for the benefit of the State because my father said it belonged to me."

She blushed.

"And what are you going to do now?" asked Monsieur de Longeville.

"I shall go to your aunt, the Canoness. She's blind and often sends for me to read to her. Now that you've come back, I think I shall go and live there."

Monsieur de Longeville was standing by that very same window through which, four years before, he had seen the revolutionaries coming, while a little girl was pulling him away by the hand. He thought for a moment.

He was approaching his fortieth birthday. Monsieur de Longeville no longer wore a wig. He was going grey at the temples and he had learnt much during the last four years. He had known fear and hunger, had seen the discords among the *émigrés*, and the conspiracies of parties, only to find on his return to Paris a frenzied search for pleasure and a longing to forget which shocked him.

Marguerite was nineteen.

"I'm compelled to go away again for a while," he said. "But the first thing we must do is to put our affairs in order. We shall do so tomorrow. You must summon your relations."

"I no longer have any."

"Then your friends, all those who were present four years ago."

"It was the whole village, Monsieur le Marquis."

She spent an appalling night, the last of the dream she had indulged in her loneliness. But next day, when Monsieur de Longeville appeared, her eyes were dry and she was prepared, as it was in her nature to be, to face events.

She had had no need to summon the village; it had summoned itself as a result of a word she had dropped to a neighbor.

And now, what she had always foreseen was going to happen. She had to go to the Town Hall to undo what she had done that evening in her childhood.

As she went to meet Monsieur de Longeville, she was unaware of the bright day, of the atmosphere of happiness that seemed to lie quivering over the countryside.

He took her hand and she ceased to think. For a few moments they walked side by side, in silence.

Then, Monsieur de Longeville said: "I've been thinking things over all night, so as to make no light decision. I think you will make an excellent Marquise de Longeville, Marguerite. You are already my wife according to your law. I wish you to be so according to mine. The priest has been summoned and is awaiting us."

She was never able to remember whether the church bells rang that morning or not.

As Monsieur de Longeville had foreseen, she made an excellent marquise. It merely took her a little while to get out of the habit of calling her husband "Monsieur le Marquis."

She gave him a daughter with round calves, auburn hair and eyelids like rose petals, who made a very distinguished marriage and, after their death, sold the château.

A MATTER OF LUCK

TO GEORGES KESSEL

❧ ❧ ❧ It was eleven o'clock in the morning, and Monsieur Mawar had just got out of bed in green silk pajamas. An immense, a monstrous figure, he seemed to overflow the fake Louis XVI chair. His belly sagged between his thighs and the lobes of his ears hung low, while a twelve-carat diamond ring sank into the flesh of his little finger.

You may, if no others have been available, have bought Mawar cigarettes. They are short, flat and Egyptian. They smell of hay; and you may well have said: "They're not as bad as all that." You may even have read, in an absentminded sort of way, under the gold medals awarded at International Exhibitions in the nineteenth century: "Manufactured in Alexandria, Brussels and Zurich. Make sure that the signature *Mawar Brothers* is on every box. Imitations are liable to prosecution." But it is unlikely that it will occur to you that there is in fact a Monsieur Mawar, the heir to the two gentlemen in fezzes, whose profiles adorn the inside of the lid. But there *is* a real Monsieur Mawar made of flesh and fat. Every day of his life, he benefits from a small royalty paid him by some five hundred thousand smokers spread over the world, and so he is able to spend the spring of every year in a luxurious suite in the Hôtel de Paris in Monte Carlo, where, every evening of his stay, he leaves several million francs on the gambling tables.

Huge bunches of lilies were spreading their sweetly suffocating scent; the sun was warming the windows of the corner drawing-room, from which could be seen the gardens, the Casino and the sea.

On the table lay an oblong mahogany box from which his soft white hand, that looked as if it was molded in lard, was drawing cards one after another, pairing them, turning them up, pushing them away and slipping out new ones. And at every pair, Monsieur Mawar sighed deeply. For he was winning.

"A hand eleven times running!" he said to himself in a low voice. "And it never, never happens in the evening. It's really too exasperating."

He knew that he would enter the Casino at about eleven o'clock that evening, with a flower in his buttonhole, while the employees bowed particularly low. He would take his re-served place at the big table; a servant would push his chair under him, and another place a whisky and soda at his left hand, while the money-changer placed a pile of chips in front of him. He would hear the whispering: "Mawar, it's Mawar, Mawar's here . . ." People would gather round to watch him play. He would note the varied expressions of covetousness. And then, as yesterday, the day before and every other day, he would turn up a five or worse, and his opponent would turn up nine.

The worst of it was that Mawar's mistress *de louange* this year was an agreeable creature with golden hair and plenty of passive goodwill, but she was not in the least interested in the Casino. She loved pearl necklaces and diamond bracelets but she was bored at the gaming table. Neither cards nor roulette meant anything to her. She was quite maddening.

Mawar pushed the baccarat shoe to one side, and tried to forget his imaginary opponents and magnificent cards.

"What's it all about?" he asked. He had not really understood what the porter was trying to explain on the telephone, and had replied without thinking: "Send him up."

He did not need to raise his eyes far to understand what it was about. The socks, the worn cloth of his trousers, even the way he held his knees, told him all he needed to know about the man who had just come in.

Wearily, he took the letter the man held out to him, read it with bored indifference and dropped it on the floor. He turned his head away toward the window; and his left cheek fell into three rolls of fat on the collar of his pajamas.

The slowness of Monsieur Mawar's movements was very trying to the man standing there. He was about fifty years old, frail and weak in appearance, and had that air of obsequious humility which results from long years of adversity. He was wearing a mourning-band on his sleeve. He had spent a hundred francs on a close shave and on having his single wispy lock of hair oiled into place across his bald head. He could still feel the smarting of the razor on his cheeks; he would have a rash for the next forty-eight hours. And Monsieur Mawar had not even looked at his face!

The little man felt as if his clothes were too big for him, and sweat was trickling down his back. His nervousness made his morning coffee come back on him.

Still gazing out of the window at the palm-trees in the garden and the façade of the Casino, Monsieur Mawar said in a sharp, high-pitched voice which seemed odd coming from such a monument of fat: "I don't know why Monsieur Oudry sent you to me. I don't like letters of recommendation. Why hasn't Monsieur Oudry given you a job? I've got nothing for you! I'm not a charitable organization. If I listened to everyone, I'd have two hundred people waiting at my door. I can do nothing for you, nothing at all."

The room with its windows, lilies, and carpets seemed to reel about the little clerk. He sadly shook his head, which disarranged the lock of hair and revealed a large purple

birthmark on his bald skull. It had an odd shape, rather like
an egg, or perhaps like an imperfectly closed zero. It might
have been the symbol of his destiny, a rubber stamp with
which Fate had marked him at birth.

"I understand," said the little man. "I can see it's no use
persisting. I've never had any luck."

"That's right, my friend. It's never any use persisting."

The little man bowed vaguely and went to the door.

Mawar reached out his hand toward the baccarat shoe
again, but paused, and suddenly, just as the little man was
about to close the door into the passage, he cried: "Hey!
Come back! What's your name?"

"Florentin."

"Is that your surname or your Christian name?"

"My surname. On my father's side, my family were of
Italian origin, Fiorentini. . . ."

"All right, never mind about that. You say you've never
had any luck?"

Mawar stared at the little man's grey, pimply face, the
scrawny neck in the ill-starched semi-hard collar, and the
purple birthmark.

"Honest," he thought. "Certainly honest. Not intelligent,
of course; he could hardly be both."

He never made a mistake about men when he took the
trouble to look at them attentively for a moment.

"Well, Monsieur Florentin, do you want to earn twenty
thousand francs a day?"

"Oh, Monsieur!" cried the other. "That's impossible!"

"I'm not joking. But I shall require you at night, only at
night."

Such a salary as that made Monsieur Florentin wonder
whether he was required for some vile and illicit purpose.
There was so much gossip about the depraved pleasures of
the very rich! Twenty thousand francs a day, six hundred
thousand francs a month, when for a tenth of that sum

he would have run and lit a candle to St. Rita, patron saint
of those in desperate straits. What frightful task was he
being asked to do in return for such a salary? Or had there
been some mistake?

"A day . . ." he repeated.

"Yes. And it won't be difficult. This is what I shall want
you to do. You will come and meet me every evening at
ten o'clock wherever I happen to be dining: here, or in a
restaurant. I shall give you two hundred thousand francs.
You will go to the Casino. . . . Have you ever been to the
Casino? Have you ever gambled?" asked Mawar, suddenly
aware of Monsieur Florentin's astonishment. "Of course
not. It's quite all right, just what I expected. You will go
to the Casino then, and you will lose the two hundred
thousand francs. You will *lose* them, do you understand?
You will lose them as quickly as possible and by any method
you please. And it'll do you no good to cheat and put some
of the money in your own pocket. As you may well imagine,
I have means of checking up on you. And then, when you've
done, you'll come back to me and you'll say: 'Monsieur
Mawar, I've lost the lot.' I shall give you your twenty thousand francs and you'll be free till next day. That's the job.
Like it?"

Florentin looked at Mawar, his flat ears, his fat breast
that could be seen between his jade green pajamas, as if
he were looking at some frightening oriental god with supernatural powers. What was the secret? Monsieur Mawar was
ugly, but he did not look in the least mad.

Monsieur Florentin bowed very low and said: "Very
well, Monsieur Mawar, thank you very much. When do I
start?"

"Tonight," said the fat man.

Monsieur Florentin made his way into the gambling-room.
He was struck by the height of the ceiling, the melancholy

opulence of the decorations, the deathly hush that lay over this place that seemed half-temple and half-morgue, and by the atmosphere of nervous tension that seemed to emanate from the several hundreds of people who stood in rigid, if controlled, excitement round the tables. One might well have wondered whether chance was undergoing a post-mortem or being committed to the grave. Impassive, black-clothed men were performing mysterious rites with the precision of surgeons, carving incisively into piled lengths of chips long as intestines on the green cloths of the tables; while voices, sonorous and indifferent as archdeacons', announced mysteriously: *"Le sept! Impair, rouge et manque. Six cents louis à la banque. Avec la table."*

Balls spun in circular ebony troughs, cards were laid out in long rows as if in hasty divination of a future which seemed to content no one when it came, wooden shoes passed from hand to hand about a table which, as if at some failure of a séance, the adepts seemed unable to turn. Everyone could apparently select his own cult, his particular Black Mass, his favorite sorcery.

For some time Florentin wandered among the silent crowd, trying vainly to understand and initiate himself. He saw a man behind a counter receiving bank-notes and giving people chips in return, which they then threw on the tables. He followed their example, and held out his wad of notes.

"Chips of what value?" asked the money-changer.

"I don't mind."

He was given a heap of assorted bakelite and filled the pockets of his old coat with it. Then he went to a table, and found that he was standing next to an old woman with a hump.

"Hunchbacks bring good luck," he thought. He hesitantly placed a chip marked "1,000" on the cloth. The ball ceased moving in the ebony trough. The croupier's rake had gathered up the chip with many others. Florentin gave a start of surprise and disappointment. But then he thought: "It's all right, I'm supposed to lose."

He noticed that the hunchbacked woman was given back her chip with a few more too. He shrugged his shoulders, moved to another table, threw down a chip marked "5,000" and saw it raked away like the first. For a time, he went on doing the same thing, though the whole performance was a mystery to him and he felt as if he were wandering through a dream, some curious scene of utter unreality. Figments of the night and of the day became confused in his mind. Surely this was all a nightmare: hunchbacked women, unreal croupiers? He was simply dreaming that he had gone into a Casino and was gambling. He was dreaming that a buddha in green pajamas had ordered him to lose.

As his coat-pockets began to empty, Florentin felt an absurd but insistent terror. Could it really be true that the green buddha was going to pay him for losing two hundred thousand francs? Or was there some hideous plot behind it all? "Suppose he's been making me spend forged bank-notes? Will they arrest me on the way out? But that's ridiculous; in that case he wouldn't have insisted on my losing."

He felt his pockets. They were empty. It was midnight. Florentin made his way out of the Casino; the lamps cast a soft light over the palm-trees in the gardens. The Milky Way looked like a fisherman's net full of bright little fish spread across the sky.

As he made his way toward the restaurant where Monsieur Mawar had told him to meet him, Florentin felt even more ill at ease than he had that morning at their first interview. For ten minutes he walked up and down in front of the door, not daring to go in. The commissionaire stared at him suspiciously. In the end he managed to pull himself together.

Monsieur Mawar was wearing a splendid white dinner-jacket adorned with a red carnation; his stomach hung low between his thighs; his ears stuck out each side of his head; and his diamond was glittering on his little finger. He had finished his dinner and was drinking champagne with a few friends. Beside him sat a young woman with a pale expressionless face; her neck and ears were laden with pearls, and from time to time the fat man stroked her slender arm.

Florentin crossed the restaurant. He felt ashamed and he swallowed nervously.

"Well?" Mawar asked.

"I've done it, Monsieur Mawar, I've lost the lot," Florentin replied. He dared not raise his eyes from the ground.

"You've taken your time about it!" said Mawar. "However it's only the first day. No doubt you'll manage better tomorrow."

He took twenty thousand francs from his pocket and handed them to Florentin.

"There you are. Tomorrow at the same time. Good night."

The next day, Monsieur Florentin took no more than fifty minutes to complete his task. And on the following days he made even better time.

He learned just as much as he required of the technique of gambling, for he very soon realized that the results demanded of him could be obtained quite quickly and with very little trouble.

A few *en pleins* at Roulette, a couple of shots at Trente et Quarante, and a *banco* or two; and it was all over in ten minutes, a quarter of an hour at most. He divided his capital into chips of five, ten and fifty thousand. If, on occasion, he doubled his stake on an even chance, he left it for the next turn of the wheel and the croupier's rake inevitably gathered it in.

And if he foolishly won a *banco*, he just said "*Suivi*" and it all went with the next cards. It was both easy and sure.

He had then only to walk a short way through the bright, warm night.

"Good evening, Monsieur Mawar."

"Good evening, my friend. Here are your twenty thousand francs. See you tomorrow."

"See you tomorrow, Monsieur Mawar."

It was a well-paid job.

Nevertheless, Monsieur Florentin soon discovered how easy it was to live at the rate of twenty thousand francs a day, particularly in Monte Carlo. He took a room in a decent hotel, ate his fill, bought some new clothes, enjoyed the leisure of his days. Every shop-window and every smile tempted him. He went in a taxi to see the sights for ten kilometres around. His hair seemed to have more life in it now and hid the violet zero on his skull with greater success. Now that he could entertain them he made several friends. He even thought of getting married.

It never occurred to him to keep a penny of the money Mawar gave him every day. The two sums seemed to him to belong to two different currencies. The twenty thousand francs were ordinary money for common use, the sort of money people used in business and paid you for your work. But the two hundred thousand francs were made of quite different stuff; it bore no relation either to your work or to your needs. It was a sort of imaginary abstraction: gambling money!

At the Casino, the little man with the funny lock of hair, who looked like a bailiff's clerk in a hurry to get the inventory finished, came, said not a word to anyone, changed two hundred thousand francs, lost them every night, and went off rubbing his hands, was becoming quite a figure. He aroused curiosity, even in a place so accustomed to the eccentric, the obsessed and the crazy. Besides, everyone secretly hated him. "There's the little fellow in black who brings bad luck," the gamblers would say. As for the croupiers, they had noticed

that Monsieur Florentin, whenever he did happen to have a
lucky break, never left anything for *le personnel*, which gamblers normally do, not necessarily from generosity but because it brings good luck. They also noticed that since he
had come, Monsieur Mawar had left off visiting the Casino.

This had been going on for twenty-three days when Monsieur Florentin happened to throw ten thousand francs *en
plein* on number 34. It might just as well have landed on the
32 or 35. It mattered not at all. Monsieur Florentin had
already turned away and was moving off, so he failed to
hear the croupier announce: "*Le trente-quatre.*" The croupier
called after him.

"Monsieur, it's yours, you've won."

"Very well, leave it on," Florentin said automatically.

"It can't be done, Monsieur, the maximum is ten thousand, your original stake."

And Florentin was handed three hundred and sixty thousand francs.

"*Rien ne va plus . . . le trent-quatre,*" announced the
croupier for the second time.

"Oh!" sighed the crowd round the table in stupefaction,
and Florentin received another three hundred and sixty
thousand francs.

Monsieur Florentin was quite taken aback. Wondering
how to lose his winnings as quickly as possible, he went to
the Trente et Quarante table where the maximum stake was
five hundred thousand. And six times running a chip for
another half-million fell to him.

"*Fin de la taille,*" announced the croupier.

"This table's no good," he thought. "I shall have to
hurry. Monsieur Mawar will be waiting for me." He had
nearly four millions in his hands; and four millions are not
so easy to lose as all that.

That evening the Casino witnessed a very extraordinary
sight. A little man with a lock of hair across his forehead

and an aubergine-colored zero on his bald skull was running
from table to table, playing with a mad fury that took no
account of any of the rules or systems of gambling. He never
even left himself the opportunity of doubling up; he staked
suicidally and yet never stopped winning. If he threw a chip
into the air, it turned into a rain of chips. If he lost a stake
at one table, he found it quadrupled on another. Chips
flowed toward him like a river in spate, with little tributaries,
also suddenly swollen, pouring into it, so that the level never
stopped rising.

It was as if the numbers themselves were fantastically in
league, all the thousands of numbers on all the tables,
wheels, cards and chips. They seemed to have some mutual
understanding and to be multiplying each other. And among
them all, Florentin spun like a soap bubble.

Time was passing and Florentin's chips were accumulating; he had constantly to go to the money-changer for chips
of a million francs, which were more convenient.

He went to the *tout va*, and put four millions on each
of the two tables. His mouth felt dry and he drank a glass of
soda-water for which he paid with what remained to him
of his yesterday's twenty thousand francs.

When he came back there was a crowd around him; but
he did not realize why. In the moment that he had been
away his eight millions had produced thirty-two. The shoe
was empty. The banker took fright and called the game to
an end.

Florentin was driven to the big Chemin de Fer table, at
the place which used to be reserved for Monsieur Mawar.
He thought for a moment he was losing, and then saw the
pile of chips opposite him assume prodigious proportions.
He then did something which is never done. There was a
huge sum at stake and he held an eight. He drew a card
instead of turning one up. It was an ace. The bank had
eight. His angry, disgusted opponents left the table. Flor-

entin never knew he had been playing against the Maharajah of Pendura, the millionaire Marielli, the Duke of Marascal, and Constantin Sardak, the greatest film producer in the United States.

The gambling-rooms began to empty. The gamblers, the croupiers, everyone seemed utterly shattered. It was the finish; the Casino was closing down. Florentin alone seemed still alive, intoxicated by the miracle. His brow felt hot, his nerves were tingling. He was full of a joy he had never known before. He wanted to go on playing.

"No Monsieur, no more play tonight."

Florentin looked at his watch, the new watch he had bought two days before. It was five o'clock in the morning. In all, he had won forty-seven millions, besides "chicken-feed." Lavish for the first time, he left the "chicken-feed," a hundred and twelve thousand francs, *pour le personnel.* "Monsieur Mawar would certainly approve."

Then, weighed down with the fortune that overflowed his pockets, he hastened out of the Casino to the all-night restaurant. "Monsieur Mawar is bound to have left," he thought.

But Monsieur Mawar was still there, sitting motionless on a banquette, his stomach pendulous as ever, with his mistress beside him, dripping with emeralds. They were among the last customers. Two couples, exhausted from lack of sleep, were still dancing in the subaqueous light.

Florentin hurried in, nearly fell as he crossed the dance floor. "Look, Monsieur Mawar!" he cried. "Look what I've won!"

He was exultant and stammered in his excitement, as he laid the notes and chips on the table.

The fat man, with his dark eyes, never moved, never gave even so much as a quiver. He simply gave a slight smile.

"This is what I've been expecting. I knew it was bound to happen. I know that gambling doesn't interest you," he added, turning to his mistress, "but now you can see that it *is* interesting. This man told me that he had never had any luck. So I sent him to lose. I made him play against his luck. You see, when one plays to win every day, as I did, one invariably loses, so I thought that if he played every day to lose, a day would inevitably come when chance forced him to win. . . . Two hundred thousand times twenty-three, that makes an outlay of about five millions, in exchange for some fifty millions. You must admit that it's not so much. . . ."

Florentin was not listening. "What will he give me as a bonus?" he thought. "He ought to give me five per cent, or perhaps ten."

"Thank you, my friend, good night. I shan't need you any more," said Mawar, wrapping the money up in a table-napkin.

"Do you think, Monsieur Mawar . . . Could you, perhaps . . ." stammered Florentin.

The fat man stared at him in surprise. "Well?" he said, calmly tying the corners of the napkin together, and Florentin suddenly felt himself growing pale.

"But Monsieur Mawar, my twenty thousand francs? Not even that?"

"Oh, no, my friend," replied Mawar. "I gave you the money to lose, not to win. Thank you. I shall have no further need of your services."

Monsieur Florentin went out. His head was bowed, his brain numb. He shivered in the early dawn. His elation had suddenly turned to utter misery.

He still had a few notes left over from yesterday's pay. He went and drank a coffee in a little bar to which the croupiers went, when the Casino had closed, and where gathered chauffeurs, tramps, flower-sellers, and the more unlucky gamblers. Everyone stared at him, and everyone whispered about him. He did not finish his cup.

The legend of Monte Carlo is full of tragedies, and they have given up counting the number of people, whose last chance having faded, opened their veins in their bath, put a bullet in their brains, or drowned themselves in the sea. But nobody could understand the suicide of this little man with a zero on his forehead, who was found that morning at the foot of the famous rock, a shattered corpse. He was the only gambler who had ever killed himself after a run of luck.

AN OLD LOVE

❦ ❦ ❦ For nearly ten years, Mother Léger had been saying to her husband: "Léger, you're the oldest man in the village now; it's going to be your turn next."

And old Léger, knocking his pipe out against a fire-dog, would reply: "It'd only be just, wife; I've had my time. I'll go and wait for you up the hill."

The hill was where the cemetery lay, and their cottage was on a corner of the road leading to it. Funerals were bound to pass the door.

Old Léger had long passed the allotted span. He was the only inhabitant of the village who had seen the calvary on the Quatremare road without the cornel-tree shading it. Unless it was his father who had told him about it. But Anatole Léger's memory went back so far that his own and his father's recollections often became confused. He was sure of one thing, however, and that was that as a boy he had picked cornels. And no one knew how many years it was since the tree had stopped bearing.

Old Léger had worked all his life on the same farm, first as a boy, then as a farm-hand, and finally as headman. He had known three generations of masters, and had left only when the land had changed hands.

Now he was blind and scarcely moved at all. For the last ten years, his wife had dressed and undressed him, shaved him twice a week and led him by the hand whenever he had to take a step or two.

He spent his days sitting very straight on his straw-bot-

tomed chair, his hands on his knees, by the corner of the
fire which burnt winter and summer in the cottage's single
room.

On this July day, Mother Léger was weeding in the garden.
She suddenly saw black spots before her eyes; there was a singing in her ears; and she had to lean on the rake so as not to
fall down.

"It must be the heat," she thought.

She sat down for a while in the shade.

But the black spots continued to flicker before her eyes. She
was stifling. She returned to the house. She wanted to iron one
of Léger's smocks; but, as she was arranging the folds, the
whole room began to swing round her.

"Surely, wife, it's the day for my shave," said old Léger.

"I'll do it this evening; I'm not feeling well."

She was suffocating, and felt as if her neck were about to
burst.

About the middle of the afternoon, a neighbor became concerned about her dark flush and went to fetch the doctor.

The doctor found Mother Léger collapsed on a stool and
unable to loosen her stays.

"I've never been ill. I've never been ill. It won't be anything
serious," she muttered.

The doctor tried to bleed her. But her blood was black and
coagulated, refusing to flow.

"Mother Léger," he said, "I never hide the truth. If you
have any particular wishes, you shouldn't delay."

As she did not seem to understand, and he had no wish to
suffer the family's reproaches—"the notary wasn't summoned;
the priest wasn't sent for"—he added gently: "My poor
Mother Léger, you're going to die."

When old Léger heard the doctor's words he stopped thinking about his unshaven beard, and his twisted old hands began
trembling.

He had married the beautiful Marie when he was already

headman. She was sixteen years younger than he was, and their marriage had aroused a lot of talk.

He had watched Marie grow old beside him day by day; but he had a start on her. And, during these last years, when Marie Léger's face had become a mass of red veins, the skin of her scalp had begun to show through her worn hair, and she had suffered from "dropsy in the stomach," as she called it, Anatole Léger was already blind.

Since his most distant memories were the clearest, the image of Marie growing old had vanished, and, when he thought of her, it was her face at twenty that he saw. And now he could not understand at first how God could allow so beautiful a girl to die. He had to make a great effort to remember that she was—what was it?—ninety-three less sixteen . . . He could not make the calculation; but his hands stopped trembling because he dozed off and forgot that his beautiful Marie was dying.

Marie was in bed; her lips were violet, and her huge stomach made a mound of the eiderdown. Through a sooty fog, she saw the priest arrive, followed by a choirboy carrying a bell. The priest had no more success in getting a word out of her than had the doctor in drawing blood. While he was questioning her, she began gasping for breath through her half-open mouth. She could hear a sort of vague whispering and a black rain seemed to be falling on the priest's face and the boy's surplice.

That evening, Marie Léger's harsh breathing ceased; she seemed to feel stronger, and she heard a grave voice saying: "Mother Léger, you're going to die."

She no longer knew whose voice it was, nor when the words had been uttered; but there was panic in her heart and the soot began to fall again. She called: "Léger! . . . Léger! . . ."

For some time old Léger had been expecting Marie to come and undress him. But then he had fallen asleep, his pipe in his hand.

His wife's cries half-awakened him.

Marie Léger was delirious. She was going up the hill. She seemed to be lying in bed and yet walking at the same time. A big black bird was pecking at her chest, and the bird had the frightful head of a demon with a parrot's beak, and the beak was laughing. Mother Léger felt as if she were enormously tall. And it was raining.

She stopped at the cornel-tree by the Quatremare calvary, which meant a considerable detour on the way to the cemetery. There the bird pecked her less hard and Mother Léger's feet became tiny and seemed to be a long way off. She felt less pain.

"The storm has broken a branch off the cornel-tree," she said.

"It's like us, wife, growing old; but it's holding out just the same."

At the sound of her husband's voice, Mother Léger came down the hill again in her bed. Through the open window she could see the July night; the bright moon lit up old Léger at the chimney corner, sitting upright on his chair, his white moustaches standing out each side of his face.

The black bird had begun pecking again. It had the wicked face of Ferdinand the cowman. That was why it hurt so much! Ferdinand the cowman followed her everywhere. Even in the laundry she found him standing behind her. He had one eye closed and a satanic laugh. And the day he had tried to assault her in the sunken lane, she had told Anatole. Ferdinand the cowman was tall and strong, but Anatole was still taller and stronger, and much more handsome. She had never deceived him. And Anatole had taken his headman's whip to him in the farmyard. Ferdinand the cowman was growing old, and the bells were ringing.

"For whom are they tolling the knell?" asked old Léger.

"For Ferdinand the cowman."

Old Léger no longer bore Ferdinand a grudge. And Mother

Léger led her husband to the church for Ferdinand's funeral.

"Léger, you're the oldest man in the village now; it's going to be your turn next."

It was cold. Old Léger thought it was morning, and could not understand how he came to be already dressed. As he did each morning, he took an old pig's bladder from his trouser pocket and slowly filled his pipe.

Then he replied, once more: "It'd only be just, I've had my time. I'll go and wait for you up the hill."

The church clock began chiming in the distance. Mother Léger did not hear it because there were already too many bells ringing in her ears. But old Léger counted the strokes in a whisper, as he always did . . . Three . . . four . . . He stopped at seven; but the church went on to eleven. And then old Léger became anxious. It was far too chilly to be eleven o'clock in the morning. How was it that he was still awake so late at night?

He heard: "Anatole, Anatole!"

That was what his wife used to call him in the early days of their marriage. Then he remembered that all his life had slipped away; he felt unutterably sad, and his hands trembled so much he could scarcely hold his pipe.

Meanwhile Marie Léger had reached the hill, to lie there beside old Léger. But it was Ferdinand the cowman who was waiting for her at the gate.

"Anatole!"

Her legs felt like lead and she could not get away. Struggle as she might, she was caught by the feet, like a blackbird in bird-lime. And Ferdinand was coming closer. He was laughing his wicked laugh; she could see the inside of his hairy nostrils. Ferdinand's hand was growing bigger, becoming huge, and Mother Léger felt it crushing her breast. At last her legs grew lighter and she fled, which made her heart beat terribly. She heard the sound of clogs pursuing her. She turned and saw the cowman running toward the cottage in the moonlight.

"Anatole, close the window!" she cried.

"Are you cold, wife?" replied old Léger. "You know very well I can't see; you'll have to guide me."

His sorrow weighed heavily on him. Was Marie so near her end that she had forgotten he was blind?

He felt he must do something for her. He knocked out his pipe, put it in his pocket and got up from his chair. And then he just stood there, not daring to move.

When Mother Léger saw her husband on his feet, she started. Her delirium turned to anger. Léger had lied to her: he would not be waiting for her up the hill. "Mother Léger, you're going to die. . . ." And here he stayed while she was dying. That he should have passed up his turn for all the other old people in the village made her proud and happy. But not when it was for her. He had sworn never to leave her.

She wanted Anatole to go up the hill first. If he did not, the black bird and Ferdinand would never leave her in peace. If only she could push him up in front of her.

"Walk," she said. "I'll guide you."

Old Léger obeyed. With his hands held out in front of him, his feet scraping along the floor, and his tall body bent in the moonlight, he crossed the room, bearing his own night.

"Is there nothing in front of me?" he asked.

"Go straight on."

Anatole's hand's touched an obstacle.

"Wife, I've reached the table."

"Turn left. That's right. Go on, Léger."

From her bed, the dying woman watched every movement the old man made. It was using up the last of her strength. And the black bird was pecking and pecking.

Old Léger had come to a halt and was fumbling the empty air.

"Am I still far from it?"

The edge of the open window was half a pace from him.

"Go on. Don't be afraid!"

The old man's hands passed each side of the pane, and his head bumped the wooden frame. For a moment he was stunned. He could no longer remember why he was there.

"Where must I go now?" he asked.

"Up the hill," replied Mother Léger.

Old Léger was seized with panic. He wanted to get back to his chair; but he banged his thigh against the corner of the table. He started off again, wandered about for a long time, feeling his way along the walls and round the furniture. At last, he found the chimney-piece and then his chair. He sat down exhausted.

There was no sound but the ticking of the clock's pendulum. Old Léger knew now that his wife would never again lead him by the hand. He knew, too, that all his most exquisite memories of Marie—Marie on the road, one autumn evening, when they played at who could walk the faster, and he had kissed her for the first time; Marie in her veil on their wedding day; Marie haymaking early in her pregnancy, before it showed—he knew that these memories would not long be his now, and that they would dissolve in the universal sleep.

"Mother Léger . . ." Was she dozing or had she lost consciousness? She felt as if she were floating up from the bottom of a lake. "Yes, Doctor, I know. But who's going to shave Léger? He won't stand any hand but mine. And who'll prepare his food?"

The thick Turkey red eiderdown, on which the moonlight was playing, formed a mound over her as at the time of her pregnancy.

"Anatole, give me my sewing," she said.

Then she remembered. Anatole could not answer. He had killed himself by banging his head against the window. At his age, it was bound to be more than he could bear.

Yet, here was Anatole standing up and saying: "Where is your sewing? You must guide me, you know!"

But then what about the hill? Had he forgotten? At meals,

he was served first. At church, he went in before her. Always
and everywhere she had followed him, happy merely to walk
behind him. She would find some way of making him die
first.

"Go on, there's nothing in front of you."

Old Léger knocked his shin against the edge of the stool.

The church clock was striking midnight. Old Léger
stopped to count the strokes.

"But you can't see to guide me; it's too dark," he said.

"Oh, yes. I can see; there's plenty of moonlight. There,
you've reached it. Can you feel it? It's the dresser. Open
it. At the bottom, on the left."

Slowly, jerkily, the old man bent down.

"She must be able to see all right," he thought, as his
fingers found the work-basket. He straightened up even more
painfully.

"Follow the wall. Go on, don't be afraid."

It seemed to old Léger that it was not the right direction
for the bed. Nevertheless, he went on. His hands were engaged in holding the basket. He heard the ticking of the
pendulum quite close to him. He tried to make a detour
round the clock. He thought he had passed it, when he
knocked heavily against it.

It was a tall old grandfather clock, and it reeled on its
unsteady, worm-eaten feet. One of them must have been
rotten through and through, for it gave way and old Léger
felt the long case topple over against his shoulder. He dropped
the basket and struggled with the clock. The strike, which
had not worked for years, suddenly began sounding. The
weight fell with a lunatic noise of cog-wheels, and the clock
struck all the hours of the day.

Old Léger gave up the struggle; he was beaten as much
by the noise as by exhaustion. His head ached; his forehead
felt as if it were on fire. Let the clock fall and break if it

wanted to. It, also, had come to the end of its time and its usefulness.

The clock stayed as it was, leaning a little to one side because of its rotten foot, but a great deal less than the blind man imagined. Old Léger could hardly stand up now. The whitewash flaked off on his hands as he felt his way along the wall. Then he came to a change of surface as he groped his way across the wood of the door. He had circled the room and was almost back to the chimney-piece.

It seemed to Mother Léger that the bed was collapsing under her, sometimes even capsizing. She felt as if she were trapped beneath it and suffocating. Then the bed would turn right way up again and she had a moment's respite to stare at the palely gleaming colored post office calendar which hung beside her from the same nail as the sprig of box.

"Do you realize, Léger, that it was our Golden Wedding yesterday?"

In fact, it had not really been yesterday, but eight years ago. But old Léger's thoughts were cast so firmly in the mold of memory that he replied in precisely the same words he had used eight years before: "It's just as well it should have come and gone without our noticing it, wife; now that the boy's dead, we've nothing more to hope for."

The boy. Mother Léger had been at the grocer's when Mother Joly, the postwoman, had given her the telegram. To think that the boy had gone through the whole war with nothing worse than pneumonia, only to get himself crushed by scaffolding when he was forty-nine, and not even at home.

Mother Léger could feel the girders crushing her chest. Really, there was no justice in the world; God had no compassion. And the price they demanded for a sealed railway-truck. The boy had been healthy enough, so why a sealed railway-truck? Poor people could not afford things like that. But there it was, and he would not be lying up the hill. One had to resign oneself to it.

"Léger, give me the boy's certificate."

And then she muttered about the black crepe veil she had put away in the cupboard. She would need it again now, when old Léger was carried up the hill by six Brothers of Charity dressed like archdeacons.

"What do you want, wife? Your veil or the certificate?"

"The certificate. You know where it is, on the ledge of the chimney-piece above you. Don't be afraid, just get up."

But old Léger wasn't going to get up just like that! He knew that chimney-piece; it was his own special corner. He knew its every dimension, its every projection; the corner of the ledge was immediately above his head.

Why did his wife want him to get up? "It's not normal," he thought. There had been the window, then the stool, then the clock. "Is it that she can't see, or is she doing it on purpose?" he wondered, as he got prudently to his feet.

His fingers found the thin rough frame containing his son's certificate of primary education on the ledge of the chimney-piece. He remembered how the boy had made the frame himself. Marie had later slipped the photograph of an infantryman with a fair moustache into a corner of it.

Old Léger groped his way over to the bed.

"There, Marie," he said, "there's the boy."

He thought she had taken the frame from him, but he heard the glass shatter on the floor.

"It must have been the veil she wanted," he thought.

The cupboard was quite close to the bed. Old Léger remembered the feel of it from the past. The door opened easily enough, just as he remembered. He did not open it wide. His hands wandered over the shelves. He felt a pile of sheets and behind it a rosary and a boy's school smock.

He continued to fumble about and found a thin, carefully folded piece of stuff. Mother Léger seemed to be talking at random; but old Léger heard her say: "Up the hill. You must go up there, Léger. Why won't you wait for me there?"

Then her voice lapsed into an inarticulate gurgle.

"Marie Mouchet," he thought, remembering suddenly, as if it had some specially appropriate significance, his wife's maiden name. He was beside the bed now, his knees leaning against the mattress.

His fingers moved in an old gesture of tenderness; he wanted to stroke Marie's forehead. But his hand found only her mouth from which there was issuing something hot and sticky; he automatically wiped his hand on the veil he believed to be black. Then he went back to the chimney corner and his chair. On the way, he dropped the veil.

He kept repeating to himself: "Up the hill . . . up the hill . . ." It was indeed true that he had always promised to await her there! And perhaps the clock and the window had been to remind him of it. Because when Marie once got an idea in her head . . . Poor, beautiful Marie! What would he do without her? They would put him in the home in the county town. And then they would bury him all by himself in another cemetery, like the boy.

"Marie, I have no light but you!" he murmured.

He could no longer think clearly. He had a headache and felt terribly sleepy. He listened to Marie's breathing. All that remained of his capacity to think was concentrated on this last evidence of the fact that his wife still lived.

Marie's breathing was short, whistling and intermittent. Old Anatole made his own breathing chime with hers, his own breast rising and falling to the same uncertain rhythm. For a moment the whistling stopped; then began again for a little; then stopped again. There followed a gentle sigh.

As silence fell, he knew his beautiful Marie was dead. Once again, he saw the road in the autumn, when they had raced each other.

"I can walk faster than you, Marie; I'd have got there first . . ."

He had kissed her. Had it been on the road leading up the

hill? He thought he was getting to his feet. But he sat there motionless.

When day broke, the neighbors looked in through the still open window and saw Mother Léger lying on her bed, the whites of her eyes showing.

The clock, which had stopped at midnight, was leaning to one side. The room was in such disorder that one might have thought people had been fighting in it. A bridal veil was lying on the floor, and cotton-reels had rolled all over the place.

Old Léger was sitting in the chimney corner, his head bowed, his hands on his knees. He was cold; his body collapsed rigidly when they touched him on the shoulder. He had a little cut on his forehead and his beard, which had not been shaved, was still growing.

The next day, they were carried up the hill, the husband in front, as was proper.

Part Two

GONE AWAY!

TO RENÉ JULLIARD

I

❦ ❦ ❦ The hunt was going home. A thin, misty drizzle of October rain mingled with the acrid smell of wet horses and the evening scents of the forest.

There was one man riding alone in the lead. The shape of his bony, slightly sloping shoulders showed beneath the soaking red cloth of his coat. He carried a hunting-horn across his chest.

He was stroking his big bay mare's streaming neck with the handle of his whip. She twitched her ears as she picked her way among the puddles.

"On you go, Queen of Hearts, on you go," he muttered.

Then he began humming the "Gone Away!"

It was hardly the time for it since they were going home. But he was not using his horn, merely humming the notes automatically to himself between thin lips that had been trained to the horn since childhood; and indeed it was not so much a humming as a little private fanfare whose phrases died away in the forest.

The wet seemed to have drowned all talk among the hunt servants following behind him. There was no sound but the squelching of mud beneath the horses' hooves and the brief call, repeated over and over again, from the man's thin lips.

He suddenly fell silent and reined in Queen of Hearts.

From the wood on the left came the howls of a hound in pain. He bent his head to one side and listened.

A very young man in rat-catcher rode up to him.

"Monsieur de Serremuids?" he said shyly.

"Monsieur?"

"Did you hear that? It sounded as if a dog . . ."

"It's time you learnt, Monsieur, that a hound is not a dog."

The thin lips scarcely opened; the short greying moustache hardly moved.

The young man was new to the hunt. To make up for his lapse, he stammered: "I'm sorry. Would you like me . . . to go and see?"

"See what? I'm old enough to take care of my hounds myself."

Leaving his guest rooted to the spot, Baron de Serremuids put his mare into a gallop, jumped the ditch beside the road, and disappeared into the wood.

The skirts of his coat fluttered behind him. Water spurted up from the moss. He pressed the flanks of his mare with his booted legs, guiding her between the beeches which were in places so close together that they endangered his knees. He crossed a patch of heather, jumped in and out of a sunken road, and galloped on, bending low under the hanging branches. The rain dripped from them onto his hunting-cap.

The howling was closer now, more urgent. He came out into a clearing littered with felled trees.

At the farther side, he saw a kennelman in livery belaboring a hound with a crop. The hound was tied to a tree by a lead, pressing itself close to the ground and howling.

Serremuids galloped straight across the clearing and, taking his boot from the stirrup, kicked the kennelman on the shoulder and sent him sprawling.

Queen of Hearts had come to a halt. The kennelman, shaken by the blow, made no attempt to get up, and lay staring stupidly at his bleeding hand. The hound broke the lead and leapt at him, baying furiously.

The man's face seemed to sag; he curled himself into a ball. He was the hound's enemy; he was on the ground like an animal; and he was bleeding. He knew no hound forgave these things.

"Falot!" shouted Serremuids. "Bike here! Bike!"

The hound bayed once more, hackles raised, eyes bloodshot, and then came quietly to heel behind the mare.

The kennelman got heavily to his feet. He was quivering with both fear and anger. He was a dark, broad, tough-looking man.

"The hound bit me," he said.

He held out his bleeding wrist. He was still holding the crop.

"Because you're a brute," said Serremuids.

"He bit me," repeated the kennelman, "and it's not the first time either."

He advanced on Serremuids, brandishing the crop by the stock. For an instant his eyes met those of the Master, narrow and grey as flint beneath their dark brows.

Queen of Hearts shied. Serremuids, in one quick, strong movement, loosed the thong of his crop and cracked it in the kennelman's face. The man stood quite still, his arm raised.

"You deserve to be horse-whipped, do you hear?" said Serremuids. "I've had enough of you. This time you're definitely sacked."

He turned the mare and, cutting back through the wood, regained his place in front of the pack. Falot followed at the mare's heels, part of the leash still round his neck, and the weals of the whip showing up on his damp coat.

"La Brisée," called Serremuids.

The head huntsman trotted up. He was short, red-faced and no longer young, but he still looked physically fit.

"Monsieur le Baron?"

As he came up with the Master, he doffed his velvet cap and held it very straight across his chest. The rain dripped onto his bald head.

"Put your cap on," said Serremuids. "I've just sacked your son, La Brisée."

La Brisée saw the long angry crease that ran from the Master's nose to his chin. Then he looked at the hound.

"It's because of Falot, isn't it, Monsieur le Baron?" he said. "I thought as much. You can't help knowing the hounds' voices, particularly that one's. I ought to have gone myself."

Serremuids made no answer. He was staring at the steam rising from the mare's sweating neck. The huntsman still held his cap across his chest.

"It was bound to happen," he said. "Ever since Falot was entered, Jules and he have never got along. Hounds have their likes and dislikes. I've often told Jules he mustn't get across the hounds. It's a pity, because he's good enough at his work."

"No. I won't keep him," Serremuids cut in. "Not so much because he raised his hand to me . . ."

"He dared do that? To you, Monsieur!"

"We were boys together. It's not the first time I've knocked him down."

They fell silent, each lost in his own thoughts. Château and kennels—their lives had run closely parallel for over thirty years, from the Master's infancy and the huntsman's prime.

"Monsieur has always been very kind to Jules," La Brisée said.

"Yes, but it's over now. You don't tie up a hound to beat it."

La Brisée suddenly sat up very straight in his saddle.

"Monsieur le Baron's quite right there. It's a disgraceful thing to do."

The rain was laying his scant grey hair smooth against his skull.

They were coming to the edge of the wood. Beyond it was a wide plain where the rain would beat down even more heavily.

"Put your cap on, I said."

La Brisée made as if to do so, but did not.

"I can understand that Monsieur no longer wants him with the pack," he said.

"Neither with the pack nor at the Château! Your son will leave tomorrow. I never want to see him again."

"Nor at the Château . . ." repeated the huntsman. "Monsieur le Baron will excuse me, but for all his faults Jules is all I have left. So, as far as I'm concerned . . ." he said hesitatingly.

He saw himself, old, a widower, his son sacked, all alone in the little cottage by the kennels, lighting his paraffin lamp tomorrow night for no one but himself.

"My dear Bernard, you must do as you think best."

Addressing the huntsman by his Christian name, instead of by his nickname by which he was known in the hunting-field, was deliberate on Serremuids's part, though it was also not devoid of affection. He began quietly humming the "Gone Away!" again.

La Brisée knew he was too old ever to accustom himself to another pack. He thought of all the things he would miss so badly: his red coat, the hounds, the forest and the sound of the "Gone Away!" which was like his daily bread to him.

"Well, as far as I am concerned," he said, "if Monsieur le Baron wishes it, I'll stay."

The bare-headed old huntsman, his eyes moist at the decision and sacrifice he had made, reined his horse in at the edge of the forest to let the Master take precedence in riding out into the plain.

II

When Baron de Serremuids received his mobilization papers, he went straight up to his room where his uniform of a lieutenant of the Reserve was laid out for him, and his kit stood ready, packed.

"Send for La Brisée," he said to his valet.

While changing and putting up his papers in his tunic pocket, he looked at himself in the looking-glass. The sight gave him no pleasure; he was too tall and too thin.

"Am I not too old to go to war?" he wondered.

Not at thirty-six, surely. The only sign of age was the thick lock of grey hair above the middle of his forehead.

"Men may think you're handsome, but not women," his first mistress had said when they were quarrelling one night.

Since then, he had had affairs with other women; but he had never forgotten that remark. It had never occurred to him that his grey eyes, his overlong nose and his thin unsmiling mouth could be attractive. Well, now he could be handsome for men. He flexed his muscles under the uniform, and spent a moment or two getting used to himself again.

He was putting on his belt when the huntsman came in.

"Is my army saddle ready?"

"Monsieur le Baron's orders have been carried out."

Serremuids took his pistol from the drawer of a desk.

"Uniform suits Monsieur very well," said La Brisée. "It makes him look younger."

"Does it?" said the Baron, turning round.

He saw that the huntsman was moved.

"You'll saddle Queen of Hearts at eleven o'clock," he went on, "and be at the Cavalry Barracks in Alençon in the afternoon. If anyone asks you, say she's my charger."

"Very good, Monsieur le Baron."

"And now see that my luggage is put in the car."

He went down the great white staircase, casting a glance at the hunting trophies on the wall: dozens of slots of stag and boar mounted on oak shields. All the staff of the Château was gathered in the hall. Serremuids, who had no wife or children, suddenly felt a sharp pang of loneliness.

He shook each one by the hand.

"Come back soon, Monsieur le Baron," said his steward. "You'll find everything in good order."

"I'm counting on you, Valentin."

He went out onto the stone steps. This last morning of August seemed to welcome him. A few dead leaves were already beginning to dry on the grass of the park. He knew every variation of this Norman air and recognized the first scents heralding autumn. The hunting season would soon be beginning, and he would not be here.

He walked across to the Chapel. The sun shining through the windows cast a glow of armorial bearings on the flag-stones. Serremuids knelt for a moment. His family lay here, under the worn stone. He had no one but the dead to whom to say good-by.

The car was ready waiting when he came out. La Brisée was holding the door. Serremuids turned to his people once again.

"Good luck to you all, my friends," he said.

He let in the clutch and drove down the gravel drive bordered by orange-trees in tubs. But instead of going out through the gate, he turned to the left in the park and stopped at the kennels. He went in, crop in hand. He stood looking at the hounds for a moment, as they came up to smell him.

"Falot!" he called.

Falot came to him with the sad eyes of a hound being left behind, and put his head against the Master's knee.

III

In the first squadron stables, men in fatigue dress were already grooming the horses. Few of them were working with much enthusiasm. As far as they were concerned, mobilization had begun with a job of hard work.

Only Corporal Jules Brisset seemed to have any taste for it. He had taken off his new fatigue-jacket; his thick striped cotton shirt hung in stiff folds over his belt; and the rolled-up

sleeves revealed strong hairy arms. With quick, precise movements, he passed the brush first over the horse and then over
the curry-comb: brushed up the wrong way, the horse's coat
showed the dirt; and this rhythmic alternation of horse, curry-
comb, horse, curry-comb produced in Jules Brisset a complete
absence of anger which in him was a sign of happiness.

There were beads of sweat on his forehead. The white scurf
rose in a cloud from the horse's rump. And Jules was singing
tunes which seemed always to end with: "Taïaut . . . hô!
Taïaut . . . hô!"

"You seem to like the job well enough, Corporal," said a
tall red-headed chap with high cheekbones, who was called
Duval.

"Oh, you don't have to be so formal these days, my lad,"
said the Corporal. "There's a war on."

"Not yet," said a thick-set peasant who was collecting dung
in a barrow.

"It's just like it though," said Duval. "If anyone had told
me I'd be called up again!"

He stood with his arms crossed on the back of his horse to
talk more comfortably.

"And what were you doing in civvy street?" he went on.

"I was a farmer near Argentan," said the man with the
barrow in a strong country accent. He had taken the question
to himself because he had been thinking of his farm.

The Corporal hesitated before replying.

"I used to be a kennelman," he said slowly, "with a pack
of hounds. You know, for hunting . . . It's not a bad job,
when you know it. I was with a baron, fed, lodged and
clothed so that you ought to have seen . . . But I left."

"Why?"

"We had words."

He hadn't liked to say that for nearly a year now he had
been a butcher's boy. He had taken the job to live and had
done it with neither pleasure nor pride.

Behind the smell of the horse under the August sun there seemed to lie the more acrid odor of the kennels, and behind that again, as if it contained all his childhood, the damp scent of the woods in the morning.

"I oughtn't to have done that to the hound," he thought. "My trouble's always been my temper. And then I certainly oughtn't to have raised by hand to the Baron . . . That was really the proper job for me."

He started humming again: "Taïaut . . . hô! Taïaut . . . hô!"

The non-commissioned officer in charge came up.

"You three," he said, "go and report to the Lieutenant. Your turn's coming up."

In the passage outside the squadron office, there were already a dozen men waiting, lined up along the wall. Orderlies were going to and fro carrying papers.

A soldier came out of a door on which was written in chalk: "B Troop."

They all began questioning him.

"What did the Lieutenant ask you?"

"Oh, all sorts of things! My age, if I had my medical certificate, where I lived. He doesn't look an easy customer."

"Is he the fellow with the long nose we saw a while ago?"

"That's him."

"Seems to be a lord. Calls himself de Serremuids."

"Just my luck!" thought Jules Brisset.

"Next!" cried the Sergeant. "You go in first, Corporal."

And he pushed Jules into a little bare, whitewashed room. Serremuids was sitting writing at a table in a corner. Jules felt his heart beating at sight of that severe, remembered profile and the grey lock dividing the hair.

He clicked his heels together and said: "Corporal Brisset, Jules!"

Serremuids was still bent over his lists.

"Perhaps I ought to take the first step," thought Jules. "After all, I owe him an apology."

With a great effort, which was in itself something of a relief, he managed to bring out: "Monsieur le Baron . . ."

"Date of birth?"

Serremuids did not even look up.

"Come on, my lad," said Serremuids, "don't you know
when you were born?"

"March 11, 1906," Jules muttered.

"Parents?"

"Only my father living."

"Mother deceased," said Serremuids, writing. "Address of
next of kin?"

"M. Brisset, Bernard, huntsman, Château de . . ."

Jules felt like shouting: "You damn well know all this
yourself! You might at least show you recognize me."

But he went on: "Château de Serremuids, Orne."

And he began to hate.

Serremuids impassively entered his own name.

"Your profession before being called up?"

Jules's thoughts were concentrated with such an intensity of
anger on the hounds, the stables, and the hunt, that he replied: "Hunt kennelman to . . ."

For the first time, the flint-grey eyes looked up at him.

"I said: 'before being called up.' "

"Butcher's boy," said Jules.

"My lad," said Serremuids, laying down his pen, "I'm
going to repeat what I've said to such of your comrades as I've
already seen. I shall expect implicit obedience from you all.
We're not here for fun, but to do our duty. You're a non-
commissioned officer, and you must set an example. I shall
expect to be able to count on you. If you want to see me about
anything at any time, I shall always be available and will do
anything in my power for you. Thank you. Dismiss! Next!"

Jules felt he was beaten, just as he had been in the forest,
and he wanted to hit out.

"I said: 'Next!' "

Back in the passage, Jules felt as if his neck were bursting.

"What was he like, Corporal?" the others asked him.

"Like he often is. I know him. I was his kennelman. And I can tell you, he's better with animals that he is with people. You just wait and see."

Jules went down into the barrack square.

Baggage and forage wagons were going to and fro. Cars kept arriving with officers in blue *képis*, setting them down, and going off again. And above the shouts, the orders and the rattle of wheels, sounded trumpet-calls; the dusty air seemed as restless as boiling water.

And yet one felt that the chaos was only superficial; the noise, the tumult, the apparent disorder formed merely the essential brew from which the groups of men hanging about the square, the horses being watered and the heaps of unloaded equipment would emerge as mounted squadrons in proper rank.

In front of the barrack buildings was La Brisée, mounted, with Serremuids's mare on a rein.

Jules showed no great pleasure at seeing his father.

"I suppose you've brought Queen of Hearts for the Baron?"

"As you see, my boy," replied La Brisée. "I didn't think I'd run into you so quickly in all this crowd. It's a bit of luck!"

"Why didn't he have Falot brought too, while he was at it? Then we'd all be together again."

"Why do you talk like that, Jules?"

"No reason."

There was a shout of: "B Troop, on parade!"

By way of saying good-by to his father, Jules muttered: "I'll pay him back!"

IV

Letellieux, the Argentan farmer, had been selected as Serremuids's groom. He was the least impertinent of men and knew his place. But he felt a continual need to talk of his byres, cows and fields. He soon had to admit that the Lieutenant was not very forthcoming.

When he discovered that Corporal Brisset had been a hunt servant with the hounds that used sometimes to come past his farm, he began to tell him about his past life; and Jules became a hero to him.

As for Jules, he told everyone who would listen that the Lieutenant "was better with animals than he was with people."

He said it when the troop was billeted in a little village on the edge of the Forest of the Ardennes, and Serremuids saw to the stabling before looking to his men's quarters.

He said it again on exercises, when Serremuids forbade them to gallop their horses when carrying full equipment, and made the men double across muddy ground on dismounted training.

And he would say it at mealtimes too; and the soldiers, for whom *la soupe* at midday and *la soupe* in the evening were far and away the most important events in the day, were easily persuaded that they were less well fed than the horses.

Little by little, Jules's animosity spread slowly like oil through the troop by mere force of repetition.

One evening in December, after *la soupe*, Jules said: "We've had just about enough of this frozen meat. We'll have fresh meat tomorrow, my lads; and it's Corporal Brisset who says it."

"That's fine by us," they said. "What are you going to do?"

"You're not going to complain to the Lieutenant, are you?" said Faivre, the roadman, who was a giant of a man.

Jules disliked the suggestion; it was the one thing he felt incapable of doing.

"I'm not going to tell you," he said, making a mystery of it. "Got to be careful."

Then, turning to Duval, he said: "You're the sort of fellow

who knows his way about. Can you find me some old leather laces?"

"New ones, if you like," said Duval.

Letellieux, for whom the conversation had been somewhat obscure, suddenly beamed with understanding.

"I know!" he said, giving Jules a wink.

He made a circle with his fingers and topped it with an imaginary knot. "I know what you're up to," he said. "Because I've done it myself. You see, at home, in my fields near Argentan . . ."

Faivre, who wanted to make his name with the Corporal, asked: "Can I come too?"

"No, some other time," Jules replied, as if some particular favor were being asked of him. "You can't have a whole damn crowd. Tonight, I'll take just Duval and Letellieux."

When night had fallen, the three men made their way silently out of the village.

It was the hour at which the squadron officers, Captain Noyères, Lieutenant de Serremuids, the two second-lieutenants and the *aspirant*, came out of dinner.

They came onto the porch in a group. It was a big brick house, which the peasants pompously called the château, and was now being used as the headquarters, the Mess and the Captain's billet.

A car was waiting by the steps. The silhouettes of the five officers stood out against the dim light of the hall.

"Well, good night to you!" said the Captain, and there was a certain irony in his voice. "I know nothing about it, of course. All the same, don't run into the Colonel and don't break too many bottles."

Three of them laughed and they all four said: "Good night!"

As the Captain turned back into the house and the lamp in the hall went out, the others came quickly down the steps.

The *aspirant*, who was hopping from one foot to the other in the cold and wrapping his greatcoat about him, said: "Well, Serremuids? No regrets? Won't you really come with us?"

Serremuids thought Dartois, the *aspirant*, far too familiar. He said dryly: "Thanks. I've already declined."

But Dartois insisted: "After all, the Captain said he was shutting his eyes to our . . ."

"So he may be, but he's staying in billets himself."

Second-Lieutenant des Aubrayes was annoyed, and interrupted in a slightly mocking voice: "Leave it, Dartois. If it doesn't amuse Serremuids . . ."

Serremuids, who was aware of the local town's resources, said: "My dear chap, I like a good hound, and I like a good horse; but I'm damned if I'm going to have to reproach myself with an ugly woman."

Upon which he set off down the dark drive.

"We really might have been a bit luckier in our second-in-command!" said Dartois, as he got behind the wheel of the car.

"You shouldn't cheek him," said des Aubrayes, from the back seat.

"Serremuids has only one good point," said Forimbert, the other second-lieutenant. "And that's when he imitates a hunting-horn in the Mess. I've never heard anyone do it better. But apart from that . . ."

The car passed Serremuids as he was going out of the gate. He crossed the church square and went down the High Street. He walked with long strides, unaware of the cold.

"I must walk for a while before going to bed," he thought. "I'll take a turn round the billeting-area."

He often did so. And on nights such as this, when the other officers, with the squadron commander's tacit permission, had gone off to finish the evening in the local town, Serremuids made a point of going close by the troop's billets, so that the men should hear his step.

He had no difficulty in finding his way in the dark, for he could see almost as well by night as by day. He noticed a girth lying on the ground outside a building and, farther on, a stable door not properly shut. He went in and told the guard to close it.

"I suppose it hasn't occurred to you that the horses' heads are in a draught? Don't let it happen again."

Serremuids knew he would be unpopular next day for staying behind and making a night round. His troop would no doubt be saying: "If only we had the *aspirant* or Lieutenant des Aubrayes . . ."

He had already overheard on more than one occasion the remark they made about him: "He's better with animals."

He came to the end of the village. He thought he saw three shadows moving across the fields toward the forest.

Serremuids was not an imaginative man. It did not occur to him that they were spies or parachutists. Nor did he draw his pistol from its holster.

He simply set off across country, humming the "Gone Away!"

Jules's determination to set snares was not due merely to a desire to increase his popularity. In the same way that Letellieux was unhappy without the feel of rich grassland or plough beneath his feet, Jules needed the woods, the damp winter smell beneath the branches, and the warm touch of the fur of game.

Besides, now that he was subject to the Baron's authority again, nothing could give him any pleasure but doing something that was forbidden.

Duval, behind him, was far from sharing in his satisfaction. In the first place, he could see nothing at all in the moonless night, and he had to cling on to Jules's coat to keep direction;

and, in the second place, he was frightened, for he was as cowardly as he was boastful.

"In case it gets known," he said breathlessly, "don't you think it would be a good idea to give the Lieutenant a rabbit tomorrow?"

He had come only so as to be able to boast of it, and Jules had brought him to publicize the exploit.

"If we catch any, that is," added Duval, who was also afraid of being laughed at should they return empty-handed.

"Never you fear," replied Jules. "I had a look round during the exercise yesterday. Do you see that big beech on the edge of the wood, higher than the rest?"

"I can't see anything at all."

"Well, there's a run full of droppings just below it. That's where the rabbits come out into the fields."

Letellieux was bringing up the rear. The tufted grass beneath his feet had revived a whole series of memories.

"If it were the partridge season," he was thinking, "we could take them with horse-hair. Like that day up on the high ground at home . . ."

They went into the wood.

When they reached the big beech, Jules sniffed the scent of wild rabbits that clung to the mossy slope of the run. Then, crouching down, with Letellieux beside him, they both began making snares. Duval, whose eyes could not adapt themselves to the dark, started whenever they broke off a twig.

"Someone's coming," he whispered.

"Oh, shut up! Don't be so damn nervous," replied Jules.

"I tell you someone's coming. I can hear him."

Jules turned. He saw a long figure in a coat, scarcely less dark than the night, coming through the trees.

"Take cover, fellows! It's the Lieutenant!"

Serremuids heard him.

"It's no use! Stand up all three of you," he cried.

They obeyed.

Serremuids was standing quite still a few paces away. The only sound was the quick slapping of his whip against the leather of his gaiters.

"Brisset . . . Letellieux . . . Duval . . ." Serremuids said as they stood up one by one. "Why are you outside the billeting-area without permission? Answer me!"

"Tell him it is because of the meat," Duval whispered into Jules's ear.

But another idea, a crazy temptation, was stirring in Jules's mind. It was night, and they were over five hundred yards from the billets. There were three of them, three against one.

Serremuids walked past them and went to the run. For a moment his back was turned to them as he kicked away a snare.

"If only I had brought Faivre; he's as strong as an ox!" Jules thought.

Serremuids turned and faced them.

"You ought to know I don't like poachers," he said, coming to a halt in front of Jules. "As a non-commissioned officer, I hold you responsible, Brisset. You'll do eight days' detention."

Jules came automatically to attention. The opportunity for revenge had gone. "It'll have to wait," he thought. "This is just one thing more to add to all the rest."

"As for you two . . ." Serremuids went on. He was going to say: "You'll do four days"; but it occurred to him that Queen of Hearts was used to Letellieux, and that during the four days she would almost certainly be badly cared for.

So he said instead: "As for you two, I award you the same punishment, but suspended. Go back to billets."

v

The eight days Jules Brisset spent in detention were hell for Letellieux. Everyone treated him as if he were responsible for the Corporal's punishment.

"It's because you're the Lieutenant's favorite that poor old Brisset's in detention all by himself. If it weren't for that, we'd be there too, wouldn't we, fellows?" said Duval, who found that ingratitude earned him a quiet life.

"If I were his groom," said Faivre, the roadman, "I know what I'd do."

"But what can I do?" said the unfortunate Letellieux. "After all, you can't go killing the mare!"

"It's not the mare, it's the man," said Duval, smoking his pipe. "But, of course, fellows like you have got no guts, not even to avenge a comrade."

Letellieux was so bullied that by the end of the week he was ready to promise to do anything.

When Jules came out of detention, where he had had plenty of time to incubate his resentment, he was welcomed like a martyr.

"We've been putting things off till you came out," said Faivre. "We've got something special for you. . . ."

Outside the stables, which opened onto a big farmyard, the troop was waiting. The men were standing in rank at their horses' heads. It had been raining.

Serremuids came on parade and made his usual inspection. When he raised Brisset's saddle-flap to see if the girth was clean, he noticed Duval giving the Corporal a wink. He gave the saddlery a particular rigorous inspection but could find nothing wrong. He went to mount Queen of Hearts, who was being held by Letellieux in front of the troop.

He placed his foot in the stirrup but, as it took his weight, the saddle turned and he fell in the mud.

He got up at once. His coat was covered with mud and manure. He heard the men laughing behind him. When he looked at the saddle, he saw that the two girth straps were still in the buckles but had been rather roughly cut through. He remembered Duval's wink to Brisset and realized that Letellieux had made no attempt to help him up.

He turned to face the troop and the laughter stopped at once.

"Letellieux, pick up that saddle. Jump to it!" Serremuids said.

Letellieux hurried to obey.

"Take the girth off."

Letellieux was fumbling helplessly. There was a cramp in his stomach. "My God," he thought, "he knows. He's realized!"

"Put the saddle on again."

The troop watched and held its breath.

"And now you'll damn well wipe it clean."

Letellieux raised the skirt of his coat.

"No! With your arse! Go on, mount! Jump!"

Letellieux was heavy and squat. His wet clothes impeded him, and fear seemed to make his legs even shorter. He made five or six vain attempts. He could hear the Lieutenant's whip flicking at his boot. The mare was growing restless, turning and backing away.

Letellieux was clinging helplessly to the mare's withers. He was breathless and scarlet in the face. "Mon Lieutenant," he cried at last, "it isn't my fault . . ."

"I told you to jump on."

Letellieux made a supreme effort and succeeded in hoisting himself across the pommel and getting astride the saddle. The stirrups were too long for him and his feet felt for them in vain.

Brutal to his mare for the first time in his life, Serremuids gave her a sharp cut on the rump with his whip. Queen of Hearts went off at a gallop.

Letellieux reeled in the saddle, clung to the mare's neck, and slid down her flank. A buck sent him flying to the ground.

"Go on, get up!"

But Letellieux lay still. Queen of Hearts came back to join

the other horses. The men, forgetting they had hoped the Lieutenant would suffer Letellieux's fate, began muttering.

"Two of you go and pick him up."

Jules, Faivre and Duval made no move.

When the men reached Letellieux he was as white as a snuffed candle. The veins stood out in a thin, pink network on his cheeks; he sat trembling in the mud, clutching his broken leg with both hands.

VI

After that day, and while the troop remained in billets, there was no further incident.

Whenever the men said to Jules: "Something's got to be done," he replied: "Don't you worry. Wait till we get into the line. That'll be the pay-off."

In April, Letellieux came back and conscientiously resumed his job as groom.

When the German offensive opened at the beginning of May, the reconnaissance group, of which Noyères' squadron formed part, advanced into Belgium.

Nothing happened during the first two days as they rode mile after mile across the Flanders plain in the spring sunshine. On the third morning, as Serremuids's troop was riding through a village, it came under machine-gun fire from the windows. It took an hour to clean up the village and winkle out the enemy patrol. The troop had two wounded, of whom one was Duval with a bullet through the shoulder.

"You see," the men said, "how right he was to be afraid. He was the first to cop it."

Throughout the skirmish Serremuids had issued orders as precisely and with no more thought of taking cover than if he had been on the barrack square.

During the morning of the next day, when Serremuids's troop was acting as advance-guard to the squadron, his leading scouts reported an armored car coming down the road toward them.

It could be seen quite clearly through field-glasses. It was driving along with its turret open. It had either got lost, or was making a solitary reconnaissance. There was certainly none behind it. It was some seven hundred yards away. And then the trees hid it.

The troop had no weapons to deal with it, and could only disperse and let it go by.

Serremuids nevertheless hesitated for a moment before giving the order. He took a quick look at the lie of the land, the hundred yards of straight road in front of him, the trees bordering it, the ditch, and the turning.

He called up Brisset.

"Give your horse to someone," he said. "Bring your sub-machine-gun and a box of magazines, and come with me."

Then he shouted: "The rest of you take your own line and disperse at the gallop!"

He jumped off his horse and threw the reins to Letellieux, who led Queen of Hearts away. The road was empty in a trice. Serremuids and his former kennelman were alone.

"Get in there," Serremuids said, pointing to the ditch. "When the armored car reaches that white milestone—do you see it?—fire at the road in front of it. If it continues to advance, lower your aim and go on firing, but always in front of it! Understand?"

Jules thought: "A sub-machine-gun against an armored car! The bastard's mad! Or he's deliberately trying to get me killed."

The armored car appeared round the bend. It came on between the trees like a big wild boar.

"Remember, in front!" Serremuids said once again. "You slow it down, and I'll dispatch it!"

Drawing his pistol, he started running up the road.

"I'll dispatch it"—the phrase Serremuids used out hunting,

when the stag was at bay, and he drew his long knife from its sheath. And suddenly, Jules realized that the Baron had addressed him in the second person singular, as he used to do. And, as Jules used to do out hunting, he obeyed him without question.

Fifty yards up the road, Serremuids had also taken cover in the ditch. His one fear was that Jules would not open fire at the right moment. If Jules hesitated, they would fail to make the kill.

The armored car was coming straight on, the noise of its engine growing louder every second. With his eyes at road level, Serremuids saw the wheels pass in front of him. And opposite the white milestone, the road suddenly began to crackle; the ground in front of the armored car rose in clouds of dust.

The driver applied his brakes. The machine-gun turned in the turret, as the gunner searched for the source of the fire.

Serremuids jumped out into the road, pistol in hand, and ran toward the armored car. Bullets were whistling very close to him. Jules had not sufficiently lowered his aim, and was uselessly trying to hit the enemy himself.

"The damned fool will kill me," Serremuids thought.

But as he ran on, he saw the bursts of fire retreat before him till the dust reappeared in front of the vehicle's wheels.

The armored car was still moving forward, but very slowly.

Serremuids jumped onto the back step, put his arm into the turret opening and emptied his pistol into the interior. The crew had no time to close the hatch. They saw two grey eyes in a hawklike face, and the sudden glow of the shots.

Serremuids watched the three round helmets collapse one after the other; he felt a jerk against his stomach as the armored car tried to go into reverse; then it stopped, dead.

As he got down off the step, he was aware of a curious sensation of weakness in his legs; and it occurred to him that it required a considerable physical effort to dispatch an armored car with a pistol.

Brisset got to his feet. He was very pale. He had just realized that, during the moment of fear in which he had forgotten his orders to lower his aim, he had very nearly killed the Baron.

And though he believed he hated him as much as ever, he was still trembling at the thought five minutes later.

VII

The reconnaissance group's retreat was an unhappy episode. For eight days and nights the troops, sometimes dispersed, sometimes grouped like so many errant swarms of bees, rode back across the country through which they had advanced, and then farther still, while along parallel roads the enemy's motorized forces continually outstripped them. These were eight days of hopeless fighting, of enormously long fronts held with derisory fire power to cover huge withdrawals, and eight nights of miraculous escapes from the closing pincers of the armored columns.

Of the four squadrons, one had been annihilated, and the others reduced by a half or a third.

On the last evening, what remained of them had succeeded in concentrating in a forest in the Argonne. The enemy held all the exits.

There was a false sense of peace as the red glow of the setting sun shone through the trees.

"What are we doing here? What are we waiting for?" Serremuids asked Captain Noyères.

"The Colonel's trying to make contact with Division. He's waiting for orders."

"If they get through," said Serremuids.

He went back to his troop.

"You can eat your haversack rations," he said. "There won't be a hot meal tonight."

The field kitchen had been hit by a shell that morning. The

men took the last of their bread and tinned meat from their haversacks.

"Would you like some, mon Lieutenant?" Letellieux asked.

"No thanks, I'm not hungry."

He looked at the men sitting on the moss, at the tired horses, grey with dust, hungrily browsing the sparse grass at the foot of the trees, at the doffed helmets and the scant weapons. He remembered the Alençon barracks on the day they had been mobilized. What hopes they had all had amid the chaos of that day!

Orders had arrived from Division.

The Colonel assembled the officers; there were twelve left out of the original thirty. Of Captain Noyères's squadron officers only Serremuids and *aspirant* Dartois remained. The two second-lieutenants had been killed.

The Colonel was pacing up and down. He was a rather short man. His stylish buff breeches were spattered with mud. The stripes on the sleeves of his tunic were tattered. He had a scratch on his chin, though he could no longer remember how he had got it; and the chinstrap of his helmet had been torn away. But an eye-glass, thick as the bottom of a bottle, was firmly fixed in his right eye.

"Well, gentlemen," he said. "We're completely surrounded . . ."

He paused.

". . . and in far greater depth than we suspected. Divisional headquarters is itself out of action."

The Colonel paused again, and clasped his hands behind his back to hide the fact that they were trembling.

"I have just received orders. It seems that our mission is concluded."

There was a moment's silence, during which nothing could be heard but men breathing and leaves rustling.

"We're to stay where we are, destroy our weapons, and kill our horses. Those are the orders."

"Christ!" someone near Captain Noyères cried.

"Yes, I know, Serremuids," the Colonel said, turning his eye-glass on him. "It's very hard. But there's no chance of the group getting through. We can make the enemy a present of our lives, but not of our horses and such weapons as we still have. Pray believe this order does not originate with me. Gentlemen, I want to thank you all for what you have done under my command."

They all realized that this word of thanks, brief as an order, meant that as a group they had not only ceased to fight, but had ceased to exist.

"Mission concluded! But we've not done a thing," cried Dartois, who had held a farm with five men for eleven hours till he was relieved.

"Mon Colonel," said the veterinary officer, "shall I ask for fatigue parties for the horses?"

"No, Doullins, there will be no fatigue parties for that. Every man will kill his own horse."

The Colonel drew his revolver and was the first to kill his charger.

The officers went sadly back to their men.

Serremuids stood stock still.

"Well, Serremuids, what about it?" said Dartois.

"There's Forimbert's horse too," Serremuids said, as if to himself.

"Don't worry, I'll see to it," Dartois said, giving him a tap on the shoulder.

For the first time Serremuids was grateful to him for his familiarity.

Shots were already ringing out in the forest. Twilight was falling. Serremuids could see the red flashes from the pistols flickering on the underside of the branches.

The dark bulks of horses were falling. From time to time, a wounded horse galloped madly away, only to run head first into a tree. Others were writhing on the ground and needed a second shot to finish them off. The wood was alive with the long screaming of their agony.

The air was heavy with the stench of blood and cordite. The butchery was reaching its climax.

A blinded horse galloped past Serremuids and nearly knocked him down. A man came running behind it, carbine in hand. The horse tripped on a stone, staggered, and fell to its knees against a bank, humble in its last agony. The soldier fired point blank, and the horse fell on its side, its skull burst open. And the long clamor of panic and pain rang on through the forest, as if the whole breed of horses were neighing in chorus.

Serremuids put his hands to his ears to shut out the sound.

When he got back to his troop, he found Jules Brisset shooting the horses of the men who had not the courage to do it themselves. He had the horse held by the bridle, and shot it in the ear with a pistol. It was painlessly done; there was merely a last convulsive twitching of the hooves, and the horse was dead. As Serremuids watched him at work, he thought: "A butcher's boy."

The men had never seen their Lieutenant look so defeated, his head bowed, his shoulders stooping.

Serremuids stared at his dead horses. There were dark rivulets of blood amid the moss at his feet.

"Brisset!" he called.

The Corporal turned to him.

"Here, take this," Serremuids said, handing him his pistol. He jerked his head toward Queen of Hearts.

It had required no less than a general disaster for Jules Brisset to gain at last the advantage over the man who had always been his master.

"If you mean your mare, mon Lieutenant," he said, "you must do it yourself. Everyone his own horse, those are the orders."

And he set about shooting Faivre's horse.

The men were expecting an outburst of anger from Serremuids, an incisive order.

But he said nothing at all. He went slowly across to Queen of Hearts. When he put out his hand to pat her neck for the last time, the mare shied away, white showing in her eyes. Serremuids recognized the panic of it, when she had been so steadfast in battle.

"You know what's going to happen, my pretty; you know what I'm going to do," he muttered.

Queen of Hearts started to neigh and, for Serremuids, her neighing drowned the screams of all the dying horses.

He suddenly stood back. There was a look of determination on his face; his mouth had become a hard line.

He hurried to the Colonel.

"Mon Colonel," he said, "since our mission is concluded, I request you to give me my freedom."

"I still have the right to do that," replied the Colonel. "We're faced with the whole group being wiped out to no purpose. A few men may possibly get through. I wish I were in your place. There's no obligation on you to share my fate; but I'm obliged to share my command's. Go on, Serremuids. Be quick. And good luck to you!"

Serremuids went back to his troop. The horses were all dead. Some of the men were already beginning to destroy their carbines by banging the butts against the trees.

"I'm going," he said, and his voice was as firm as it had ever been. "I'm going to try to get through. If any of you want to come with me, come on. This is not an order. You can do as you please."

He went to saddle Queen of Hearts.

The men discussed it.

"He's mad," said Faivre. "I'd damn well rather be a prisoner than get killed."

"Besides we're too damn exhausted. We can't do any more," another said.

They all looked at Jules. They knew his decision was the one that counted.

"Well, Corporal? Do you agree?"

Jules nodded his head in agreement. He said: "As far as I'm concerned, fellows . . ."

At that moment they heard a hunting call through the trees. Serremuids was in the saddle and singing the call as loud as he could to cover the sound of the horses dying in the neighboring squadrons.

Jules's answer was still hanging in the air. He took a deep breath and smelled again the true scent of the forest; there was almost no struggle in his mind at all.

He picked up his sub-machine-gun, put his arm through the sling, and said: "As far as I'm concerned, fellows . . ."

He went over to join Serremuids.

Letellieux followed him; Faivre came behind him; and then the others too.

The Colonel was leaning against a tree. He saw one of his troops disappear into the night, with a horseman at its head singing the "Gone Away!"

THE HAUNTED HOUSE

❧ ❧ ❧ During the day the weather had turned a little milder and it had begun to thaw. But it was bound to freeze again during the night.

In the beech and pine wood, through which the patrol was advancing in single file, there was no sound but the ceaseless dripping of water from branch to branch, and the squelching of the thirteen men's boots on the sodden ground. The uniform cloth hung soaked and heavy from their shoulders, each greatcoat a second body to be carried on their backs.

Rémi Hourdou, a native of the Perche, who was almost a giant, was bringing up the rear and could sniff the scent of the whole file in front of him.

"We smell like wet dogs," he said.

No one answered him. There was nothing but the drips from the trees, footstep following footstep, and the icy mud squelching under their boots.

Hourdou could see immediately in front of him the wide back of fat Butel, and farther along the path, Corporal Cruzet's sloping shoulders, and farther on again, where the mist began, the seventh helmet from the rear, which belonged to Diriadec, the Breton, who never spoke.

Wet to the waist, their collars turned up, they all walked with a stoop, except Rémi Hourdou, the giant, who stood up straight because it would have tired him to walk in any other way.

It took them half an hour to reach the edge of the forest. The village was below them, in a hollow. It had recently been bombed. They could see the bare timbers of the roofs, the joists showing like the ribs of skeletons, and other roofs that had merely been holed, and others again with their tiles turned up on edge and still holding traces of snow.

"They're like a pigeon's wing, when you blow against the lie of the feathers," said Rémi Hourdou.

Night had fallen by the time they entered the village. They passed shattered doors, shutters hanging askew, and the glass from the broken windows crackled beneath their feet. The silence of the forest is normal and bearable; nor is it ever a true silence for there is always a branch cracking or an animal moving. But the silence of dead houses is a poor welcome to men numbed with cold and fatigue.

In the center of the village, in front of the Mairie, a bomb had made an enormous crater which the rains had filled. The dark, opaque surface of the water, polished as marble, with a coronet of snow still about its edge, added to the desolation of the place.

The sergeant, who had studied his map well, led them through the streets without hesitation. They turned into a farmyard and walked past several outbuildings.

"This is it," said the sergeant, pushing open a door.

He switched on his torch, and the men followed him in. The little bluish light flickered along the walls, and momentarily lit up the corners of the room, the leg of a table, the motionless pendulum of an old clock. On the floor, there were a dozen mattresses left by their predecessors.

"Is everyone here?" asked the sergeant. "Cruzet, see that the shutters are properly closed. The rest of you, barricade the openings. And see you do it properly!"

Hourdou dragged over a huge table and set it against the door. Then, with Diriadec, who said not a word, he carried over a kneading trough and put a chest on top of it. They put crossed benches against the windows.

The torch made a blue circle on the floor at the sergeant's

feet. The men instinctively dragged the mattresses as close as they could get to the dim circle of light.

A tin-opener squeaked against a tin; their hands fumbled in their haversacks for a damp piece of sausage or a half-melted bar of chocolate.

"If we hadn't seen the smashed roofs from up above, you'd almost think we were in a safe shelter," muttered Levavasseur, simply to say something.

"Why do you lower your voice like that?" Hourdou asked.

"I don't know, I wasn't thinking," Levavasseur replied.

An odd constraint lay over the room and lent the least word, the most ordinary sound, a curiously exaggerated importance in the silence: a heel scraping on the tiles, water swilling in a tin. Then Corporal Cruzet said: "So this is what they call a 'haunted house,' do they? For a lot of ghosts, I'd say we're doing pretty well, eh men?"

All along the Lorraine front, in the no-man's-land between the lines, there were evacuated villages to which the standing patrols retired at night. They came in at dusk, shut themselves into a house, and made neither fire nor light. And these derelict houses, in deserted and often ruined villages, from being inhabited by shadowy figures between dusk and dawn, were known as "the haunted houses."

Sergeant Lalande's patrol had already spent long weeks in the advance posts. But it was the first time they had ever had to take refuge in one of these houses.

"What about the fellows opposite, Sergeant?" asked Chambiron. "Don't they ever come here?"

"Occasional patrols," the sergeant said, cutting slices from a loaf of bread. "Sometimes there are two haunted houses in the same village. But it's unusual."

"Well, men," said Levavasseur, after a moment's silence, "I tell you they'll come tonight. I've got a presentiment."

"What you've got is cold feet," someone said.

They laughed, in the way soldiers do when they are tired

and are beginning to digest a meal. And then they suddenly stopped laughing. No one moved, and they all held their breath.

"There's someone upstairs," said Corporal Cruzet in a whisper. "Do you hear him, Sergeant?"

"I hear him," said the sergeant. "Shut up!"

He switched off his torch. All their heads were tilted up toward the ceiling in the dark as they listened to the heavy footsteps upstairs. From time to time the footsteps stopped, then moved on toward the back wall. Below, the men turned their heads in sympathy, as if the heavy footfalls had clutched them through the ceiling by the hair.

"Funny, wouldn't it be, if they'd chosen the same house as us?" muttered Levavasseur, a quaver in his voice.

"We'll go and take a look," said Sergeant Lalande, putting his helmet on. "And don't make a row, see? Don't all of you come."

The little blue circle of light showed on the floor again. Rémi Hourdou, Corporal Martin and Diriadec got silently to their feet, took their rifles, and followed the sergeant. Corporal Cruzet fumbled a magazine into his sub-machine-gun, doing his best to muffle the click. He whispered: "You just give a shout, Sergeant, and I'll fire through the ceiling."

The rest held themselves ready. Lalande went out of the room and slowly climbed the stairs. Behind him came Rémi Hourdou, doing his best to walk lightly, but the boards groaned beneath his weight.

"Who goes there?" the sergeant shouted abruptly as he reached the top stair.

Down below, Cruzet's finger tensed on the trigger.

"It's me, Sergeant, it's me," a voice said.

And fat Butel's silhouette appeared on the landing.

"I was looking for something to drink," Butel said.

"You've had a damn lucky escape! We've come to look for you in force!"

The sergeant angrily seized Butel by the shoulders and sent him spinning down the stairs.

"Get the hell out of here! I'll teach you to play the ghost next time! You deserve a damn good beating up! And now, if you'll just stay quiet, we might try to get some sleep."

They all stretched out on the mattresses. From Chambiron's direction the sound of breathing soon became a long whistle. Butel muttered: "I'm sure as hell there's something to drink up there."

Then he fell asleep.

He started awake to the sound of an appalling crash.

"Get your weapons!" cried Levavasseur, instinctively reaching for his rifle.

The men all started up.

"What's going on?" Butel asked.

The noise had come from inside the room. The sergeant switched on his torch. One of the benches barring the windows had fallen down.

"It can't have fallen of its own accord," said Rémi Hourdou. "I know I fixed it properly."

"Could someone have pushed it in from outside?" said Corporal Martin.

Hourdou put his hand through the broken pane; the shutters were tightly closed and the fastenings had not been moved. He had to admit that the bench had fallen of its own accord. He put it back in place and lay down again.

Quiet was restored. The only sound was of men occasionally turning over. Outside, the drips had ceased falling from the roof; it was freezing again. Their clothes grew colder and stuck to their bodies.

"It's funny," Chambiron said suddenly; "I'm dead tired but I can't get to sleep."

They felt surrounded by hostile, impalpable influences. They were all waiting for something to happen. A brick suddenly fell down the chimney into the grate, with a cascade of falling plaster. Hourdou leaped to his feet.

"I can't take any more of this," he cried. "I can't take it! The whole damn house is on the move, cracking up, falling to pieces! No one can say I'm the sort of man who's afraid" (he gave himself a hard blow on the chest); "but this whole damned thing's too much. Can I go and have a look round, Sergeant?"

"No," said Lalande. "You'll stay here. Understand?"

Hourdou was pacing up and down. He went to the back of the house, stumbled into the furniture, banged against the doors. He seemed calmer after a while, and there was silence in the room. But only a little later they again heard footsteps on the floor above.

"Hourdou!" cried the sergeant.

"It's not Hourdou, it's Butel. This time I've found the damn brandy. You just wait a minute."

He came down the stairs.

"Come on, men, bring your mugs. Don't you worry, this is proper stuff."

"That'll do, Butel!" said the sergeant. "I warn you, if you get drunk . . . Butel!" he shouted.

The torch caught Butel in its blue beam. He was drinking from the bottle, with little chuckles of pleasure. The sergeant knocked the bottle out of his hand and it broke on the floor.

For a moment, Butel was dumbfounded.

"To hell with it, Sergeant, you can't do a thing like that to a man!"

The sergeant instinctively took a step backward.

"Now, now, Butel!" said Corporal Martin.

Butel uttered a great deep roar of rage, as if his anger had come up from the depths of the earth before finding issue. The torch went out, and Butel was left standing there with his fist raised in the dark, breathing the odor of alcohol rising from the tiled floor.

It was at this moment that the church bells began ringing. First a single stroke, a great brazen clang that hung on the freezing air. Then a second, and a third. Then silence.

Then the bell rang out again, once, twice, thrice, long echoing vibrations. The sergeant switched his torch on. The men looked at each other. Butel had forgotten his anger; they had all forgotten it.

The bell rang again three times, then all the bells pealed out together in a great clangor that seemed almost to come from next door.

"The angelus," muttered Butel. "The angelus at midnight. The devil's angelus."

"They say bells sometimes ring on stormy nights," said Cruzet, without much conviction.

"Bells don't ring of their own accord when there's no wind," someone said. "And even the wind can't ring the angelus."

"The Germans are in the village, men," said Corporal Martin.

"Come on! Get your weapons!" ordered Lalande.

There was an element of panic about their scrambling for their weapons in the dark.

"But if they are in the village," said Chambiron suddenly, "why are they ringing the bells like that? Don't you think, Sergeant, it might be just one of their tricks to frighten us, and that they'll ambush us when we come out?"

"We shall soon see," Lalande said. "Come on! Patrol order. Out by the back door!"

Butel seized the sergeant by the arm as roughly as if he wanted to hurt him.

"No, Sergeant, let me go first."

He would have liked to add: "Because of the bottle." But he didn't know how to say it.

When they opened the door, the bells sounded even louder and more terrifying.

"They're ringing for coming out of Mass now," Butel said.

He hastily crossed himself, striking his forehead and his heart, dashed out into the farmyard and took cover against a wall.

"You can come out, men," he said a moment later, "there's no one here."

The clangor grew ever louder as they approached the church. The whole air seemed to be reverberating in their ears with a brazen sound of bells.

Butel, Gruzert and Chambiron were all wondering how many men there were ringing the bells.

They split up into two parties, one section going round the right of the square and the other the left, keeping level and advancing slowly. The church was at the end of the square, and they could see the dark porch between the trees and the gates of the cemetery, in which the crosses gleamed in the shadows. The pealing grew slower and came to a stop.

The two sections halted instinctively. The atmosphere seemed suddenly to have become heavier; the silence did nothing to lessen their foreboding. All was quiet in the church and the village. Diriadec, the Breton, who never said anything, almost began to believe that it was the dead who had been ringing the bells.

The sergeant ordered the sections to continue advancing. Corporal Cruzet stopped at the corner of an alley and looked back to see if his men were following. As he turned to his front again, he found himself face to face with a German. They both started. The German jumped back into the alley, and Cruzet backed against the wall.

There were indeed two "haunted houses" in the village that night.

The bells began their clamor again. They rang out wild, joyous and terrible.

The two patrols stalked each other for a while, each trying

to surprise the other. The battle began in front of the Mairie, round the great bomb-crater and its dark water.

The sub-machine-gun clattered, projecting a flickering red light across the ground.

"But why are they still ringing?" Sergeant Lalande, like everyone else, was wondering.

Butel suddenly gave a cry and dropped his rifle.

"That's done it!" he said, as if something had happened he had been expecting for a long while.

He had got a bullet in the arm. It did not hurt, or at least less than he had expected; but his shoulder was trembling and he could not stop it.

Both sides were firing rather at random, the brief flashes of shots coming from dark corners. Corporal Martin had his calf grazed by a bullet. He put his hand to it. There was no blood, merely the smart of a burn. The leather of his gaiter was cut through, but not the flesh. "Luck!" he thought.

Suddenly a tall shadowy figure without a helmet detached itself from a wall and ran toward the Mairie. A burst of fire stopped it; and the man fell into the crater. On the instant, the whole light in the square changed. The surface of the crater turned white. Stupefaction seized on both patrols and they stopped firing. The sudden milky pallor and the unceasing, infernal tocsin were so abnormal that some of them began to wonder whether it was really a man who had been killed, and if there was not in fact something supernatural about the village.

Soon afterward the German patrol withdrew, carrying two wounded. There were a few more shots in the darkness, and then the French were alone.

"They're still ringing," said Chambiron, "so it can't be the Germans."

But none of them felt brave enough now to go to see what was happening in the church.

As he passed the crater again, Diriadec, saying nothing as

usual, held his rifle at arm's length and felt the surface with the butt. It was ice. There was no doubt that it was a man who had fallen in. The water had frozen suddenly on the impact of the body. Diriadec remembered having seen the same thing happen on occasion at home in winter, when the thermometer stood at four or five degrees of frost and you threw a stone into ponds that were not yet frozen over.

They went back to the house, entered by the back door and barricaded themselves in again. They put a field-dressing on Butel's shoulder. He seemed all right; he talked, and indeed seemed to be the only one of them capable of joking.

"If you hadn't gone and bust my brandy, it would have done me a power of good now."

But his shoulder went on trembling, and nothing could stop it.

While they were still bandaging his arm, the bells rang out in a long peal, then the sound gradually diminished as if they had been left to swing to a stop. The medium bell stopped first; then the little one. The bourdon died away last, leaving a long vibration that went on for some time after it had fallen silent.

"I don't understand it," said the sergeant. "The Germans never attack at this time of night. They do the same as us, wait for dawn to attack the patrols when they're leaving. It must have been the bells that made them come out into the open, as they did us. They would certainly have attacked us in the morning."

The men were eating, for hunger takes precedence over all else; but they ate in silence. Suddenly, there was a noise at the back door.

"Oh, it's not going to begin again, is it?" cried Corporal Martin.

Someone was trying to get in, knocking and pushing at the door.

"Come on, men! Open up!" a voice shouted.

"Surely everyone's here, aren't they?" asked Lalande, shading the torch with his hand.

There was no time to check up. The door gave way, and fell in with the bench that was barricading it. A huge figure appeared at the end of the room. As it came forward, stretching its arms, it turned into Rémi Hourdou.

"Ah, that did me good, men," he cried. "But why did you shut me out?"

There was a short silence before the sergeant spoke.

"When did you go out?" he said.

"Well, it was when you told me not to, Sergeant. And then, when I got outside, I thought: 'Well, now, I'll just go and give those bells a ring for the fellows.' I thought it would cheer you all up. It reminded me of when I was a choir-boy!"

And big Rémi Hourdou, the company's hard case—three civil convictions and seventy days' military detention, though never by evil intent—began roaring with laughter.

The men looked at each other. In all the tumult that had followed on the incident of the bottle, no one had noticed Hourdou's absence.

"And you, you bastard, of course you heard nothing while you were ringing?" said the sergeant. "I'll give you choir-boys!"

Then Diriadec, the Breton, who hadn't uttered a word for the last twelve hours, said calmly: "If it comes to that, Sergeant, the Germans were in the village. So, perhaps, if it hadn't been for Hourdou . . ."

He stopped there, having said enough for one day.

MOURLOT

TO AYMAR DE DAMPIERRE

❧ ❧ ❧ Mourlot was cleaning a motor-bicycle and sidecar. He was doing it carefully and honestly, as if he were cleaning his carriage at home on his farm in Brittany. An officer came up.

"What's your name?"

"Mourlot, mon Colonel."

Mourlot stood up but, even at attention, he seemed to grow no taller; he was low and thickset like a clod of earth.

"From tomorrow you will drive my car."

An unaccustomed expression of pride, or perhaps even joy, passed over Mourlot's face which bore marks of hardship in childhood. He replied: "Very good, mon Colonel."

But the Colonel, who never gave an explanation, had already gone on; and Mourlot, who never made an unnecessary gesture, stopped his salute halfway.

And this was how he became—though without knowing why he had been chosen—the Colonel's driver.

Lieutenant-Colonel Auvray de Vigneul went up to the advance posts each morning. In the early days, when the sector was still quiet, he had gone up by car, and he still continued to do so. He was a cavalryman and had no liking for a long walk. He would have Mourlot drive him right up to the line, even when the enemy was less than two hundred yards away. The door would open; a cap, a stick and a length of fawn gaiter would emerge in turn; and then the Colonel would slowly alight. When a shell fell near him, he would give its caliber as if mentioning a horse's pedigree.

More than once, the big green car became a target and as they drove home Mourlot would say: "Mon Colonel, I thought we'd had it today."

"Mourlot," the Colonel would reply, "you know why I chose you!"

Mourlot had no idea; but it was enough that he had been chosen. "Yes, mon Colonel!" he would say.

And each evening the staff would say: "Auvray's crazy. He'll get himself killed in the end. Someone ought to stop him!"

But next morning the green car would go up the line again, for everyone knew that the reconnaissance unit's morale might not have been half so good if the men had not seen Lieutenant-Colonel Auvray de Vigneul's cap, stick and fawn gaiter emerge from the door.

On 10 May, Auvray's regiment led the Army Corps toward the Belgian frontier. Contact had not yet been made by the morning of the twelfth. It happened to be the midday halt, when the Colonel went forward to see what was going on. He told Mourlot to drive up to the leading squadron.

The squadron was resting in an apple orchard beside the road; motor-bicycles and sidecars were parked under the trees and had been camouflaged with branches in blossom. The men were sitting about, eating; they had loosened their thick leather chinstraps and pushed their mica goggles up onto their helmets. They were stretching their limbs that had been so long cramped on the machines and letting their faces, burnt with dust and wind, relax.

The fawn gaiter and the cap emerged as usual, almost at the same instant as a little black arrowhead appeared in the sky. Behind the arrowhead was another, and behind that a third.

The men looked at each other, their mouths hanging open in surprise.

It was as if the noise threw them suddenly flat to the ground. Surely one of the aircraft must fall among them. For a twentieth of a second their hearts stopped beating as they waited for the falling thunder to crash. They could no longer think in words; images filled their minds. For the rest of their lives, if they escaped the diving aircraft, they would see that patch of grass before their eyes. They had not known that grass could have so many colors.

The ground shuddered. They pressed their heads closer to the grass, because what was happening to them was not the casual result of chance, but the deliberate ill-will of man. They began to think in words again, and at once one word sprang to everyone's mind: "Machine-gun."

The first aircraft regained height; but the next was already roaring down, stuttering at them; and the second was followed by a third.

After this, the droning in the sky was almost silence. A wounded man cried aloud, astonished. For a moment their muscles relaxed, only to tense once more. The men who had rashly raised their heads dropped them again at once. There was another arrowhead upon them.

The stuttering of the machine-guns, which seemed to be seeking out the very stones beneath the grass, was unlike usual descriptions of it. It was not a rattle or a coffee-mill. It could just as well have been a thrashing-machine accelerating as it smashed the ears of wheat, or even a monstrous hailstorm beating against the windows of life.

A third, a fourth . . . a fifth arrowhead was regaining height again.

But Mourlot did not try to place the noise. He lay flat on his face, trembling, biting the earth as he thought: "We're going to die."

The first arrowhead circled round and then came in to drop its bombs.

There was a noise like a circular saw driving into wood, followed by an explosion and a violent shock every man felt in his stomach; then another whistle and another shock, while the interval between the bombs seemed far longer than the time it really took. And now, as they waited, the machine-guns were merely metronomes beating to a lunatic rhythm.

Life in the orchard seemed to have changed, now. A hundred and thirty silent voices, a hundred and thirty voice-less cries told the earth: "This one's for me! This one's for me!"

And at each explosion, a hundred and thirty bodies waited to be hit. They instinctively clasped their arms over their helmets, desperately protecting their brains and their senses with a thin shield of flesh.

There was no need to be particularly devout to pray: "Oh God, save me! O God, save me!"

For now there was not only the enmity of man attacking them from above; the very earth beneath them was exploding and casting them off.

After each bomb, there were fewer of them to wait for the next. And between each explosion of earth, those who were left listened to the racing pulse of their own blood.

During a moment's quiet, while one of the arrowheads was making its circuit, the men heard their commanding officer's voice, a long way off as if he were giving an order in the riding school: "Lie on your backs!"

The prostrate bodies did not move. No one at that moment could believe that the voice could come from an unwounded man.

"That's done it!" thought Second-Lieutenant Galtier. "The Colonel's been wounded."

But then the voice came again: "What the hell's going on?

Don't you obey orders any more? Mourlot! Lie on your back!"

Mourlot was an obedient man. He made a great effort and was surprised to find that his muscles still obeyed him. He turned on his side. But, as he did so, he opened his eyes and saw an aircraft diving at him, and rolled over on his face again.

"I said on the back!"

This time Mourlot turned completely over. The aircraft had passed. Another was coming. Mourlot thought he was going to die. Then he saw the aircraft climbing again and realized that you were no more likely to be killed on your back than on your face. He also saw his big green car burning on the road.

Then the next man, Nicolas, raised himself on one elbow and saw Mourlot looking upward. He turned over too. And Nicolas's neighbors followed his example.

"Come on, my lads! All of you on your backs!"

Then, little by little, hesitantly, sometimes falling back, with slow, patient movements, or uncertainly as if their courage were coming back in fits and starts, they all turned face to the sky under the tornado of steel, all that is except those who would never move again. It was like a circular ripple spreading out from Mourlot across the orchard. And so they began to get used to looking hell in the face.

They saw the Lieutenant-Colonel, standing very straight and irritably tapping his gaiter with his stick; beside him, Captain de Navailles was watching the bombers through his field-glasses; at the other end of the field, leaning against a tree, Sergeant-Major Koueric was firing his pistol, and there was nothing, except the fact that he was firing at aircraft with a pistol, to show that old Koueric was not perfectly normal.

Second-Lieutenant Galtier stood up.

There were still fifteen aircraft dancing their somber ballet above the trees.

Galtier, who had just come from the military academy, suddenly remembered his training; he ran to the motor-bicycles and seized a sub-machine-gun. He was trying to remember the drill. "When the aircraft dives straight at you, don't lay off your aim. When the aircraft dives . . ."

The aircraft was diving straight at him. Galtier aimed.

"Don't aim off!"

Galtier fired. The aircraft went on diving.

"Don't aim off!"

Suddenly Galtier could no longer feel the weight of the sub-machine-gun. He wanted to feel his hands, but he had no hands now. There was a huge weight against his side and it threw his body to the left. He fell, repeating: "When the aircraft . . . don't aim off . . ."

Mourlot, who had seen the lieutenant fire and fall, reached for his rifle. And Nicolas did so too. Lying on their backs, they both began firing into the sky.

Captain de Navailles shouted an order: "N.C.O.s! Open fire with sub-machine-guns!"

Soon the three automatic weapons were giving their regular rattle.

The Colonel's voice rang out again.

"Go on, my lads! Fire! Fire! Fire, all of you! Well, Mourlot?"

The whole field suddenly bristled with a new noise which grew louder and louder. There was a shout of joy when the aircraft gained height. Every weapon in the squadron was firing now. The aircraft dived again but soon gained height once more, obviously put out. Their bombs were scattered more widely. They came in another two or three times, but not so low. And then the thunder went back into the sky and one by one the arrowheads disappeared.

"That lasted twenty-seven minutes," said the Colonel, looking at his wrist-watch, as if he had been timing a competitor in a gymkhana.

His voice sounded very loud in the silence.

"That was a good idea, mon Colonel, making them turn over," said Captain de Navailles.

And he put his field-glasses back in their case.

The men got to their feet. Beneath the powder, earth and dust, fear had molded their faces into tragic masks.

A petrol tank blew up, and several threw themselves back onto the ground. Smoke was rising from the shallow craters. There were groans among the blossom and splinters of metal in the orchard. Branches and steel, cloth and flesh were all mingled. Leaves were still falling, like drips of rain after a storm. A twisted motor-bicycle hung from the shattered trunk of an apple-tree. A soldier, who could still stand, did not understand why he had been spared and why his comrade beside him lay still. One of them had gone mad and was running round and round a tangled mass of motor-bicycles.

A third of the squadron had been wiped out.

Suddenly the Colonel heard someone calling him. It was Nicolas, dragging himself along with a wounded leg.

"Mon Colonel! Mon Colonel! Mourlot! Mourlot!"

"What's the matter with Mourlot?"

And the Colonel went over to the tree at which Nicolas was pointing.

Mourlot was lying there, his unhappy, childish face turned up to the sky. A burst of machine-gun fire had drawn a red band across his chest.

"Better than in the back," said the Lieutenant-Colonel for all to hear.

Then, as if to himself, he murmured: "Mourlot! You know why I chose you . . ."

And Mourlot, who was not quite dead, gasped: "Yes, mon Colonel."

NIGHT PATROL

❦ ❦ ❦ Officers were forbidden to move about alone between the lines at night.

Lieutenant Serval, who had been visiting his outposts, came out of the isolated farm held by Sergeant Dercheu's patrol.

"Damn! It's got dark very early," said Serval.

"I'll send a couple of men with you, mon Lieutenant," said the sergeant.

"No, Dercheu, not today. No one here has slept for three nights. The men are quite tired enough as it is. I'll go back on my own."

"It's not right, mon Lieutenant," said Dercheu. "There are a lot of enemy patrols about."

"Don't worry. I know the way. There's still enough light to see by. Besides, I've got my pistol."

And he slapped the holster like an old friend.

It was the end of January. The sky was black, but a little light came from the snow. Serval, a sheepskin coat over his uniform, walked along the ditch beside the road to deaden the sound of his steps.

"Two kilometres, that's nothing," he thought. "But it would have meant four for the men . . ."

From time to time his heavy boots crushed a frozen tussock of grass and the noise made him start in spite of himself. The snow and the darkness made the distances seem greater.

"After the beech, the hut; after the hut, the white telegraph pole; after the telegraph pole, the turning . . ."

Serval watched the familiar landmarks appear slowly out of the night.

The turning was the most dangerous point on the route. Several encounters between patrols had taken place there. Serval stopped a moment to have a look round.

Nothing.

He went on again. He was wearing his holster in front, in the middle of his belt, with the flap turned back so that he could draw the pistol more quickly.

It was a heavy automatic, and Serval was much attached to it, because it had belonged to his father in the other war.

"Even if you hit a man in the hand with it, the shock will knock him down," Commandant Serval had said when giving his son the weapon. "Take care of it. It saved me twice at awkward moments. Bring it safely home as I did. That's all I ask."

As he walked on, Serval stroked the ribbed butt with his hand.

He had passed the turning now. He need not have walked so quickly or felt that twinge in the stomach . . .

Serval could see the hedge now. Then, after the hedge, there was the ruined wall at right angles to the road.

A few yards from the wall, he suddenly threw himself into the ditch and drew his pistol.

A faint gleam of light had appeared for an instant to his left, the dimmed glimmer of a pocket torch. It had been at ground level and immediately extinguished.

But it was enough for Serval.

"An enemy patrol!"

He was surprised to hear himself whisper the words, as if there had been someone behind him to warn tonight.

He tried to make out how far away it had been. About a hundred yards. The patrol could not have seen him, because he had kept in the shadow of the hedge ever since the turning.

He'd merely have to spend a few minutes lying in the ditch, and then he'd be able to go on again. Unless, of course, the patrol . . .

There was another gleam of light, nearer now. The patrol had moved some way toward him. How many men were there?

Staring like a sailor on watch in the deceptive light of the snowy field, he made out three dim shapes crouching by a silo; three shadows, one behind the other like the fins of sharks.

As Serval pushed off the safety-catch, there was another gleam of light. The silo was close to the road, just beyond the wall. That was where the enemy patrol would come out. But he realized he would still be invisible: a sheepskin lying in the snow.

"The first man to fire has the advantage," he thought.

He gathered himself together, like an animal about to spring.

The advancing shadows stopped for a moment; then the patrol began to move forward again and was hidden by the wall.

He watched for them to appear again at the other end. He could feel his heart beating in his chest. But he was not afraid.

"Some people are frightened before," he often said to his friends, "some during, and some after. I'm frightened after."

This time he felt sure that though he was only one against three he had the advantage. Unless . . . unless another patrol was coming up behind him to reconnoiter the other side of the wall.

It seemed to him a perfectly logical maneuver such as he might have decided on himself. But the only line of advance for the second patrol, if it existed, was the ditch in which he was lying.

The longer he waited, the more wildly his imagination worked. He longed to look behind him. But to move now would be to give himself away. He merely dug his boots into the snow so that the nails should not glisten.

Then, thirty yards away, a figure appeared beside the road. Serval could clearly see its shoulders and the squat steel helmet.

The man advanced a few paces along the ditch, signaled with his arm, and the two others appeared behind him.

Serval watched them come toward him; he could hear the rustling of their boots in the snow.

"I'll get them," he thought. "I'll get them!"

He had now completely forgotten the possibility of a second patrol. He was wholly concentrated on the game of life and death that he must play out with the shadows in front of him. He knew he was a good shot. He calculated the chances.

"There are three of them. There are nine rounds in the magazine. And I've got the advantage of surprise."

There was a clink of metal from the patrol. Serval started.

"Damn fool!"

It was a purely disinterested reaction, like shrugging off a friend's mistake.

"When they reach the corner of the wall," he thought, "not before. If I fire too soon, I may miss them and they'll have time to get away."

He could see only the first figure at all clearly. Behind it, only parts of the others were visible: a helmet, a torso, a leg . . .

"If they'd only get out of single file!" he thought.

Then, as if at his orders, they did so. Two of them came walking side by side down the ditch.

"When they reach the corner of the wall I'll put four bullets into them. Then I'll jump up and fire three more. I might even take a prisoner."

The moment for action was coming very near.

"At the corner of the wall," he repeated to himself to contain his impatience.

Under cover of his left sleeve, he raised the pistol.

The ticking of his watch was like thunder. The forearm of his pistol hand had gone rigid. He forced it to relax. He settled the second joint of his forefinger on the trigger. Another four yards . . . another three . . .

The patrol came to a halt. He could hear them whispering. Yes, he must certainly take a prisoner.

He was just going to fire when the leading shadow jumped out onto the road, dashed across it and slid into the ditch on the further side. The other two joined him.

Serval felt his flank had been turned. The enemy now had the advantage. He would have to fight for his life. But when he looked over the edge of the ditch he saw he was wrong: the patrol was walking silently away.

There was a gleam of light, then another, then nothing. The sharks' fins disappeared into the still waves of snow.

Serval was very angry when he reached headquarters. He told them what had happened.

"Like a stupid fool, I waited too long before firing. And they slipped through my fingers."

"And lost you a jolly good *croix de guerre*," said Second-Lieutenant Dumoutier with a laugh.

A few days later, when they were in rest billets, the officers put up a target against the wall in the courtyard of the Mess.

"Go on, Serval, take the first shot," his Captain said. "Imagine you're at the corner of that damned wall of yours."

Serval took up his position fifteen paces from the target. He raised his pistol to his shoulder and lowered it slowly as he took aim. He pressed the trigger. There was a loud snap.

Dumoutier turned to him.

"If you'd made a noise like that the other day, they'd have got you."

Serval had gone very pale and his hands were trembling.

"What's up? Aren't you going to fire?" the Captain said.

"Up? It's just that I'm more frightened after the event than I've ever been in my life before. It didn't fire."

He took out his knife and unscrewed the pistol butt.

The spring had broken.

THE KNIGHT

TO JEAN-PIERRE LE NÉE

❧ ❧ ❧ "Monsieur le Marquis should take his boots."

"You think so, Albert?"

Monsieur le Marquis de Bourcieux de Nauvoisis was drawing up his will; he was sitting at his desk and his little feet hung an inch or two above the floor.

"This mobilization is really very tiresome!" he said.

"Particularly," went on the valet, "since Monsieur le Marquis will certainly not find army issue boots to fit him. Besides, the instructions say that an allowance will be made to persons providing their own boots."

"Very well, then. And fetch the sword hanging in the gallery."

"The late Monsieur le Marquis'?"

"That's right. I remember that when I was doing my military service I found the regulation swords too heavy for me. And also, Albert, there's my cross, don't forget to get my cross out!"

The Marquis de Bourcieux, who was now approaching forty, was really very small indeed. Though he wore high heels on his boots and brushed his curly hair, which was carefully parted in the center, upward from his head, he failed to achieve normal height.

He went on drawing up his will, which began with the words: "At the moment of leaving for the Armies of the Republic in which one cannot tell what may happen to one . . ."

By this will, the Marquis, who was a bachelor, bequeathed to his nephew, the Vicomte de Nauvosis, the whole of his fortune, "or rather such part of it as those rascals of lawyers have left," which meant that what with mortgages and other debts he was leaving almost nothing at all.

He melted a little wax onto the envelope with his short, dimpled hand and said once again: "This mobilization is really very tiresome!"

Then, equipped with his two best pairs of boots and his father's sword, he set out for the cavalry depot at Carcassonne. The Marquis was a non-commissioned officer on the reserve. On arrival, he was given a form to fill in. He wrote his name and then his Christian names: Urbain Louis Marie. Having searched vainly for somewhere to enter his titles and distinctions, he wrote opposite the word *Profession:* Knight of Malta.

And that was all for that day.

No one said anything about making him an allowance for his boots, and he would not have accepted it anyway. But he mentioned it for the principle of the thing; it was clear to him that all army quartermasters were rascals.

On the other hand, he was made to take a heavy, clumsy sword though he told them he had brought his own.

Two days later, as he was crossing the barrack square, a red-faced commandant called him over. "Have you been a member of the Cadre Noir?" he asked.

"No, sir."

"Have you ever been a Spahi?"

"No, sir."

"Then why are you wearing gold spurs?"

"It's my right, sir. I'm a Knight of Malta."

"Oh, so it was you who wrote *Profession*: Knight of Malta, was it? Well, I'm sorry! There's nothing military about a Knight of Malta!"

"I beg your pardon, sir, the Order of Malta is a religious and military order. . . ."

"All right. It may have been military once, but as far as I'm concerned it counts as civilian. I can't go into all that now. But you'll wear ordinary nickel-plated spurs like everyone else."

The Marquis de Bourcieux made no attempt to explain to this oaf, who happened to be his superior officer, that when he had been made a knight "in the name of Monsieur Saint George, vigilant and pacific, and in honor of knighthood" gold spurs had been placed on his feet because they were "of the richest metal than can be found and therefore symbolic of honor."

The Marquis could have quoted fifty lines of the ancient text; but it was not easy to say these things when standing to attention.

He changed his spurs, but to make it clear that he was in no way abandoning his position he pinned his Cross of Malta to his tunic.

The cross caused a certain amount of confusion in the garrison. The first time Sergeant Bourcieux passed the gate wearing it, the sentry presented arms. And several times in the town, after dark, officers saluted him first because they saw the white cross gleaming and did not know who he might be.

In barracks, the gossip among the men was that he had been an officer in a foreign army, while the officers avoided talking to him because it was embarrassing to give orders and reproofs to a man who had his sixteen noble quarterings pinned, as it were, to his chest.

Nevertheless, one day, Captain d'Haquinville sent for him and said: "Listen, Bourcieux, couldn't you just wear the ribbon, like we all do for our decorations?"

"Sir," replied the Marquis, "I am a Knight of Justice and Devotion and only my cross . . ."

"Yes, I see," interrupted the Captain, "but I assure you, Bourcieux, it looks a trifle ridiculous."

"It surprises me to hear you say such a thing, sir!"

"Listen, Bourcieux, do as I say. You see, the Knights of Malta are a little obsolete these days."

"Sir, you're insulting the sovereign Order of St. John of Jerusalem."

"Very well, if you're going to take that tone, I shall have to remind you that you're not in Jerusalem here, but in barracks!"

"I'm among a lot of rascals here, sir!"

"You'll take fifteen days confined to barracks!"

"Sir, I shall send you my seconds!"

The colonel smoothed things over. There was no duel, nor was the Marquis confined to barracks. They gave him an office job. After a while, however, he declared that he had come to fight and not to make "nil returns."

He was transferred to the first squadron which was preparing to leave for the front.

"I should have waited another fortnight before making my application," Bourcieux thought when he realized that he was under the command of Captain d'Haquinville.

The Captain made no comment on the cross the Marquis still insisted on wearing, but simply allotted him the tallest horse in the squadron.

The Marquis was a very good horseman; but when he wanted to mount, he had to be given a leg up, like a woman, which made everyone smile. But he paid no attention; for, after all, it was a perfectly normal way for a gentleman to get into the saddle.

From the first engagement, Sergeant Bourcieux de Nauvoisis was a surprise to the squadron. He always dismounted last so as to avoid having to mount again in case there were counter-orders. But when he did dismount, the first thing he did was to unfasten his father's sword from the saddle, for he never allowed himself to be parted from it.

"Really, Bourcieux, what are you doing with that toothpick of yours?" cried the Captain, while the troops were taking up their positions and the machine-guns were beginning to rattle.

The Marquis made no reply as he walked unhurriedly on, his head high, his helmet tilted up on his brow, his Cross of Malta gleaming white on his chest and the hilt of his father's sword almost in his armpit. He never took off his gloves, and he never lay down even under the heaviest fire; though he was, on one occasion, seen to stoop on the pretext of removing mud from his boots. He seemed to lead a charmed life. When anyone mentioned it, he simply shrugged his shoulders. He was not really interested in this sort of war.

"You don't know whom you're killing and you don't know who's killing you," he said. "Shells and bombs arrive from God knows where. The enemy's above you, beside you and behind you; I don't see how anyone can expect to die face to the enemy these days."

One evening, when the squadron, whose strength was already reduced, was retreating, it reached an abandoned village which it had orders to defend. The doors and windows had been left open. The sun was setting. The bright red rays shone through the windows and showed up the chaotic interiors of the houses. Chattels the inhabitants had been unable to take with them littered the farmyards. The poorer the house, the later and the more hurriedly it had been abandoned. A patrol sent on ahead reported nothing suspicious.

As the Captain and his headquarters reached the square they were received with a burst of machine-gun fire which seriously wounded two men. The village was searched at once. The enemy must still be there. Every alley was explored. Shots were fired into the basements of the houses but drew no response. The whole place seemed empty. The Captain returned to the square by the church. There was no sign of the enemy. He issued orders for the defense of the village.

"Don't let's waste time over the bastard; he's probably de-decamped already," he said.

But at that very moment there was another burst of fire that only just missed the squadron's second-in-command. The Captain and the men with him took cover against the wall of the church, in the shelter of one of the side porches.

"Don't stay there, sir! Don't stay there!" a man shouted. "The fire's coming from the presbytery."

The presbytery was surrounded, entered by the back and searched from cellar to attic. The men appeared at the windows. They signaled there was no one there. But another burst of fire swept across the front of the house.

"This is too damned much," the troops said. "The bastard's got the hell of a nerve. We must draw him out." But where was he?

The men, and even the Captain himself, were becoming rather concerned. Their positions might be attacked at any moment. Enemy motorcyclists had already been seen a little way up the road. And during the coming battle, the mysterious machine-gun would be right in the center of the village, covering the junction of three main roads, interfering with communications, and generally creating confusion where calm was required.

"Oh, the rascal!" suddenly cried Sergeant Bourcieux, who had just been greeted by a burst of fire as he rode his horse round the back of the church.

He galloped across the square.

"Oh, the rascal!" he repeated.

"What's the matter, Bourcieux, are you wounded?" the Captain asked.

"No, sir. I'm all right. But I've found the fellow. He's in the church, and firing through the windows of the choir."

"Are you sure? It won't be easy to dislodge him."

Captain d'Haquinville gazed at the squat old country church with its gothic apse pierced by dark, narrow windows, separated from each other by thick stone buttresses.

Clearly the man with the sub-machine-gun could move from window to window and, knowing every corner of the place, could fire either to the right or to the left from behind good cover. When attacked, he could climb into the bell-tower and it would be a hell of a business to dislodge him.

The Captain did not want any more casualties and he had no ammunition to waste firing at the stones.

"It would be a different matter if we had some hand-grenades," he said.

There was no alternative to entering the church. The troopers looked at each other. They were not lacking in courage but they were reluctant to fight in a church.

Sergeant Bourcieux de Nauvoisis came forward.

"Sir," he said, "will you permit me to deal with this business in my own way?"

"What do you propose to do?"

"I'm a Knight of Malta, sir."

"So what?"

"I have the right to enter churches on horseback, sir!"

And without waiting for a reply the Marquis called two men over, placed them each side of the great door, and told them to throw it open when he gave the signal. Then, in front of the astonished squadron, he buttoned up his gloves and drew his sword.

The sun was behind him, a red sun on the horizon which lit up the church door and glinted on the blade of his sword.

"Open!" he cried.

And he galloped forward.

The Marquis had both surprise and the sun on his side. And he had luck too.

The man with the sub-machine-gun was prepared for anything except a horseman, sword in hand, appearing suddenly out of the brilliant, dazzling light. He lost his nerve and tried to take cover behind the altar. But he slipped on the steps and dropped his weapon.

His surprise lasted no more than three seconds. But during those seconds, as he lay on the floor of the church, he had time to see a round, blood-red sun between horse's hooves pounding the flagstones. It was a vision he might have remembered all his life. He just had time to get to his feet and pick up the sub-machine-gun. His finger was on the trigger. But he had no time to fire. The sword point took him full in the chest.

When the Marquis raised his eyes, he saw in a niche above him a stone "Monsieur Saint George," spurs on his heels, the dead dragon at his feet. The saint seemed to be looking down at him.

The Marquis then realized to whom he owed his luck. He dismounted and fell on one knee.

Then he mounted his horse again, though he felt a curious weakness in his legs, with the help of a pew.

He walked his horse out of the church. The sun lent the Cross of Malta on his breast a rosy glow.

Sergeant de Bourcieux de Nauvoisis, a Knight of Justice and Devotion, saluted his Captain and then wiped his sword on the leaves of an elm which grew nearby.

THE FAIR-HAIRED GIRL

❧ ❧ ❧ Night had fallen when they lifted them out of the ambulances. Their captors' guttural tongue, of which they understood not a word, increased the feeling of unreality they had had ever since the ground had suddenly rushed up to hit them, or they had fallen into sudden darkness with just time to think: "This is it!"

Since then, a series of ill-connected images, like dotted lines on maps representing doubtful paths, had marked their passage from fit men to their present dubious state. Stretcher-bearers in uniform, enemies standing over them like executioners—though at that moment they would have felt a surge of hope and brotherly affection even at the approach of the hangman himself—lapses into unconsciousness, regimental aid-posts, sniffing gas through cold masks, the strange painlessness of surgeons' scissors cutting at their flesh, plaster pouring round their limbs, transit hospitals where they had seen nothing but the stains on the ceilings, the rubber-deadened jolting of trolleys against their necks, the smell of formaldehyde, ether and dirty linen, dark ambulances and bright sparks of pain—all these had ultimately led to a nurse with heavy breasts and a crudely shining white room in which all eight of them had been laid in beds side by side.

Only two of them already knew each other, if belonging to the same regiment could be called that.

They could at least mention the same officers' names and say: "Oh, yes! That tall dark one, who always looked half-witted!"

And this gave them a welcome illusion of friendship. Failleroy and Louviel managed to persuade themselves that they had often passed each other on the barrack square and drunk side by side in the same bar and gone to the same brothel on the same day.

"Didn't you once turn me back because my overcoat was dirty when you were on gate-guard?"

"Quite likely. Yes, I remember . . ."

"Funny, isn't it?"

Failleroy's foot had been blown off by a mine, and the bone of his leg had been opened like a lily. Failleroy lay in the first bed, nearest the window hidden behind a black curtain.

Fat Louviel was lying flat on his back; his chest, neck and head were encased in a breastplate and helmet of plaster. The ceiling lights hurt his eyes. He was sorry to be separated from Failleroy by another bed. Renaudier, most of whose face had been removed by a bomb, did not yet know he was blind; he had the irritating feeling that his hair had fallen over his face and had been carelessly caught in the dressings.

"It's queer to be shut up in a room like this and not even know where you are," said Mazargues, who occupied the sixth bed.

What was the name of the town? What was the shape of the building? What was it built of? Indeed, was there a town at all, or was this some country house that had been turned into a hospital with a big red cross on the roof? Yet, they thought they could hear the noises of a town outside.

"Anyway," continued Mazargues, "have you seen the nurse? She's got a front on her, by God! Ugly as she is, I could . . ."

He told them obscenely just what he could do. Mazargues came from the south of France, had bright eyes, and sticking-out ears. Half a dozen shell splinters had been removed from his back and buttocks. His wounds had aroused in him a strange state of priapism. It was continual and almost unbearable.

The lights were dimmed. Those who could went to sleep. The others dozed fitfully on waves of pain, listening to the blood hammering in their wounds.

Failleroy stared for a long while at the black curtain that hung beside him and entirely obscured the window; it was like the dark veil through which you must talk to a cloistered nun and, in this milk-white cube of a room, seemed to be masking the entrance to death's domain. The foot Failleroy had lost was absurdly painful.

Mazargues had difficulty in controlling his groans at the mere contact of his nightshirt.

In the morning, the nurse with breasts like melons came into the ward and drew the curtains.

Light flowed into the room. The wounded men became conscious of its evil stench.

Failleroy raised himself on his hands a little. His short brown hair was wet with sweat and his feverish flush gave him a deceptive appearance of health.

"Well, Failleroy, what's it like outside?" Louviel asked from within his white breastplate.

"Outside?" repeated Failleroy.

He rubbed his eyes.

"Damn this hair over my face!" muttered Renaudier; only his mouth was free of the bandages. "It's a bit of luck they put someone by the window who can see out. I hope in a few days' time . . ."

They all felt rather embarrassed. Failleroy looked out of the window and said: "It's not too bad outside. Can't complain. We're in a fairly decent sort of place. There's a little garden with a street beyond it, and then more houses."

He went on describing the view: the houses were low and built of brick. A little old man was walking down the street, reading a newspaper. Housewives were going out shopping.

The wounded men listened with silent attention.

The passing of a vehicle made the windows shake.

"It's a big military truck with fellows with rifles," said Failleroy.

"What are the women in the street like?" asked Mazargues.

Failleroy laughed and showed his fine white teeth.

"They're nothing to get excited about, my lad," he said. "They've not got much in the way of looks, I promise you."

"I don't care a damn whether they've got looks or not," cried Mazargues. "I just want a woman, do you hear, a woman!"

"You'd better get your bottom cured first," said Louviel.

"And you're not the only one, you know," said the deep voice of the last man in the row. "The only thing is, *we* don't make so much fuss about it."

Failleroy retreated under the bedclothes and closed his eyes. But a moment later he sat up, and began looking out of the window again. Suddenly, he cried: "At last, here's a pretty girl!"

"Is there?" said Mazargues. "What's she like?"

"Fair. And her hair's done up in a bun at the back of her head. But she's pretty, all right!"

But then the doctor came in on his rounds. Since he had no common language with the wounded, he was like a vet who has to question by touch and supply his own answers. The nurse nodded as she noted his orders. While he was examining the wound of the last man in the row, who had drainage tubes in his stomach, they heard a stifled groan from behind the clenched teeth.

"I'm damned if I'll squeal in front of these bastards," he muttered, when his dressings had been renewed.

"Bastards or not, they look after us pretty well," another said.

"Yes, funny, isn't it?" said Louviel. "They do all they can to blow us to bits, and then . . ."

"The human race is all crazy!" said the man with the drainage tubes sententiously.

The morning went by without incident. But a few minutes after noon, Failleroy said, "Ah, there she is again! She's looking this way."

He smiled and raised his hand and waved, as if to say hello.

"The little bitch, she turned her head away on purpose," Failleroy said, lying down again.

At about two o'clock, he saw the fair-haired girl go by again; she avoided looking up.

"I think she must be a typist," Failleroy told Louviel.

At six o'clock, she appeared again and, this time, Failleroy was able to announce triumphantly that she had looked up at the window for a long time.

He had to describe her in detail. What were her breasts like, her legs, her bottom?

"Her ankles? Oh, I didn't notice her ankles."

"It's always the fools who have the best seats," said Mazargues in exasperation.

Night brought its own pain and weariness. But with the morning came reassurance once again with the drawing back of the black curtains. And for the next few days, apart from the rhythm of temperature-taking, doctor's rounds, dressings and meals, they lived by strange time divisions of their own, marked by a clock whose face recorded the passing of the fair-haired girl.

"Failleroy, you're in love," the others said.

"Not at all. Can't you see I'm simply amused?"

But the other seven were in love too. It was as if the intrigue that was developing through the window was their own. They felt as if they had been there for an eternity, and that the fair-haired girl, invisible to all but one of them, had already passed by a thousand times.

Nothing else interested them. If, by chance, Failleroy was

dozing at noon, one of them would shout: "Wake up, Failleroy! It's almost time!"

They knew that Failleroy had been a tailor before he had joined the army.

"You could dress her," they said.

But Failleroy thought: "How shall I be able to sit cross-legged on my bench without my foot?"

Mazargues could bear it no longer. He was rent with desire, jealousy and wounded pride. He would have committed any betrayal, could he have done so. He longed to get out of hospital before Failleroy. "Anyway, he won't look much hobbling about on crutches," he thought. Whereas he saw himself strolling through the streets of the town, his arse still a bit stiff perhaps, but square-shouldered, arrogant and carrying all before him.

He kept on telling wild and obscene stories in order to attract attention.

And they kept interrupting him to shout: "Shut up, Mazargues!" Particularly when he brought the fair-haired girl into them.

"It's a pity we don't even know a single word of their damned language," said Louviel to Failleroy. "Or I'd be able to write something nice on a big piece of paper and show it to her."

Then Failleroy had the idea of cutting a heart out of an old leave-pass. And three times he held it up to the window as the fair-haired girl went by.

And the next morning, as she passed, Failleroy smiled broadly. His smile contrasted with the puffy pastiness that had begun to spoil his good looks.

"She's wearing a heart-shaped brooch on her dress!" he cried.

"Which dress is she wearing?"

"The one with the green flowers!"

Another two days went by. Then, one morning, Failleroy replied to their usual questions: "No, she hasn't come by."

It so happened that it was the very morning the doctor, on feeling Failleroy's leg above the stump, nodded his head in an interested way, gazed attentively at the temperature chart, and looked meaningly at the nurse, as much as to say: "Didn't I tell you so?"

That evening, when Failleroy was looking out of the window, he murmured: "It's not really surprising."

"What?" asked fat Louviel.

Failleroy didn't answer.

"Do you mean your girl hasn't gone by tonight?" Louviel asked a moment later.

"Oh, yes! She's gone by all right. But with another man."

"Perhaps it's her brother!"

"To hell with that! They're all whores, the whole lot of them!" said Mazargues with satisfaction. "It's not paper hearts you want to show them, it's . . ."

"Shut up, Mazargues!" cried the man with the drainage tubes.

There was sadness in the ward.

"After all, it's perfectly natural she should have a boy-friend," thought Louviel. "But she might at least have been decent enough not to pass under our window with him."

Failleroy groaned a good deal during the night, though he was not conscious of doing so. He seemed to spend all the next day dozing; not once did he look out of the window, and the ward respected his sorrow.

And then, to everyone's surprise except the doctor's, that night he died.

His corpse was carried out and clean sheets were put on the bed.

Mazargues beckoned to the nurse with the big breasts and gave her to understand he wanted to be moved into Failleroy's bed.

The nurse was obviously sympathetic; and Mazargues was moved.

Mazargues hardly closed his eyes all night. His mind ran on green flowers, fair hair, and rosy, freckled flesh . . .

The nurse came in and drew back the long black curtains at the very moment Mazargues had at last fallen asleep.

He started awake, sat up like an exclamation mark, and looked out of the window.

"Christ!" he cried, and fell back on the pillows.

"What's up? What's the matter with you? Feeling bad?" the others asked.

Mazargues did his best to put a good face on it.

"Of course, I knew from the start that Failleroy was putting one over on us," he said. "I just wanted to make sure, that's all!"

Beyond the window there was nothing but a high grey wall and a rubbish heap.

And fat Louviel, imprisoned in his plaster helmet, felt the silly dampness of tears upon his face.

THE COLONEL

TO FREDDY CHAUVELOT

❧ ❧ ❧ "You're asking me what La Marvinière died of?" our comrade Magnan said. "I don't know. He died in my presence, in a few seconds, on the night of the Armistice. I'm no doctor and I couldn't tell you what it was exactly. I believe he may have had a bit of a heart. He used to say so himself. He was an odd person. I saw him only three times in all, but I shall never forget him.

"The first time was in Normandy, below the Seine, in a little village called Reuillenville. I was doing a liaison job at the time. I asked how to find him and was told: 'Colonel La Marvinière? You'll find him at the General's headquarters. You'll know him because he's tall and thin and very pale . . .'

"The headquarters was in the priest's house. You can imagine what the divisional headquarters was like, when I tell you that it had come in the night before and was almost certain to move again that day; there were motorcyclists making a filthy row all over the priest's garden. I went in. The General was there, leaning over a map with half a dozen senior officers round him. He was drawing big circles with a red chinagraph. An unfortunate non-commissioned officer was tapping away full bat on a typewriter; orderlies were hurrying in and out. And there, in a corner, all alone, an enormously tall man was standing against the wall. Indeed, he was so tall that there seemed to be no end to him. He had five stripes on his cap and was staring abstractedly straight in front of him. It was La Marvinière. He was leaning on a walking-stick that was as long as Louis XIV's. It had brass fittings, though what they were for I don't know. He looked bored, and as if he were taking no interest in what was going on round him.

" 'Good morning,' he said, raising two fingers from his walking-stick. 'What's this you've brought me?'

"I watched him while he was reading. It was really one of the most singular faces I ever saw: very long with a broken, squashed nose, and above it two big blue eyes, which seemed to pop out at you like snails. It was Morange who used to say: 'When La Marvinière is eating, one's always afraid his eyes are going to fall into his plate.' He had scars, too, on the jaw and at the temple; and his whole face was quite extraordinarily pale, the complexion of a delicate twelve-year-old.

" 'Have you had lunch, my dear fellow?' he asked me. 'No? Well, come along with me. We might as well go and have it for all the good I'm doing here. May I fall out, mon Général?'

"And off he went. We'd hardly got outside the headquarters when there was an air raid. The dive-bombers were overhead and came in again and again. Bombs were bursting all over the place, and a house collapsed. There were two hundred vehicles crammed into the village. A truck burst into flames thirty yards away. Panic. The men threw themselves down flat in the gardens. Meanwhile, La Marvinière stood with his back to a low, half-ruined wall, leaned on his stick, and waited for it to stop. His helmet was still hanging from his belt. It's far from agreeable to be with a colonel who insists on remaining on his feet when all you want to do is to throw yourself flat on the ground—discreetly of course—like everyone else! When he heard a bomb coming rather too close, he merely sank his head a little between his shoulders till the explosion, and then began to look up in the air again. I suddenly heard him shout through the hubbub: 'You lie down, my dear fellow! It's different for me. I prefer standing because I've got a bit of a heart.'

"The bombing lasted ten or twelve minutes. The anti-aircraft came to life at last and the dive-bombers flew away. The men got to their feet. One man ran past us yelling as if he were crazy. The colonel stopped him with his stick and said: 'What's the matter? It's all over now. There's no point in running, my lad. Look, I've not moved, and I'm still alive, you see.'

"He gave a crooked smile with a twitch of his stiff red moustache. But the man cried in a panic: 'Mon Colonel! Look at that! It'll go off!'

"A few yards from us, on the other side of the wall, was an unexploded bomb. It was lying on the grass like a big wild boar, its steel tail a little farther off. The ground round it was still smoking. Instead of moving away, La Marvinière put his arm over the wall, and poked at the bomb with the brass ferule of his stick. 'How very odd!' he said. 'Very odd, indeed!'

" 'I think we've had a damned lucky escape, mon Colonel!' I said.

"He nodded, and went on poking his stick at it. Then, still smiling his crooked smile, he said: 'It might perhaps be wiser not to touch it, don't you think? I'm told some of them have a delayed action. What's your view?'

"I saw to my surprise that the soldier was still standing beside us, absolutely hypnotized. He was breathlessly watching the colonel, but he'd stopped yelling and seemed quite calm."

Magnan paused for a moment, lit a cigarette and then went on: "Yes, La Marvinière was quite a man. You couldn't explain it, but you felt it. Indeed, yes, a great man! Well, now the raid was over, we got into our cars. He had a splendid apartment with a standard in his regimental colors. He first made a tour of his squadrons to see what damage there was; then we went to the house where he had set up his mess.

There wasn't a pane of glass left in the windows, but the table had been properly laid and the waiter wore a white jacket. I couldn't help asking, 'Have you been here long, mon Colonel?'

" 'No, we arrived this morning,' he said. 'Oh, you're surprised by Taupard's white jacket, are you? I insist on his being properly dressed. I really don't see why one should discard all the little decencies of life merely because there's a war on. After all, when one can have them, why not? Don't you agree? Taupard's a very good lad. He gets my bath ready, and he knows my habits. Taupard, have the others had lunch?'

" 'Yes, mon Colonel.'

" 'Good, bring us ours.'

"During the meal—and it was a meal such as I had not eaten for a long while, accompanied by an excellent claret La Marvinière brought out from the boot of his car—he noticed I was looking at him with some curiosity and said: 'You think I look a bit odd, don't you?'

" 'Not at all, mon Colonel!'

" 'Oh, yes, you do; be frank about it! You see, my poor mother gave me a face that wasn't particularly handsome. Still it was more or less passable. I hope she can't see what I've done with it from up above! My nose is due to a fall steeple-chasing. My horse had a heart attack jumping a big fence. He fell stone dead. And that' (he pointed to a sort of hole in his jaw) 'was an Uhlan's lance in 1914. You see, I've actually been in a cavalry charge! Oh, I'm an old-fashioned sort of fellow, I know! And that' (it was a pink, hairless patch above his temple) 'was a graze from a bullet in Morocco. The rest's only minor stuff. Anyway, I can say I carry all my memories in my head.'

"When talking, he closed his lids nearly completely over his eyes, which seemed as it were to overhang his flat nose. Then lunch came to an end. 'Good-by, mon Colonel!' 'Good-by, my boy!' And off I went.

"A week later, and a river farther back—this seemed to be the rhythm to which we lived—I was sent to find La Marvinière, who had remained somewhere out in the blue, fifteen kilometres away, with what few troops he still had left. My orders for him were to come back across the Loire as quickly as he could. The roads were almost empty, not a vehicle to be seen, merely a few stray groups of men making the best of their way south. Farther on, even these ceased, and there was nothing but the cows in the fields lowing to be milked. I was on my guard against being caught like a rabbit in a trap at each bend I came to. At last, I heard firing on my left. 'La Marvinière must be somewhere over there,' I thought. Eventually, I reached a village and found some of his men.

" 'The Colonel's in the big farm over there,' they said.

"I went to the farm. And what did I find there? La Marvinière having a bath in a huge tub in the middle of the farmyard. Beside him on a chair were his tunic, his breeches and his Louis XIV stick. His servant was standing in front of him holding out a mirror. La Marvinière was calmly shaving. I discovered afterward that it was a ritual; he had to have his bath every day. His servant's first duty on arriving at new billets was to find a receptacle large enough for the colonel to immerse himself completely, which, considering how tall he was, cannot always have been easy. That morning, he greeted me with the words: 'Hullo, delighted to see you! I always wonder what has happened to the fellows I've had luncheon with. Tell me your name again. Oh, yes! Magnan! That's right. What have you brought me?'

"He extended a long arm, white as chicory.

" 'Orders to retreat, mon Colonel.'

" 'Retreat? I never seem to do anything else! Besides, how do you expect me to retreat? Both my right and my left are engaged. Do they want a massacre? And where am I to retreat to?'

" 'Behind the Loire, mon Colonel.'

" 'But that's not a retreat. It's a cross-country run. So they won't let me fight any more, won't they? Taupard! The mirror! Hold it higher!'

" 'It's a definite order, mon Colonel. They're going to blow the bridges.'

" 'All right, all right, I'll look into it. I can't retreat with only one cheek shaved.'

"And he went on shaving, taking great care to avoid his moustache. There was something extraordinarily contagious about his calmness. Indeed, I had scarely realized that the firing seemed to be coming closer. However, a non-commissioned officer came up:

" 'Mon Colonel, things will soon be getting pretty hot here. Captain Duchemin has sent me . . .'

" 'Very well,' said La Marvinière. 'Just tell Captain Duchemin to keep me informed. I'll come to see him later on.'

"I thought he'd at least get out of his bath. But not at all. He merely said: 'Bring me a box of grenades. Put them there, within reach.'

"Then, turning to me, he said: 'It's always just as well to be prepared. I tend to be rather nervous of the unexpected. You see, as I've already told you, I've got . . .'

" 'A bit of a heart, mon Colonel?' I said with a smile.

" 'Certainly. But don't laugh. What's so odd is that no one will believe it. Well, I suppose we must get down to business. Taupard, the towel!'

"He dried his hands.

" 'My map!'

"He had only a Michelin map, and I suppose was lucky to have that.

" 'Right! Well now, Magnan, you can do something for me. Come over here!'

"I leaned over his bare shoulder.

" 'There, I shall retire on this point here, by the B—— bridge. So go and tell them not to blow it before I get there.

What's the time now? Ten o'clock? Yes, tell them not to blow it before half-past twelve, will you? Right, get off at once. And thanks, my boy. See you soon.'

"Bullets were beginning to whistle about not far away. He sank back into the tub, saying: 'I shall stay here another five minutes; it's going to be damned hot today.' "

Magnan had unconsciously been imitating the colonel's voice. He went on in his own: "I admit I went off rather reluctantly. I'd have given a lot to see La Marvinière chucking grenades at the enemy stark naked.

"By half-past twelve he hadn't arrived, of course. At three o'clock, the guard on the bridge received orders to blow it. After that, we naturally thought La Marvinière had had it. Some people said: 'Of course, he was completely crazy!' And others: 'No doubt, but if everyone had behaved as he did . . .'

"Then, on 25 June,"—Magnan paused for a moment— "and, my God, what an absolutely heavenly day it was!" he murmured. "Well, on 25 June, as I was going through a little town in the north of the Dordogne, I learnt by chance that La Marvinière was there. I found him in the notary's house. Outside, as always, were a sign in the regimental colors saying 'Regimental Headquarters,' a sentry and an orderly —the whole proper set-up. Le Marvinière, calm as ever, was sitting on a Henri II chair, with his stick beside him as usual.

"My first words were to ask him: 'What happened to you, mon Colonel?'

" 'What happened to me?' he repeated. 'Oh, nothing. We came over in boats by night; and then, as everyone seemed to have forgotten about me, I just went on with my own little war. But I've a feeling that now things aren't . . .'

" 'They're not going too well, mon Colonel.'

"He shrugged his shoulders as if utterly indifferent to the whole business.

"We talked for a few minutes, and I was just going to ask

him whether he had used his grenades, when a soldier came running in, his face radiant with joy, and cried: 'Mon Colonel, mon Colonel! It's over! They've signed the Armistice!'

"And the fool was smiling all over his face, believing the Armistice meant the end of the war, and, what's more, that the news would please the colonel.

"La Marvinière seemed not to react at all. He merely said quite quietly: 'All right, my lad, all right; thank you, you can go.'

"He seemed almost to be smiling himself. We were alone together. He said: 'Well, there it is!'

"He fell silent, staring straight in front of him. I suddenly saw him, who was normally always so pale, turn red. First his neck, then his chin, then his cheeks, then his forehead; second by second the color rose. I can't tell you the effect it had on me. He himself didn't seem to notice it. He was crimson right up to his forehead. I said: 'Can I get you a glass of water, mon Colonel?'

" 'Yes, a glass of water . . .'

"I went out and found my way to the kitchen. When I came back with the water to the dining room, La Marvinière was leaning out of his chair with his head between his knees. I pulled him up and cried: 'Mon Colonel! Mon Colonel!'

"He didn't seem to see me and muttered: 'Oh, it was bound to happen one day!'

"I don't know whether he meant the Armistice or death. His head fell forward and that was the end. . . ."

Magnan stopped, and crushed out the butt of his cigarette. There seemed nothing we could say. He went on: "I've told you that I've no other explanation except that he had a bit of a heart."

IN THE TRAIN

(12 *November 1942*)

❦ ❦ ❦ On 11 November 1942, all goods and passenger services were stopped on the Bordeaux-Marseilles line. We were not surprised. The German troop trains were on the move. The public knew that in case of total occupation or allied landings the Germans would take complete control of the French railway system for a week. For a country that had already been bled white, despoiled of its reserves, and in which the distribution of the essentials of life was already almost at a standstill, this could mean nothing but total paralysis, famine in the villages and death in the hospitals. And, no doubt, also, a profound reaction from the whole social organism in self-defense against death.

The Germans must have been aware of it, for they closed only the one main line to the south, and even then for only twenty-four hours.

"The trains have started again; the Germans are sending their troops by ordinary passenger train. It's no doubt a guarantee that the line won't be sabotaged," said the friend with whom I had been staying for the last month, at about noon on the twelfth.

I was gazing out of the window at the view. The landscapes that matter to us are not those we admire for five minutes on emerging from a car at a famous viewpoint that's marked on the map. Nor are they those we watch sliding past the compartment windows of a train. They are the landscapes we

161

know by rain and moonlight, those that have altered our very selves because they are linked forever to a love affair, a period of convalescence, or indeed a book.

"I think I shall leave tonight," I told my host.

I gazed out at the long, oily, metallic ribbon of the Garonne, at the fields on its banks, the lines of poplars criss-crossing in the valley, the greens, russets and mauves of the fine, late-autumn day. The light, the friendly curve of the hills on the horizon, the trees on the terrace through which you could see the hills, the house itself, even the window framed in branches, were all purely eighteenth century and purely French. The whole vista took on a peculiar clarity, the branches of the trees a greater density, because from the road below there came the sound of German columns moving on steel tracks down the tarmac, like overlarge jack-boots. If my plans worked out and I was able to leave France one day soon, this landscape would remain forever in my memory.

"The 'Bordelais' is an hour late," said the porter, as he weighed my luggage.

The 'Bordelais' was my train; and for nearly an hour I walked up and down the platform in the dark. The few lamps were so dim that I could not make out the faces about me.

At last, the train came curving out of the night. Lines seem always to curve before entering a station. The engine's light grew larger. The compartment windows swung past and, where the blinds were ill-drawn, they looked like so many pale, glaucous, sightless eyes.

Why was this train of 12 November to remain more permanently alive in my memory than any other train of my life? I think because there was in it a microcosm of the whole of the France in agony I was about to leave. Disaster, uniformed in green, sat side by side with France.

Even before the wheels stopped turning, the shivering

passengers, who had been standing scattered about the platform, gathered hurriedly into groups at the doors, like so
many filings drawn by magnets.

I had a word with the guard. I still believed in privilege.

"There's not a free seat anywhere till Toulouse."

So I joined the nearest group. I was last in the queue.

A hand was extended to help me with my bag.

I can still see that hand. It was large, white, and not very
clean.

"People are always more helpful in the third class," I
thought.

I looked up. Above the hand I saw the sleeve of a green
uniform. A German was helping me with my bag.

I found this intolerably disagreeable. I had been brought up
to say: "Thank you." I could not bring myself to say it to a
German.

But I could not afford to miss my train simply to stand on
dignity.

The coach I was in was reserved almost entirely for the
Occupation troops. Half the compartments were marked:
Nur fuhr Wehrmacht. You could see similar notices in
Belgium, Holland, Denmark, Norway, Greece, Yugoslavia,
Poland, Czechoslovakia and the Ukraine. Surely they had
already exported their language and their hated faces far
enough? My bag was propped on top of their luggage. There
were fifteen of them at my end of the coach, crowded into the
nauseously smelling lavatory, the corridor, the narrow space
between the two coach doors, standing, sitting, leaning, resting a foot on a pack: an army on the move.

Who had said that the German army consisted only of boys
and elderly reservists? These were tall, well built young men,
thin but tough, and there was a hard, a disquietingly ruthless
look about their faces, whether they were peasants or factory-
workers. Fair or dark, round of head or long of chin, they all
had the same look of having been dipped in a chemical solu-

tion that had given a sort of metallic film to their skins. Some
were asleep. The smell of their fatigue differed from that of
French troops; it was sourer. To be crowded among five of
them, with their belts against my coat, my feet among their
rifles, and the texture of their skins before my eyes, quickly
became intolerable. It was impossible to look away, to
ignore them. "These are men, after all—just men!" I told
myself, but the hatred surged up in me like the rising note of
an air-raid siren. The longing to commit murder is not of
much account when you cannot satisfy it. I picked up my
bag and began to make my way along the coach. Their
shoulders and their boots seemed to fill the corridor. Some
of their uniforms were worn. Others were spick and span.
They moved to make way for me. They were ten in each dark
compartment. But, in one, two non-commissioned officers
were lying asleep, each with a whole side to himself. In
another compartment two women and an old man in a cap
were sitting among the German soldiers. The women were
dozing; but their legs were tucked under them so as not to
touch the legs of the Germans. It was the same through all
the train. I saw silk stockings and cotton stockings, or none
at all, slim ankles, or ankles thickened by work or maternity,
all carefully drawn back from the black, enemy boots.

It took me about five minutes to reach the end of the coach.
Here was another heap of packs, helmets and weapons.
Twelve soldiers were standing in the corridor and the lavatory
door was open. And, hemmed in against the door, were two
French non-commissioned officers, one belonging to the
Colonial Army and the other to the Air Force. They were
no doubt on leave and strangers to each other, but their
isolation in this coach full of the enemy had drawn them
together. They typified our phantom army.

I made my way through the group of Germans blocking the
communication between the coaches. Beyond, there was a
crowd of young men, all about the same age, twenty, young

workmen and peasants, all joking, shouting and calling to each other. On my way down the corridor, I even heard one singing: *Auprès de ma blonde*. Who were these boys, each with his little suitcase or kitbag, who could still sing? I moved on and inquired of one of them.

"We're conscripts."

"Conscripts?"

"Yes, for the Youth Camps."

I had forgotten about this parody of "military service," a military service without arms to which groups of young men from the Free Zone were sent to clear heathlands or make charcoal for eight months. I had thought the government had forgotten about it too.

I knew that the Minister of Labor at Vichy, an old man with long white hair, wept often in his flat at night because the German government threatened to take these young men from the Youth Camps by force and send them to factories in the Reich. And yet, here was this new contingent, called up on the very day the Free Zone was being invaded. It was, no doubt, the better to assemble the young men to hand them over.

And here I found four boys, sitting unaware by a window, singing *Auprès de ma blonde!* They wanted to be conscripted and miss no part of their youth.

I looked for a vacant place—not in a compartment—somewhere merely to put my bag down and sit on it.

In the next coach the green uniforms of the enemy, ordinary travelers and conscripts were even more intermingled.

I found a temporary place beside a young, tired-looking woman, who was sitting on her luggage, and holding a child of seven on her lap. I heard her murmur from time to time: "Go to sleep, darling. Try to go to sleep."

If the child would only sleep, she could rest too. I could guess what that woman's day had been: queueing at the food shops at six o'clock in the morning; returning home at eleven with a few carrots and some *ersatz* sausage in her bag; two hours at the stove because the gas-pressure was so low the food wouldn't cook; doing the laundry without soap in the afternoon, using a brush instead; and, this evening, traveling, because every family was dispersed, and a relation, a brother perhaps, had fallen seriously ill at the other end of France. And all night long she would have to sit in the corridor and cope with the restlessness of a young child.

"Go to sleep, darling. Try to go to sleep."

And she pulled the little socks up the thin white legs.

The Germans in this part of the train were mostly from the Luftwaffe, the best dressed and the best maintained of the German forces. They were nearly all tall, blond and handsome; you felt they were proud of the fine cloth of their uniforms and of the long, cement-grey overcoats that reached to the ankle. Beside us, a corporal took a large sandwich from his pocket. It was of white bread and the rosy edge of a thick slice of meat showed between the well buttered slices.

"Mummy, I'm hungry!"

The reaction was instantaneous. The thin little legs beside me kicked. The socks fell down again.

"Mummy, I'm hungry!"

The child's eyes were fixed on the rosy meat. He couldn't sleep because of his hunger.

For the first time since boarding the train, I noticed the shaking of the coach and the rhythm of the wheels, to which you can sing any song in the world in three-time. For a moment I lost the thread of my thought and a tune began running through my head of its own accord. Was I, too, reacting to that slice of red meat? It was too silly. I belonged to the class that was relatively the best fed in the country. Sometimes, it made me ashamed. I had forbidden myself even to think of the hunt for food. We all lacked calories.

I looked at the German corporal again. He was biting into

the firm meat; it refused to give way. He stopped, looked at me, and said in comprehensible French, though his accent was appalling: "It won't give way. It must be English."

He laughed.

For a second I was amazed, and then it occurred to me that he had made a splendid quip. I looked away, smiled and thought that I would certainly repeat it. The German clearly mistook the meaning of my smile and I had a feeling he wanted to enter into conversation with me. I quickly took a newspaper from my pocket. It consisted of a single sheet. None of the articles was signed. It contained merely the Vichy communiqués printed in large type: "The entry of operational troops is being carried out in a perfectly orderly manner . . ." "It is the duty of the population to welcome the German forces with calm and dignity." I turned the sheet over: "Food rations for the month." Absent-mindedly, I read the column. This month we had a right to 250 grams of flour, 3 kilograms of potatoes, 30 grams of coffee, or 90 grams of *ersatz* coffee, 1 liter of wine per week, etc. . . . All subject to whether the shops could be supplied.

Two women were talking in the compartment behind me.

"So you live in Marseilles? I'm told the food situation there is more difficult than anywhere else. And now that *they* are there, it'll be worse still. . . ."

When standing earlier on the station platform, I had heard two middle-aged men, both well dressed and presumably businessmen, saying to each other: "How do you manage? If you like, I can give you the name of a restaurant in Nice. You have to eat in the back kitchen. It's pretty expensive, but the other day I had . . ."

And he detailed the dishes. A bit of fish and a slice of cheese had become miracles.

On every level of society the subjects of conversation were the same. First: "The bastards . . ."; second: food. The rich discussed restaurants, the poor grocers. The children kicked their legs at the sight of bread. The main concern of the whole population was hunger.

The train slowed down. The lights suddenly flickered and we were all thrown against each other. It was not an accident; merely the ungreased brakes. They overheated and deteriorated at every turn of the wheels.

A few travelers got out. Others got in. Everyone was talking about the Germans and reporting the situation in his own town.

"The convoys have been continuous since this morning. . . ."

"Where on earth do they manage to find so many of them . . . ?"

"The bastards took over the post office and turned everyone out of the Hôtel du Commerce. . . ."

They were no longer called the Boches as in the other war, nor the Fridolins as in 1940; the whole population referred to them merely as "the bastards."

I took advantage of the general bustle to find a less crowded coach. As the train started again, a man left his seat in a compartment and offered it to me.

"I'm going to look out of the window," he said. "It's dark and I shan't see very much of the countryside. But it's a pleasure all the same. It's two and a half years now . . ."

He was wearing a beret, and was dressed in an ill-cut suit of civilian pattern, but made of military khaki; he had a little white cloth cross on the shoulder. He was a prisoner repatriated from Germany.

There were five more repatriated prisoners in the compartment, all peasants; and also two factory-workers, of whom one, sitting in the far corner, never uttered a word, while the other, who was next to me, asked ceaseless questions.

The repatriated prisoners had a good deal to say to their fellow countrymen, and they talked for the next half-hour, while I dozed and listened to their stories. They told of

death by cold steel, of traps set for sentries, of escapes and of
the food.

"There were many worse off than we were. We worked on
the farms. Where I worked, the farmer's wife, when she heard
that her third son had been killed, took Hitler's photograph
down from the wall and put it away in a drawer. When the
fifth was killed, she went and took the photograph out of the
drawer, tore it up, and threw it on the fire.

"It's the Russian prisoners who have the worst time. There
was a camp of them near ours. I've seen the 'ghost-wagon'."

I listened. I'd already heard of the "ghost-wagon" from
others who had come back.

"They were dying at the rate of forty or fifty a day. It seems
men six feet tall weighed less than sixty pounds. The Russians
have to bury their own dead. Every night they put the corpses
into a big hand-cart; they were naked because the others had
taken their clothes; and then they put the dying, who were
still moving and groaning, on the top of the cart; but it took
about thirty of them to push it, because they were so weak.
You could see them going past at night beyond the barbed
wire. It was a cart full of skeletons, drawn by skeletons. . . ."

This memory was common both to peasants and intel-
lectuals; those who had seen it would never forget it. They
would remember it all their lives.

"Have you been freed because of the *relève?*"* the factory-
worker sitting beside me asked.

"Freed, do you call it? Just look at the papers the bastards
have given us."

The papers were passed from hand to hand. They stated
that the prisoner was on agricultural "leave" in France; that
he was still subject to the military authority of the Reich;

---

* The *relève* consisted of volunteer, or more often conscripted, French
workers sent to work in German factories. In return, a varying but always
proportionately small number of French prisoners of war was released.

(*Translator's note*)

that he might not carry arms; that he might commit no act nor utter any word against Germany; and that, if he contravened these regulations, he would be subject to "the laws of war and, in particular, to that of death."

"So you see what the *relève* does for us!" cried the repatriated prisoner. "One of us for fifty of them! The workers who go to Germany ought to be shot!"

"Wait a minute, old chap," replied the factory-worker. "You don't imagine they go of their own free will, do you? They're taken by force and herded into trains. What's more, you know how many leave, but you can't tell how many reach the other end. Lots of them escape on the way. You no doubt haven't heard that the other day a crowd of them left shouting 'Vive Stalin!' out of the train window. And you don't yet know that many of them are hiding in the countryside. But you'll find out!"

The factory-worker sitting by the window in the corner, who had not opened his mouth since the start of the conversation, suddenly turned and said curtly: "So long as there's still anything to steal in France, it's a great deal more honorable than going to work in Germany."

I had returned his seat to the peasant, who had been gazing with such sad intensity through a chink in the blind at his recovered, night-bound countryside. Indeed, our whole country was covered by the night; our whole population was in darkness, hemmed in and heaped together, as in this train, by the crushing presence of the enemy. Turning vainly this way and that, it could find no resting place and all the blinds of all the windows had been drawn so carefully that it could see nothing of the world outside.

These men who had been talking in the compartment had a courage of which they were unaware; indeed none of us were wholly aware of it, because our idea of courage needed refashioning. The burden of abnegation the period demanded was too heavy for the shoulders of one man alone. You might as well have asked an artisan to build a railway engine by himself, from mining the ore to fashioning the wheels. Apart from a few élite, there were none capable at that time of carrying through from beginning to end an act of heroism or even of mere resistance.

But the factory-worker fled the *relève* and the peasant hid him. The railway-worker paralyzed distribution by refusing to unload trucks, even when they contained food for thousands. The hostage was shot for the saboteur; the saboteur died of hunger; the railway-worker became a hostage; and the prisoner cried from his prison camp: "Don't come to Germany!" Each began a course of action for which all had collectively to bear the consequences. Courage, like labor, was widely spread; but it was the people as a whole that was courageous.

I continued my way down the train through the corridor till I came on such a crowd that I could go no further. There was an almost empty compartment but no one dared enter it, neither women nor Germans. It was marked "Reserved." There were three passengers in it, but of a particular sort: two police and a criminal, a murderer, I was told. He was young and puny, with a sharp, dishonest face; his clothes had a sordid look about them.

The police were broad-shouldered and jovial-looking. One of them had a pair of handcuffs hanging from his pocket. I opened the door and said: "Can I put my bag on the rack?"

"It would be a pleasure, Monsieur. But we've just refused those bastards there," one of the police replied, jerking his thumb at the Germans leaning against the corridor windows. "They wanted to put their damn luggage in here, but I showed them the notice. Damn it, this is our country! We've still got some rights!"

The consideration society still afforded crime was impressive. Women and Germans, indeed everyone might stand; the police themselves would be standing had they not been escorting the mean-looking character sitting in the corner with a smile on his lips and smoking a cigarette with no sign of remorse.

The only people who could still say "No" to the Germans and still had "rights" were these two policemen, not because they were policemen, but because of the criminal they were escorting. And the Germans submitted.

I looked at the Germans. They were nearly all wearing the wide black and red ribbon of the Russian campaign in the third buttonhole of their tunics. They had just come from the Eastern front and each one of them must have had at least half a dozen lives on his conscience, even if he had not herded Jews into gas chambers in Poland, or massacred children in captured villages.

Was it of this the mean little prisoner with his single murder was thinking? He could estimate the criminal values concerned better than we could. Suddenly, in a rather drawling voice, he said something that made me feel I could forgive him, whatever he had done: "When are we going to chuck the vermin out?"

The police nodded their heads. They were all three agreed that the road to the guillotine should be among Frenchmen and free of vermin. I wanted to shake them by the hand—all three of them!

Toulouse. Even before the train had come to a halt there was shouting at both ends of the coach.

"Monsieur, stay where you are! No, Monsieur, don't get out yet! Madame, take care! Let's have a little order!"

This was no riot among the passengers; merely the Communications Police, the latest Vichy police force, throwing its weight about. It was odd how the presence of the Germans seemed to give them authority. The police were taking themselves seriously; they had an example of discipline before their eyes. Besides, their black uniforms were modeled on those of the Communications Police of the Reich. But the crowd paid no attention to their shouts and threats; they were simply submerged by sheer weight of numbers.

Movement on the platform, however, was almost paralyzed by the number of police in evidence. They were of all kinds; Garde Mobile in khaki with slung rifles, Gendarmerie in blue, the old State Police, the new State Police, the Territorial Control in plain clothes, a brassard on the sleeves of their overcoats, and Communications Police. All the dozen varieties of Vichy police were present, for the Secret Police, the Marshal's Personal Police and Laval's Personal Police were there too.

The hero who had ridden under the Arc de Triomphe in 1919 was now called "the Marshal of the Police."

And, indeed, all he had left was, on the one hand, former civil servants of the Republic who reluctantly continued to do their jobs because it was all they had, and, on the other, the newly enlisted army of police, which did its best to justify its triple rations.

A considerable number of Germans got out of the train. I noticed that many of them were carrying away the cushions from the first-class carriages.

"They use them in their tanks and trucks," someone said beside me. "They've been doing it in the Occupied Zone for a long time past."

All the varieties of Vichy police looked on with indifference. Indeed, when you came to think of it, there was no reason why these soldiers should not be permitted to steal cushions, when the government allowed railway-engines to be looted every day.

The guard had promised me a first-class seat after Montpellier; in the meantime, he had found me a second-class seat which would be vacated after the next station.

The corridor of the coach was as crowded as the other, and I would have gained no advantage from the change were it not for the fact that there was a certain relief in seeing fewer green uniforms.

Beside me, a man of some thirty years of age was watching me roll a cigarette in my little machine. I had no tobacco left except some coarse bitter stuff the peasants cultivated and harvested secretly for their own use. You had to tease the tobacco out into the machine, lick the paper, press gently on the cover and, even then, more often than not, the cigarette broke. So you had to start all over again. It was a difficult and complicated technique.

My neighbor smiled politely and extended his cigarette case.

"You're sure I'm not depriving you?"

"Not at all. Please have one," he said.

I gratefully accepted a cigarette. The man had a slight Flemish or Alsatian accent. I couldn't quite place it. I felt like asking him from what part of France he came; but I did not dare. At that time, there were so many people who had something to hide. We talked about tobacco for a moment or two. To find something to smoke had become an obsession, perhaps the worst obsession of all. The ration was four cigarettes a day. A packet cost a hundred francs on the black market, when you could find it. Everyone used their butts over again.

"Your cigarettes are first class," I said. "Pre-war."

Someone touched me lightly on the shoulder. I turned.

"Oh, Pierre! How are you?"

He was trembling with anxiety, but relaxed when I called him Pierre. I was not such a fool as all that. I would never have called him by his surname. And anyone might be called Pierre. In any case, Pierre was not his real Christian name.

"What's the news?"

"As you see, I'm traveling, as usual," he murmured with a smile.

I noticed that his pale, rather ugly face looked tired.

"I haven't slept for four nights," he said; "but that's nothing. Anyway, I hope to have a good sleep tonight."

He spoke very low. I avoided asking him where he was staying. Anyway, I suspected he never stayed in the same place more than a couple of days.

Pierre was an obscure journalist who had covered theater gossip before the war. In all the four years I had known him, he had worn the same overcoat and the same nonchalant smile. Like today, I had met him by chance in a train some months before, and he had asked me with some embarrassment not to call him by his name.

"I call myself Pierre," he had said.

I had realized that he was a member of that clandestine France which was to cost Germany so dear, was indeed costing her already more than a whole army in uniform. It had occurred to me, indeed, that Pierre was probably one of the leaders of the great organizations of the Resistance. But that we were to know only after the war. He was working with trades unionists, students of the Beaux-Arts, university professors, school teachers, garage hands, typists, solicitors, engineers, carpenters, writers of the Right, communists, practising Catholics, actors, doctors, and socialist revolutionaries.

Pierre was suddenly silent, and I saw him pass his forefinger slowly across his lips as if in thought. But the gesture was too emphatic to be automatic. He wanted me to shut up. I saw his eyes flicker to my left; and I looked round.

Beside us, the man who had given me the cigarette a moment before had been joined by another who was wearing a little swastika of red enamel against a white background in his buttonhole. My neighbor saw me glance at it. He seemed embarrassed. I heard him order the other away in a low, curt voice, and in German. The Gestapo.

I felt suddenly polluted by having spoken to him. I had taken him for a Belgian dealing in black market tobacco.

I had noticed nothing wrong. But Pierre, accustomed as he

had been for months to a clandestine, hunted life, was constantly on the alert.

"Fortunately, some of them are very stupid," he murmured, while the man with the swastika moved away. "What are you doing? Do you mean to say you throw away cigarettes only half-smoked? You must be rich," he added in astonished reproach, as if I were throwing bread in the mud.

That cigarette destroyed all desire to smoke for the next hour.

"There are two hundred and fifty of them on the train," Pierre whispered. "All for Marseilles. And there are as many going to Nice and Cannes. Come and look."

Pierre pointed them out to me; they were wearing flannel trousers and tweed coats, and had respectable suitcases. There were four in the next compartment, three in the one after. The corridors were full of them. The putrefaction of the Gestapo was everywhere. I had an intolerable feeling of uncleanness, of being stifled. The handles of the doors I touched were contaminated. The night was contaminated. The noise of the wheels was contaminated. Once again, I heard the rising note of the sirens of alarm and hate.

But Pierre was smiling. He was working to destroy them; he was at peace with himself. His mere presence among them was a defiance. He risked his life every hour of the day. He might be arrested today or tomorrow. He could afford to smile.

At the first stop, Pierre changed into another coach.

I went back to my seat in the compartment. The Gestapo agent came and sat opposite me. From time to time he looked at me. I began to wonder whether perhaps he was watching me. I knew that later on, as I left the station, I would turn instinctively to see if I was being followed. It was absurd, but that was the pass we had reached. I thought of the life Pierre led.

The other free seats had been taken by two German officers and by a young girl.

The sight of German officers seemed less intolerable now. They were at least wearing uniforms; when you looked at them, you knew you were looking at the enemy.

I saw them staring at the girl. She was doing her best not to catch their eyes and kept her feet well back against the seat.

At last one of the Germans made up his mind; in an accent that was so guttural it distorted every word, he asked her: "Do you know where one can dance and amuse oneself in Montpellier, Mademoiselle?"

The girl blushed; she lowered her eyes and made no answer.

The other German officer, in perfect and slightly ironic French, said: "Mademoiselle, this officer has just asked you a question. Perhaps you did not understand him. He was inquiring whether you knew of anywhere to dance in Montpellier."

The girl turned her head away, twisted round in her seat, and screwed up the edge of her coat. Her unhappiness, her helpless anger were painful to watch. Would she answer? What could she answer? Suddenly, sitting up very straight, she looked the German in the eye and said: "I know of none in Montpellier, but it seems there are excellent ones in Stalingrad!"

Opposite me, the Gestapo agent smiled.

The corridors of the first-class were crowded with senior German officers. As I reached the coach in which I was to finish my journey, I bumped into a friend. In old days, I would have been surprised to meet anyone I knew. But for the last two years everyone had always been meeting in trains. We had never traveled so much or so uncomfortably. In a France divided and dispersed, people were always traveling on some business or other between Toulouse and Lyons or Nice and Marseilles, as in the old days they went from the Place de la Concorde to Passy or from the Champs-Élysées to Saint-Germain-des-Près.

This particular friend was very tall, about forty, though he looked younger, and his eyes were very assured behind his heavy tortoise-shell spectacles; he was one of the leading engineers in France and perhaps in Europe. He had been extraordinarily successful during the last few years. He built dams and bridges. The last time I had seen him, a few months before, he had been reconditioning a harbor. I had a great admiration for his ability, and he knew it.

"I'm going to Switzerland," he said. "I'm going to make a survey and discuss plans. . . ."

"But the frontier's been closed since yesterday. You can't cross without a personal pass from Laval."

"Oh, I shall have to see. I'll fix something. I'll get across all right."

His calm assurance surprised me. But, inevitably, we began talking about the landings in North Africa.

"You know," he said, "I don't dabble in politics. That's the business of governments."

He seemed rather non-committal. He was obviously weighing every word he said as if afraid I might quote him. Did he distrust me? Or was he, by any chance, actually making concessions? "Ah yes," he said, "the Anglo-American victory. Yes, of course we shall probably have to give them some of our colonies. In any case, that's not the immediate problem. The De Gaulle party, the Giraud party, yes, excellent, most heroic. But of course they're outside France. And these Resistance organizations about which everyone's talking are rather disquieting for the future. . . ."

His attitude gradually became clearer. It was not his custom to talk merely for the sake of talking.

"In the present state of France," he went on, "I think the best we can hope for is the exhaustion of the warring nations. The Germans are still very well organized. And, in a certain sense, their conception of Europe can be defended. A victorious Russia would open the door to a revolution. You mustn't change your conquerors too often."

I did not want to understand. I still hoped I was mistaken.

And yet, whatever his views might be, this man I admired must surely share the suffering of France on this day the Armistice was being violated and provinces that had not known the presence of a foreigner for six centuries were being invaded. I thought we would be at one at least in our indignation.

"Look at this army of Occupation moving in in mass," I said.

He shrugged his shoulders rather nervously, as if I had made some unpardonable solecism, and replied, as if it were an obvious truth: "But it's not an army of Occupation, it's an operational army!"

And then, of course, I knew for certain. I understood what sort of people held the levers of power, and pulled the wool over the eyes of the credulous, the fearful and the stupid. I understood what sort of people disseminated propaganda and fear of revolution, as they distributed Pétain's photographs and national assistance cards, among the host of sound Frenchmen throughout the country, among the weak and the retired, and the shopkeeper fearful for his business.

"The business of governments" so easily became "have confidence in Pétain; he's an old fox." "The exhaustion of the warring nations" could be construed as "let's hope the last Russian will kill the last German."

There were not many of these people perhaps; but I was face to face with one of them. I knew that this man's assurance was due to the fact that he had Laval's signature on his passport. And he very probably had a German signature too. Why was he going to Switzerland? What complicated interests did he represent? On whose behalf was he playing the invader's game? I did not know. But I underwent one of the more painful kinds of change of heart: the loss of respect for someone one had admired, the death, within the compass of a few seconds, of confidence in a friend. And a face I had always been pleased to see had become a desert. . . .

I was on my guard now, and I answered: "Yes, yes, I've no doubt you're right. . . ."

The train had stopped at a town in which I had been in garrison in the autumn after the Armistice, before I was de-mobilized. I got out to walk up and down the platform I had known so well. I remembered that I had even commanded the platoon guarding the station on two or three occasions. It had not been a popular duty. But now, it took on almost the aspect of a happy time and I smiled at my memories of it. I strolled past the office I used to occupy on those occasions. There was a German lieutenant sitting in the same chair at the same table. I could see him through the window. I knew I should never again be able to think of that garrison town and of that period of my youth without seeing a German sitting in my place.

Getting back into the train, I saw a French officer in uni-form entering the coach by the farther door. He had been in my old regiment. Though we had not always seen eye to eye in the past, I was delighted to see him now. He had been a first-class horseman and steeplechase rider. He had been a good soldier too, and had greatly distinguished himself in 1940. I had been with him in June 1940, when he wanted, as we all did, to get to England, and the door had been closed on us. And then, six months later, I had heard him in the club preaching loyalty to the Marshal and obedience to the government in the name of military discipline, order, loyalty to one's superiors and one's sworn word.

To get to me down the corridor, he had to make his way past a number of Germans. I saw his face grow hard with an intense, cold hatred; there was such loathing in his eyes, such a look of defeat, that I hesitated to accost him.

"Look," he said, "look at what we've come to."

And for the next ten minutes it was all he could say: "Look at what we've come to!"

"You see, this P—— business" (he could not yet bring himself to say "this Pétain business—" the disillusionment was too great) "has been a swindle on one's honor as a soldier for the last two years. We were told we would take up the struggle again on D-Day. But D-Day was yesterday. And nothing was done. Now the bastards are here; and I have to appear among them wearing uniform."

I looked at his regimental badges, the very badges I had worn myself. Even though I was in plain clothes, I felt the same sense of physical humiliation.

He took me by the arm.

"Don't worry. They won't get our ammunition. Or if they do, it'll be in their guts," he whispered. "We hid five tons of it out in the country yesterday. I drove the truck myself."

He did not need to tell me this. It was merely that he wanted me to know that the honor of the regiment was safe.

"And if the army's disbanded, as rumor has it," he went on, "so much the better. Things can't go on like this. I shall go to England or Africa. Or take my men into the mountains. Good luck, old friend! We'll met again."

We always said "good luck" in the Cavalry, particularly when things were bad.

Seven o'clock. A grey light was spreading over the hills and orchards. I went to the restaurant car as soon as it opened. I had some difficulty in finding a place because half the tables were reserved for the officers of the Wehrmacht and most of the rest were already taken by members of the Gestapo. I saw my traveling companion from the second-class again; he was in conversation with a loyal Frenchman, who had no suspicions.

I said not a word to the people at my table. From now on the south would be like Paris. From now on, in all France, you would have to look carefully about you before whispering: "The Germans . . . Pétain . . . Laval . . ." And most of the time you'd keep silence.

We were served with a disgusting, black, sugarless concoction for coffee, and a slice of dry, grey bread.

The German officers had sugar and butter. The Gestapo agents, like the French, had to content themselves with what they were given.

I watched the officers. They stared out of the windows at the dawn breaking over this countryside they did not yet know. They smoked with a curious air of satisfaction. No doubt this conquered landscape afforded them a proud and special savor. Among the younger ones, I noticed one with his head bent over a book. And the mere fact of this made him somehow a man. I felt he had a mother and favorite authors. Perhaps he liked going to concerts, playing tennis and riding horses. Yet, his death was also necessary.

On my way back to my seat, hurtling from side to side in the corridor past the sleeping cars, I suddenly heard a voice I knew behind me.

It was a charming voice, that of a young woman who was descended from two of the oldest and most illustrious families in France. The coat of arms she wore on a slim gold ring on her little finger had sealed declarations of war and treaties of peace. She was on her way from Paris. She was small and very elegant; and she was wearing shoes with wooden soles. They were thick and heavy, yet shaped as carefully as a Louis XV console-table. She looked as if she were walking on stilts. The most famous shoemakers in Paris had become clog-makers by force of circumstance.

It was a pleasure to sit in her sleeper for a while. It afforded a moment's relaxation. Here, at least, you could give rein to your disgust without fear. And we did; but without insisting too much upon it. She belonged to that fashionable world in which, no matter what the circumstances, it has always been bad taste to insist too much on disagreeable subjects. She began telling me the current Paris stories.

"Old Baron de N—— was invited to dine with a famous

actress—who will undoubtedly be hanged," my friend added. "As he went into the hall, the first thing he saw was a German officer's overcoat; a smart green coat lying casually over the arm of a chair. So N—— retrieved his hat from the butler and said merely: 'Will you please tell Madame that I was taken ill the moment I arrived.' Good, isn't it?"

Any other day, I would have laughed. Today, it seemed terribly trivial in the face of what was happening. However, I did not want to be outdone. I told her about the criminal and the policeman, and the German who thought the meat must be English. I knew I could rely on her; they would go the rounds. But I did not tell her of the sadder side, of the child's hunger, of the compassion I had felt for the murderer. These things were not, it seemed to me, in keeping with the woman I was talking to.

She showed me her latest purchase: a box for cigarette-butts from the finest leather-worker in Paris. She laughed and put our cigarette-ends into it.

I thought of the conscripts on their way to the Youth Camps, who had sung *Auprès de ma blonde* the night before. And now, as if this young woman's gaiety had cast a new light on their singing, I understood them.

Indeed, nothing could ever destroy the simple, and yet subtle, ability to laugh in our people; nothing could ever prevent a Parisian woman being elegant, not even wooden soles to her shoes; as nothing could stop a Cavalry officer saying "good luck" in misfortune, or prevent a handcuffed criminal wanting "to chuck the vermin out." Our heads were unbowed; the traditions of our race were still intact.

It may well be that the easy, superficial, light-hearted conversation I had with her did me more good than anything else during the whole journey.

There was a knock on the door. It opened and Pierre appeared.

I was considerably surprised. He, too, seemed to have a moment's hesitation.

But the young woman smiled at him. She started introducing us in the most natural way in the world.

"Do you mean to say you know each other?" she cried.

I admit I was very surprised she should know Pierre.

We were drawing into Marseilles and Pierre looked at his watch; then he looked at me. Though he was expert at concealing his emotions, I felt he was anxious.

"It's quite all right, Monsieur, quite all right . . ." she said with a calm, gay gesture.

I watched Pierre climb onto the seat, put his hand into a crack in the wood behind the rack and bring out a white, quite ordinary-looking, but rather fat envelope. He slipped it into his overcoat pocket. No doubt the contents of that envelope were sufficient to send us all to Upper Silesia.

"I may perhaps have to apply to you again, Madame . . ." Pierre said.

"Whenever you like," she replied, as if it were some quite ordinary kindness she could do him.

And then, turning to me, she made a final witticism: "It seems our old families are so effete, they're above suspicion."

Marseilles. The train had barely come to a stop when the Germans who, the night before, had been so obligingly helpful with my bag, burst into the first-class compartment to which I had now returned and ordered us all out. Even the travelers who were going farther were turned out. They pushed us about and jostled us. You felt they'd throw your luggage out of the window as soon as look at you. The whole coach was needed for officers of the "operational army." You wondered what particular satisfaction they derived from obeying orders which at one moment constrained them to be polite and courteous and, the next, to behave as brutes and bullies. I did not understand; I never was able to understand.

I hated them for their docility, their capacity to accept and act on such contradictory orders as these.

There was a huge crowd on the platform. The loudspeakers were already crying: *"Achtung! Achtung!"* as they were doing in Paris, Brussels, Amsterdam, Athens, Oslo and Warsaw. *"Achtung, Achtung"*—orders for the detraining German troops: Luftwaffe pilots, Reich sailors, huge and bestial with loose black ribbons at their necks, officers with daggers at their belts, long green files, long black files, and the pullulating Gestapo; they all forced their way through the crowd with some difficulty, for it never made room and never mingled with them. And France too was going by. I saw the young woman who had hidden the secret message, the murderer with his police escort, the young men who had been singing, the hungry child, the exhausted mother, still more exhausted now, the workman who would rather steal than go to Germany, the officer who had hidden his unit's ammunition, Pierre who might well be arrested that very evening, and the rest, those thousands of others, to whom I had had no opportunity of speaking, and whose hunger, singing, courage and laughter I so much wanted to know. I was weary as a result of a sleepless night and my tired brain began to form images on its own. I thought of the powder you use in guns. The grains are not all of the same color. Nor have they all the same properties. But they're all mixed and mingled; and they all catch fire together, all create a single, huge explosion. And I knew that what I had seen would explode, explode annihilatingly when the moment came that a spark was set to it.

The crowd jostled me; and I did not care.

November 12, November 13. What was there so peculiarly distinctive about those days? A train had merely traveled across France as trains so constantly did. And here was a platform similar to every platform in every station in France.

And yet, as I looked about me, noted the French faces in the crowd, I felt an overwhelming certainty that, in spite of the loudspeaker shouting *"Achtung,"* the victors were not those who were under arms.

Part Three

MONDEZ HOUSE

TO GENEVIÈVE

❧ ❧ ❧ The doors at street-level were banging. The employees of the Société du Grand Egout Collecteur were leaving their offices.

On the first floor, Canon Augustin de Mondez put down his pen and got to his feet to relax for a moment. Now that he was seventy-one years of age, the greater part of his mail consisted of announcements of deaths, and he used the backs of the black-edged cards for making notes. The announcements, fastened into bundles with elastic bands or shoelaces, or simply lying in loose heaps, had been accumulating for years on the three desks, hiding the ink-pots, propping up the lamps, encumbering the armchairs, and strewing the carpet, until in the end the room began to look like an undertaker's office during an epidemic.

Augustin de Mondez was slight of build, looked nearly as short standing as he did sitting, had a pale, wrinkled skull, no eyebrows and narrow shoulders. He walked up and down with his hands in his pockets, swinging the skirts of his soutane like a bird's tail, as he usually did when he was thinking.

He was repeating to himself the last lines he had written and was wondering how to go on.

"It was the period (the fourth century B.C.) when Pithias and Euthymenes, the adventurous sons of Massalia of Phocaea, had already set out in their ships, the one toward the white shores of Scandinavia, the other to black Senegal . . ."

The sun was beating down on the roofs and the overheated air seemed to be boiling on the tiles. The smells of frying oil, basil and charcoal floated up to him.

Like most human lives, Mondez House had two façades opening onto different worlds. The principal façade gave onto the plane trees and the aristocratic houses of the Allées Léon-Gambetta, formerly the Allées des Capucines, and which the Marseilles aristocracy persisted in calling the Allées for short. This was the side onto which faced the drawing-rooms and reception rooms. The back of the house looked out onto a maze of sordid little courtyards, mean sheds in which various minor trades were carried on, tufts of greenery that had been preserved by a miracle, windows decked with washing, and black walls adorned with wire meat-safes on which fell the soot from the Saint-Charles station.

The forty-two books by Augustin de Mondez, Honorary Canon, had been born in sight of this view.

". . . thus opening navigational routes from earliest times to the commerce of our rich and industrious city . . ."

Beyond the little courtyards, on the narrow balcony of a house, which looked clean among so many filthy peeling walls, a dark young woman appeared in a flowered dressing-gown. She looked up at the sky for a moment, spread out a white and orange striped mattress, took off her dressing-gown, and with calm immodesty lay down naked, flat on her stomach.

"Ah! Noon," thought the Canon.

For this unknown woman with dark hair and golden limbs, who appeared as punctually as a jack from a belfry, served as timekeeper to the district and no one took offense.

Everything was as usual and the day was like every other day.

The Canon had no need to be displeased with his morning. Since he had said Mass at six-thirty at the Church of the Réformés and eaten a milk roll dipped into a cup of black coffee on returning home, he had filled six sheets with his fine, regular handwriting; its lines lay as close as in a musical stave, without a single erasure. "Augustin never crosses anything out," his sister Aimée always said, as if it did peculiar honor to the family.

He went to make sure that the two doors to his study were properly closed. He always took care to lock them before beginning work; but he knew himself too well not to be on his guard against absent-mindedness.

He pushed some oak library steps in front of a huge two-piece Renaissance cupboard, the masterpiece of a Provençal cabinet-maker, which was so fine that it had been reproduced on a postcard. Tucking up his soutane to reveal violet drawers, real bishop's drawers, of which his sister, Aimée, had bought a stock at the sale of a bankrupt shop which specialized in these things—"If Augustin had wished, he could very well have been a bishop; and, anyway, they don't show underneath . . ." —the Canon climbed onto the little steps and opened both doors of the upper part of the cupboard.

Heavy gilt-edged volumes bound in red morocco, pamphlets written long ago and sold for fifty sous, booklets, miscellanies, compilations, proofs, manuscripts, his complete works, were heaped within in the wildest disorder. It was hard to understand how the same hand could have written with similar fluency a study of the dispersion of the relics of Saint Ferréol, an educational manual for blind children, a detailed catalogue of Moustiers faience in the collection of Monsieur le Marquis de Pigusse, and an anthology of eucharistic literature; nor how the same mind could have found equal interest in Arles headdresses, the traditional staging of five-act pastorals, the Delphic oracle, the import of spices in the fourteenth century, and the ethics of Christian marriage.

And yet it was so. Canon de Mondez's specialty was to have none and to be able to write about anything, provided he was given a subject. Publishers, who were unknown to the great public, often appealed to him from their provincial towns and never met with refusal, delay, or disappointment. The Canon would always complete a series that was at a standstill, or take over works that had been left unfinished by authors who had been overconfident or had died prematurely. He jibbed at nothing. His masterpiece, the catalogue in four volumes of the treasures of the Churches of Provence (crowned by the Académie Française) had for the last forty years made sure of his leading position in the literary and social circles of Marseilles; and it occurred to no one to dispute it.

Augustin de Mondez might have felt a certain vanity at so much work accomplished, but he was free of this vice, as indeed he was of all others. His mind never lingered on what he had done in the past but turned always to what he would do tomorrow; and age had in no way diminished his eagerness to undertake new work.

Perched on the third step of the library steps, he put his hand out and felt behind the books in the cupboard and was surprised not to find what he wanted. Three times he plunged into the darkness of the cupboard up to the waist, vainly moved *The Treasure of the Cathedral,* succeeded in throwing his pamphlets into still greater disorder, and finally emerged anxious, upset, and with a slightly red face. His pot of honey had disappeared.

"Has Aimée found my hiding place?" he wondered anxiously. For since Mademoiselle de Mondez had begun to think she suffered from diabetes, she had deprived the whole household of sugar, especially her brother the Canon. "Augustin always has the same maladies as I do."

Yet, the Canon well knew that sugar is essential to intellectual work and, to appease the little fits of hunger that overtook him while writing, he was accustomed to conceal a pot of honey in the Renaissance cupboard, confident that there, protected by the rampart of his works and the proper respect that was their due, no one—until today!—would dare to touch it.

From the cupboard came a sweet, an almost alpine scent, and the edges of the books were all sticky.

The Canon wiped his fingers on the bottom of his pocket. "Perhaps, being so absent-minded, I may have put it somewhere else," he thought. He pulled open the drawers of the three desks—a huge Italian table of a good period, a Louis XVI cylindrical *secrétaire* and a Napoleon III card table with moth-eaten baize—for the Canon never worked at less than three books at the same time. He vainly pushed aside the funeral announcements of some thousand of his contemporaries. "Really, I'd forgotten the poor fellow was dead," he thought from time to time, though he did not allow this to distract him from his major concern.

It was not so much the pot of honey itself that fussed him, but the prospect of having to discuss the matter with Aimée; and then there was the difficulty of finding another hiding place, and having, as it were, to reorganize his life.

He decided to mention the matter at once to his niece, Minnie, the wife of his nephew Vladimir, who was his accomplice and regularly renewed his store. But, as he was going toward the door which communicated with the pantry, he heard his sister Aimée's voice saying: "And, above all, not a word to the Abbé. He's so sensitive and we must avoid upsetting him."

The Abbé was himself. Aimée had never got used to referring to him as anything else; though he had been a Canon for more than fifteen years now, to his sister he still remained the Abbé.

"You'll brush the Abbé's cape . . . You'll buy a box of nibs for the Abbé . . . We mustn't disturb the Abbé, he's writing. . . ."

She used his Christian name only when speaking to him directly, and then only in family or intimate circles.

The Canon beat a retreat. No doubt there had been some domestic tragedy of which he would be kept in ignorance; and he would take care not to get mixed up in it. The maid must have cut her hand with the bread-knife, or perhaps the frying-pan had caught fire, unless it was that Madame Alexandre, the concierge, had been rude to the third-floor tenants again. And to all this the Canon was equally indifferent; his sister's conspiracy of silence suited him perfectly.

He went back to his desk. "It was the period when Pithias and Euthymenes . . ." A little silver spoon, its handle terminating in a fleur-de-lys, which had been given him by a pious penitent who had traveled in Italy, lay in front of him among the pencils, the sealing-wax and the pens. He kept it, so he said, as a souvenir; but, in fact, he used it to eat his honey. How useless the little spoon was now!

Walking on tiptoe, the Canon went to the door and put his ear to it in the hope of discovering what had happened that he was supposed to know nothing about. Thank God, it had nothing to do with the pot of honey!

Mademoiselle de Mondez was two years older than her brother and even smaller than he was, which meant that she was very nearly a dwarf. In any case, it was rare for a Mondez to be more than five feet tall. She had slender bones and a crumpled face. She had had no past, no love affairs and no imagination. Unlike most old maids, she did not even cultivate an illusion that she had refused numerous proposals of marriage. Nothing had ever happened to her, and it was remarkable that so dull a life should have drawn so many lines on her face.

Some people are born over a shop with the souls of princes. Mademoiselle de Mondez had been born into one of the best families in Provence with the soul of a pew-opener. It was her good fortune, which she did not sufficiently appreciate, that her brother had gone into the Church. For she was thus able to live in an ecclesiastical atmosphere and attend to her religious duties without leaving home.

Her dresses were too short, for she had renewed her wardrobe toward the end of the war, when skirts had been knee length. Since then she had refused to buy any new clothes, on the pretext that she was bound to die soon and that the expense was unwarranted.

She spent most of her time in the pantry, counting dirty dishcloths, or checking the household accounts. The pantry was her observation post, her bridge, her place of ambush. From this small room, which was all cupboards and doors, Mademoiselle de Mondez could keep a watch on the courtyard, an eye on the maid in the kitchen and waylay the visitor who rang at the door.

"And are you quite sure, Minnie, you had it last night?" she asked.

"Yes, Aunt Aimée, I'm quite sure," the Countess de Mondez replied.

"At what time did you go to bed?"

"I can't remember, aunt; about eleven o'clock, I think, but I paid no particular attention. I'd been out playing bridge with the Danselmes. When I got home, I made myself a *tisane*."

"Didn't they give you anything to drink at the Danselmes?"

"Of course they did, Aunt Aimée, but I wanted a *tisane*."

"And where did you prepare it?"

"Here, in the pantry. That's why I came to see if by any chance I had dropped it."

Countess Minnie was head and shoulders taller than all the rest of the Mondezes. She was forty-five years old, fresh-complexioned, and had a generous bosom she carried well to the fore, like a professional singer, and which she adorned with necklaces and lace. Though fairly tall, she neglected nothing to make herself taller yet, as if she were bent on dominating this family of pygmies she had entered by marrying Vladimir. She dressed her ash-blond hair in a style that was at once high and voluminous, over a pad of horsehair, though it was naturally abundant enough. Her admirers assured her that she looked "completely eighteenth century." She had created a personal style. Her hats were invariably adorned by the massacre of some rare bird, an ibis or an egret, whose wing, crest or tail quivered in the wind as she walked. The general effect gave her something of an air and she was never referred to in the town otherwise than as "the beautiful Countess de Mondez."

"You must realize, my dear," Aimée went on, "that if we had to replace that bracelet today, we should have to scrape together our last pennies."

"Who's talking of replacing it, Aunt Aimée?" replied Minnie. "I shall find it; that's all there is to it."

"All the same, you'd have done better not to lose it. You see, that's why I never wear my jewels. Even if one tried, one could never find the same again. They don't do work like that these days. That bracelet came to us through our grandmother, the Pole; it was part of her dowry. I gave it to you on your marriage, so that you should keep it."

"But really, aunt, in twenty-five years I've never lost . . ."

"I shall call on the Danselmes later on," Mademoiselle de Mondez interrupted. "The bracelet may well have slipped down behind a chair cushion; it's the kind of thing that happens."

"Not at all, aunt," Minnie cried. "I tell you . . ."

"Hush! The Abbé!" said Mademoiselle de Mondez, pointing to the door of the Canon's study. "I'm sure you don't want to upset him. It was his grandmother's, you know!"

"I tell you again, aunt, I had it on when I came in," said Minnie, lowering her voice. And as she said it, she was wondering: "Was I really wearing it when I got home last night?"

"In that case," went on Mademoiselle de Mondez, "it must

have been lost in the house. Where do you put your jewelry when you undress? Are you listening to me?"

Her eyes on the ceiling, Minnie was going over the evening in her mind. She started.

"On my dressing-table," she said.

"What dressing-table? You have no dressing-table in your room."

"I mean on the work-table I use as a dressing-table."

"And this morning, when you went to put it on, it wasn't there? Well, my dear, it's quite simple: it's been stolen. Who has been in your room during the morning?"

At the moment the only thing that mattered to Minnie was to prevent Mademoiselle de Mondez going and making a fuss at the Danselmes. "If I did lose my bracelet in their house, they're bound to find it," she thought. She therefore continued to answer her aunt's questions as tactfully as she could.

"Let me think," she replied. "Loulou came to say good morning to me as he always does before going off to the Chamber of Commerce . . ."

Mademoiselle de Mondez shrugged her shoulders indignantly.

"Poor boy, it couldn't possibly be him," she said. "You're not going to accuse your son, I trust?"

"I'm not accusing anyone, Aunt Aimée. You asked me who had been in my room. I'm telling you."

And suddenly Minnie thought: "Suppose it was Loulou?" On several occasions, she had noticed that a thousand-franc note had disappeared from her bag. And some old, broken sleeve-links, which were worth no more than their basic weight in gold, had disappeared the previous month. All the same, Loulou surely wouldn't have taken anything so big and conspicuous as the bracelet? Among the various possibilities that occurred to her, of which the most probable was also the most unmentionable, her mind became somewhat confused.

"And yet, I'm sure I had it on when I came in. Nothing like this has ever happened to me before."

"What about Madame Alexandre? She had some letters for you this morning."

"Yes, she had, but she gave them to me in the passage a little while ago."

"In that case, it must be Térésa."

They could hear the Canon walking up and down on the other side of the door. Mademoiselle de Mondez signed to her niece to be quiet. Then, when the footsteps had moved away, she went on: "What's more, if you want to know, I'm not really surprised. For several days now, that girl's had a look about her I don't like at all. She pays much less attention to her work. Only yesterday, she answered me back most improperly. She said she was feeling ill. I'm sure she's got ideas . . ."

"Do you really think so, aunt?" Minnie said, and her voice was indulgent.

"Tarradiddle! I know what I'm about and I know the kind of girl. She mustn't be allowed to slip through our fingers and take with her . . ."

Mademoiselle de Mondez broke off and murmured: "Take care!"

She pretended to be busy sorting lentils on the pans of the old Roberval scales which had in fact jammed.

Térésa came into the pantry, dragging her feet in their rope-soled shoes. She was a big-bosomed Corsican girl, who would have been pretty enough had nature given her longer legs. She didn't wash much, but scented herself with mimosa. She had heavy black hair in waves held in place with multi-colored combs, brilliant teeth, and a short but well-shaped nose. One of her compatriots, a beadle at the Church of the Réformés, had recommended her to the Canon. "A good girl from Calvi. Very respectable family." She wanted a job to save her wages for her dowry. Térésa had been in service with the Mondezes for two years and had worked like a horse. At the start, Aimée had said she was delighted, as she always did when she engaged a new maid; but then things had begun to go a little wrong. Térésa had had the mischance to say one day in front of Mademoiselle de Mondez: "What we've always needed in Corsica is a Garibaldi."

"You've had Napoleon; isn't that enough?" the old lady replied. "In your position in life, Térésa, one should avoid having opinions."

And, from that moment, she had kept a more vigilant eye on her.

"Tell me, Térésa," Mademoiselle de Mondez said suddenly, interrupting her sorting of the lentils, "when you were doing Madame la Comtesse's room this morning, did you see her bracelet by any chance—the big, gold one with the turquoises?"

Térésa backed out of the china cupboard.

"No, Mademoiselle, I didn't notice," she replied.

"You didn't notice *what?*"

Térésa looked at her uncomprehendingly. She was clearly thinking of something else.

"I didn't notice, that's all."

"Didn't it surprise you not to see it?"

"No, Mademoiselle."

"In that case, it was there?"

"I don't know, Mademoiselle, I didn't notice."

"Your mind's obviously not on your work. I very well understand why so many things get broken—or disappear," said Mademoiselle de Mondez, her lips pursed. "It's really most tiresome. Madame la Comtesse can't find it."

Térésa scowled at Minnie who, somewhat embarrassed, thought it better to intervene.

"Perhaps you moved it, without realizing it?"

"No, Madame la Comtesse, I didn't touch it," Térésa said.

And she went off to the dining room, her arms laden and her feet dragging.

"As we've got a visitor you'll put on a clean apron, won't you?" Mademoiselle de Mondez called after her.

The 41 tram stopped on the slope of the Rue Paradis. Marie-Françoise Asnais came running out of the house.

"And do take care not to talk too much," someone shouted after her from the door.

The conductor, with a sweep of his arm, gathered Marie-Françoise onto the platform.

With a metallic clattering, the tram started off again down the narrow street, which was lined with sad and identical houses.

Marie-Françoise felt as excited as if she were setting off on a long journey. She was sure her fate was to be decided today.

From the moment she had ceased to be a child, Marie-Françoise had had only one dream: to leave the Rue Paradis. She hated the way the *mistral* swept down it; she loathed the house in which she had grown up; she could no longer bear the figured walnut furniture, the dim water-colors and the glass lusters with which the flat was furnished.

Her father, who could talk of nothing but the price of ground-nuts, she thought vulgar. She despised him for having made money and because he thought only of making more; but she would have despised him a great deal more had he been poor.

Between fifteen and nineteen, life seems to move desperately slowly; and Marie-Françoise had dreamed as all girls do. She had thought in turn of becoming an actress, an air-hostess and a parachutist. She had considered creating a scandal, running away, or eloping. The cinema had been a great refuge during these difficult years. But now, she had chosen the real adventure: marriage. But not just any marriage. She had selected her district; and she was determined to marry into the Allées.

From the pocket of her tailor-made she took the string of small pearls her mother had lent her and which, in her hurry, she had not had time to put on.

For a moment she hesitated, considering the paste ladybird her old governess had slipped into her hand at the last minute. "For good luck," Miss Nell had whispered. The ladybird didn't seem altogether suitable to Marie-Françoise. Nevertheless, from sheer superstition, she decided to pin it into her buttonhole.

"He really can't have invited me to luncheon with his family for no reason at all," she thought, as the tram turned into the Canebière.

And she thought of what Louis de Mondez, his forehead wrinkled in thought and his eyes pensive, had said at their last meeting, during a bathing party at l'Estaque.

It had been the fifth or sixth time they had met. Louis de Mondez had told her how weary he was of life, how indifferent to those too easy and too numerous conquests; how he was searching vainly for that unique love which, alas, one never seemed to meet.

Marie-Françoise had told him that her state of mind was exactly the same as his; she was disappointed by the vulgarity of men today and the grossness of their feelings. As the dirty sand trickled through her pink fingers, she had even gone so far as to utter the phrase "an ideal companion." She had noticed, naturally, that Louis de Mondez was narrow-chested and pigeon-breasted; and that he seemed to sit in the sea rather than swim. But the ideal companion need not, necessarily, be an athlete.

As the tram-stops passed—Cours Belsunce, Cours Lieutaud, Allées de Meilhan—she felt her excitement growing.

She took a mirror from her bag and ran a comb through her fair hair. She had lengthened her eyebrows with a pencil and her lipstick matched her nails.

It was her cheeks that gave her most concern, for they were

round and chubby. One is not always endowed at nineteen with those facial planes that make the fortunes of Hollywood stars. Marie-Françoise had to admit that she resembled her father. In public, she could remedy the misfortune by sucking her cheeks in, holding them between her teeth, and saying nothing.

She left the tram at the crossroads by the Church of the Réformés and turned left into the Allées. The peace of the gardens, of the avenue where the noise from the Canebière was so wonderfully subdued, the submarine light under the thick planes, the coolness and, above all, the big private houses, which had been built toward the end of a rich century, showing through the fronds, all fascinated Marie-Françoise as if they were some forbidden land. She saw beauty of style where there was none and admired every façade as if Pierre Puget had sculpted it. She dreamed of the people who lived behind those high windows, had coronets engraved on their silver and handed on, from generation to generation, as if it were some mysterious recipe, the certainty that they were better than the rest of the world.

As she rang the bell, she felt as if she were committing one of the most important acts of her life.

The bell rang tunelessly and was followed by the twanging of a wire. The door of Mondez House opened of its own accord onto a dark hall.

"Who is it?" a voice called from above.

Marie-Françoise felt rather disappointed. The Concierge clearly lived in the attics, as did all the other Marseilles concierges. But that her room should be on the third storey in a private house surprised her a little.

"I've come to see Monsieur le Comte de Mondez," she replied, trying not to shout too loud.

"Whom?" the Concierge asked.

"Monsieur le Comte Louis de Mondez."

"Oh, yes, Monsieur Loulou. It's up here on the third

floor. The stairs are on your right. Take care, it's rather dark."

And the same voice cried: "Monsieur Loulou, there's a young lady coming upstairs to see you."

Marie-Françoise felt her way forward. The staircase rose with a noble curve into the shadows. "It's really very grand," she thought, looking at the wrought-iron banisters.

When he heard Madame Alexandre shouting to him, Loulou quickly put away the field-glasses through which he had been watching the unknown woman of the Boulevard Dugommier sunbathing. The field-glasses had belonged to his uncle Louis de Mondez, who had been killed at the Dardanelles, and he had found them stowed away in a cupboard. He dipped his comb into the water jug, smoothed his hair, tightened the knot of his tie and hurried onto the landing to greet Marie-Françoise.

"We have luncheon on the first floor with my uncle, the Canon," he told her.

The phrase "my uncle, the Canon" sounded delightful in Marie-Françoise's ears.

"Can I see where you live? Or would that be indiscreet?" she asked to show how interested she was in him.

"Not at all. It's along here," Loulou replied without much enthusiasm, as he led her down a dark passage.

The third storey was not the most elegant part of Mondez House and Loulou would have preferred to begin the visit elsewhere.

The accommodation on the third floor consisted of Madame Alexandre's room, Térésa's bedroom and Loulou's room; there were also some spare rooms which Mademoiselle de Mondez had let to retired sailors, widowers or old bachelors, who did their cooking on spirit lamps. The smell hung about the place.

Loulou opened a door.

"Oh, it's charming!" cried Marie-Françoise before she had even looked round.

A brass bed covered with a crochet-work counterpane, a mahogany washstand with a marble top, a place for hanging clothes ill-concealed by a curtain, and a table heaped with detective stories and illustrated magazines made up the greater part of the furniture. Even the faded flowered wall-paper had not been changed since the room had been a coachman's.

"As you see," Loulou said, "it's a real student's attic; but I prefer it because it leaves me free."

"I can well imagine that after spending the day at the Chamber of Commerce, you want to relax and be alone. You work very hard, don't you?"

"Yes, but it's interesting. Besides, my family has always had a taste for high finance."

How different "high-finance" sounded to Monsieur Asnais's market-price of ground-nuts!

"At one time I thought of going into the army," Loulou went on, "which is also a family tradition; but since the war was over it didn't seem very interesting."

Marie-Françoise listened to him with admiring attention, her eyes bright, her cheeks held firmly between her teeth.

"I thought also of going into the higher administration— the police, for instance."

"Really?" said Marie-Françoise in surprise. "The police?"

"Yes, repression must be very exciting!"

He didn't say what sort of repression; he didn't really know himself. He merely liked the word. He longed to exercise authority, no matter what authority. Unfortunately the road to the great professions was barred to him since he had never succeeded in passing his *baccalauréat*. Having failed twice to get out of the second class, he had been superannuated from school. When he mentioned the Chamber of Commerce he never admitted, at least not at first, that he was merely a shorthand clerk, the only work for which he had ever shown any aptitude.

Marie-Françoise was hoping the conversation would assume a sentimental turn; she was even prepared to submit to a kiss.

"Let's go and have luncheon," Loulou said. "It's time."

As they went downstairs, he told her how difficult it was for old families to keep up their houses, how crushing the taxes were, and how impossible it was to find staff to run such a big house.

Marie-Françoise thought that with her father's money this fine house could be restored to its original splendor. What wonderful parties you could give in it. Surely this was a better use for a self-made man's money than the constant building of new warehouses.

Minnie was sitting on the Canon's right; Marie-Françoise on his left. Mademoiselle presided opposite her brother, between her nephew Vladimir and her great-nephew Loulou.

"By the way, I've found my breviary," said the Canon, as he unfolded his napkin which promptly slipped to the floor. "Yet, I didn't tell you Aimée, so as not to make you anxious. I forgot it the other day in the Arles train. Well, the person who found it saw my address inside and sent it back to me through the post. People are really much more honest than one tends to think."

"Honest, honest! Not all of them," Mademoiselle de Mondez said loudly as Térésa was serving the melon. "Honesty has become a rare virtue these days, don't you agree, Minnie?"

"In any case, when I meet with it, I find it a heartwarming virtue. As the poet says: *Hoc juvat et melli est . . . melli est*," the Canon repeated distinctly, leaning slightly toward his niece.

But Minnie, who was thinking of her bracelet, seemed to have missed the point.

So, turning to Marie-Françoise, the Canon asked: "Have you done any Latin, Mademoiselle?"

"Yes, Monsiegneur," said Marie-Françoise, blushing.

"Monsiegneur, Monsiegneur! How nice she is! It's only in Italy you get called Monsiegneur so easily. Here, I'm simply Monsieur le Chanoine."

"All the same, Augustin," said Mademoiselle de Mondez, "you could easily have been a bishop had you wished."

"Yes, but there it is. I preferred a studious life. And so, Mademoiselle, you will undoubtedly have understood my quotation: 'It is as agreeable to me as honey.' It is a phrase from Horace."

The dining room was hung with tapestry depicting a forest scene. Around the thick tree-trunks, beneath their faded foliage, red deer and fallow deer were grazing in moth-eaten meadows. The plane-trees of the Allées, reflected through the windows, cast an aquarium light over the herbaceous walls.

On entering, Marie-Françoise had thought of her mother's advice: "Take care not to talk too much!" It was an unnecessary caution. She found she could not get a word in edgeways. For the family, who spent the rest of the day whispering about the house, shouted at the tops of their voices at meals, each in pursuit of a different subject. The Canon was discoursing on the richness of Latin syntax; Minnie was saying that she had to go to the Aubagne farm after luncheon; and Loulou, to acquire prestige in Marie-Françoise's eyes, described the beauties of the farm and elaborated his views on agriculture. Mademoiselle de Mondez addressed her remarks to them all at random. When the maid came in, she assumed an air of secrecy and began talking in German.

"It's so that the servants shan't understand," she explained to Marie-Françoise.

"Do you speak German, Mademoiselle?" the Canon asked. Marie-Françoise was embarrassed and shook her head.

"It is always a good thing to know the language of the enemy," said Mademoiselle de Mondez. "We had a brother killed at the Dardanelles."

And Marie-Françoise felt terribly middle-class, having only had an English governess to bring her up.

Since there were crests on the spoons and forks, she was not unduly surprised by the oilcloth on the table; on the contrary, it seemed to her merely a sign of aristocratic simplicity. She saw only the gold line on the plates and did not notice that they were chipped. She barely tasted the dishes, which were few and far from copious. She marveled at the tapestries.

People to whom we would pay no attention in other circumstances suddenly become the most important in the world if they are likely to have an influence on our loves. So it was with the Mondezes for Marie-Françoise. Old Aimée, to whom she might easily have given a couple of francs at a church door, the little Canon, who was absent-mindedly wiping his mouth on his watered silk sash, the Countess de Mondez, who was dressed in such a curiously old-fashioned way with her lace and her necklaces, all inspired Marie-Françoise with the greatest respect, because her fate depended on them. "What do they think of me?" she wondered.

The most impressive and alarming of them all seemed to her to be Count Vladimir de Mondez. Count Vladimir, who had a yellow complexion, drooping moustaches and his few remaining hairs arranged carefully across his skull, had a habit at mealtimes of gathering anything in the nature of pips or stones carefully into saucers. He had already collected the melon pips, and complained that the pips should have been removed from the aubergines before they were cooked.

"Please, Vlad, no arguments in front of the Abbé," his aunt whispered, and then went on conciliatingly: "There's a compote of cherries coming and I've had the stones set aside for you. *Kirschen Compote*," she added because Térésa came into the room.

Then Count Vladimir, seeing some logical connection that was apparent only to himself, talked sadly of his Polish inheritance of which he had been despoiled by revolution: thousands of acres in the neighborhood of Cracow, consisting of forests which he had, as it happened, seen only once and then at the age of thirteen.

"Before 1914," he said, "one could travel all over Europe, except Russia, without a passport."

"People who are in oil like us," Marie-Françoise said, "know all about the difficulties of customs barriers."

It was the only thing she had said, but even this was too much.

Count Vladimir stopped removing the pips from a tomato and shot her a glance of indulgent contempt from beneath his drooping eyelids.

The Countess de Mondez thought Marie-Françoise much too young and much too made-up. "It would be sheer folly for Loulou," she thought, "to marry this child whose head isn't properly screwed on yet." Yet she had to admit that she had been no older when she had married Vladimir. "And after all, that's not been such a great success." The fact was, she disliked the idea of becoming a mother-in-law, of going to visit the Danselmes, for instance, accompanied by a girl of twenty, and having to say: "Do you know my daughter-in-law?" Loulou had plenty of time.

Mademoiselle de Mondez had no particular opinion. From the moment Loulou had brought the girl downstairs, she had felt more or less favorably disposed to her. Besides, the Asnais had money, and there was no harm in that. And then, Marie-Françoise seemed to please the Abbé, who rather liked young people; and indeed, at his age, he rarely found a new audience.

Térésa, who was dragging her feet more noisily than usual and giving Mademoiselle Asnais black looks, was so consistently forgetting to serve Loulou that in the end he got quite angry.

"And what about me, Térésa!" he said loudly as she was

taking the compote of cherries away without handing it to him.

"A bad conscience tends to an absent mind," said Mademoiselle de Mondez in an aside. Then, handing a box of saccharine to Marie-Françoise, she added: "The compote is unsweetened, because of the Abbé."

"Nevertheless, it's excellent, quite excellent, my dear sister," the Canon cried. *"Hyblaeis apibus florem depasta salicti . . .* That's from Virgil, Mademoiselle, as you no doubt recognize. *Hyblaeis apibus . . ."*

And this time, Minnie blinked quickly at the Canon to show him she had understood. A Latin phrase containing the word "honey" or "bee" was an established code by which the uncle informed his niece that the pot in the cupboard was coming to an end. For the purpose, the Canon had quite a selection of quotations, ranging from the famous verse, "The bees swarming on Hybla are nourished by flowers," which he had just uttered, to the more daring image: *"Medio flumine mella petere,"* which meant: "Seek for honey in the middle of the river," or in other words: "pursue a chimera."

As soon as they rose from the table, Loulou said he had to go back to the Chamber of Commerce. There happened to be an important meeting early that afternoon which he felt he must attend. He automatically tapped his pocket to make sure he had his pencils.

"I'll leave you with my family," he said to Marie-Françoise.

But within the next few moments the family dispersed. Count Vladimir, without a word to anyone, went upstairs to his flat on the second floor, taking his saucers of pips with him. Aimée said she had things to attend to on the third floor, "while Térésa is washing up," she added in a low voice for Minnie's benefit. Minnie, as she had remarked during luncheon, had to go to the Aubagne farm, where she had things to discuss "with the tenant." The Canon caught her on the landing.

"The pot's gone," he whispered.

"Oh, I'm so sorry, uncle. I'm afraid it's my fault," Minnie replied. "I took it yesterday, when I got home, to sweeten a *tisane*, and as it was empty, I threw it away. I quite forgot to tell you."

"Oh, good! That's a relief."

"I'll bring you another later on, you can count on me."

Marie-Françoise, who dared not interrupt these asides, remained standing in the ante-room, admiring a collection of ancient chasubles and ivory crucifixes displayed against a background of velvet.

"You're in no hurry, are you?" the Canon asked her. "Come along then and have a chat with me for a minute or two."

And so it was that, on her entry into the Mondez world, Marie-Françoise was privileged to have a tête-à-tête with the Honorary Canon in the study full of funeral announcements. It lasted an hour and a quarter during which he read her the beginning of his forty-third book: *The Principles and Methods of Phocaean Colonization.*

The catastrophe burst on them toward the end of the afternoon, when Térésa realized her room had been searched, her cupboard ransacked, the basket in which she kept her souvenirs of Corsica turned out, and the shoe-box in which she hoarded her money opened. She ran down the two storeys and, breathless with anger, reached the pantry where Mademoiselle de Mondez was busy inspecting the contents of the drawers.

"I'd like to know . . ." Térésa cried.

"A little less noise, my girl, if you please," Mademoiselle de Mondez said curtly.

"I'd like to know, Mademoiselle, who's been at my things."

"I have, Térésa. I never conceal my actions," replied the old lady. "And I did it in your own interests, what's more, before informing the police of the loss of Madame Minnie's bracelet. If you have behaved dishonestly, you still have time to repent."

"You think I'm a thief, do you?"

"Not so loud, my girl," said Mademoiselle de Mondez, indicating the door. "There's no need for the Abbé to know about it. I'm not accusing you, but merely warning you that we're going to call the police in. When an object disappears from a household, it is usual to begin by suspecting the servants."

Térésa's face went dark and her eyes glittered with anger; one lock of hair had fallen loose and a green comb was hanging from the end of it. "You think I'm a thief," she said; "there's no other word for it. Well, if that's how it is, I don't see why I shouldn't talk."

"Of course, Térésa, if you know anything about it, you must say so."

Térésa drew a deep breath, hesitated a moment, and said: "Instead of looking for evil where it isn't, Mademoiselle would do better to look where it is! I'm disgraced . . . disgraced for four months. It's even beginning to show," she cried, tearing her apron off in proof.

Faced with this unexpected avowal, Mademoiselle de Mondez's first reaction was surprising enough.

"How can it have happened, my girl, since you have no day out?" she asked.

"There's no need to go out for that."

"What? Do you mean to tell me you brought a man into the house? Ah, he must be the thief, of course!" cried Mademoiselle de Mondez, for whom the bracelet remained the principal preoccupation.

Térésa burst into tears.

"No, Mademoiselle, I haven't brought anyone in. It's Monsieur Loulou. Monsieur Loulou did this to me. There, now I've said it!"

For weeks she had been anxious and unhappy. But she had

said nothing for fear of being sacked. "I can't go home in this state and show my shame to the whole village. My father wouldn't even take me in." She had suffered many mornings of misery. "I shall speak to Monsieur le Comte this morning; it's no use going on, I shall speak to him. Well, no, perhaps I shall tell Monsieur Loulou. After all, it's his fault. My God, what's to become of me?" And yet the days went by and she said nothing; but the time was approaching when the evidence would need no words of avowal.

To be accused of theft at such a time had made her furious and given her the courage she lacked. And now, delivered of her secret, she burst into tears. With wet and shiny face, red nose, and breast heaving with sobs, she fled to the kitchen.

The study door opened.

"What's going on?" the Canon asked quietly, though he had in fact heard every word.

"Nothing, my dear, nothing at all," Mademoiselle de Mondez replied quickly, spreading her hands wide. "Merely the maid being silly again."

And she closed the door.

Mademoiselle de Mondez, who had spent her life inventing dramas to give herself importance, found herself totally at a loss now that there was a real one. She felt faint, sat down on the pantry chair and thought that what she really needed at this moment were a few drops of menthol on a lump of sugar, had there been any sugar in the house.

Then, recovering herself a little, she was carried away by her natural aptitude for suspicion. Térésa might very well have lied and accused Loulou of a fault he had not committed. Poor little Loulou! He was such a good boy, went to work so regularly and was thinking of getting married! If he had adventures—and, after all, boys would be boys, and wild oats had to be sown—he conducted them with the greatest discretion and gave no cause for scandal.

It was blackmail and calumny, that was what it was! Besides, an immoral girl who stole bracelets was also perfectly capable of blackmail; it was all of a piece. And Mademoiselle de Mondez immediately went up to the third floor to question Madame Alexandre.

Alas, the Concierge's revelations destroyed all Mademoiselle de Mondez's illusions.

"If you put a young man and a young girl next door to each other like that, it's bound to happen. Oh, I saw what they were up to and, what's more, I heard them at night, saving your presence, and I must say that Térésa . . ."

"It was she who seduced my nephew with her immodest tricks, no doubt?"

"Oh no, Mademoiselle, quite the contrary! She did all she could to ward him off. But Monsieur Loulou was what you'd call enterprising, you know. So the girl got a taste for it as the days went by. It's very understandable at that age. Besides, she's Corsican. They're pretty hot-blooded over there."

"But why didn't you warn me, Madame Alexandre?"

"Oh, that's not my job, Mademoiselle. I've got quite enough to do with Monsieur le Comte always throwing his rubbish and those old pips of his into the courtyard just after I've finished sweeping it; and then there's all the fret and worry this house gives me, what with the stairs, the post and all. It's always better to mind your own business, don't you think? If it had been anyone else but Monsieur Loulou, I don't say but what. But there . . ."

"Well, now we're in a pretty pickle," said Mademoiselle de Mondez.

"And that's certain," replied Madame Alexandre with a glint of enjoyment in her eyes. "Particularly, since that Térésa's in a bit of a state at the moment. Things aren't going to be all that easy, believe me."

Countess Minnie reached home about half-past six, her face glowing pink, and the pheasant's feather waving aggres-

sively in her felt hat. She had had time, on the way back
from Aubagne, to call in on the Danselmes and also to go on
another errand of which she said nothing. She seemed completely relaxed.

"You know, Aunt Aimée," she said, "I'm not quite certain
I was wearing my bracelet when I got home last night. And
I'm beginning to be of your opinion. It must be Térésa."

"My poor Minnie, I've got something terrible to tell you,"
said Mademoiselle de Mondez with a sigh. "You're going to
be a grandmother."

The Count and Countess de Mondez hardly ever saw each
other and to all intents and purposes never spoke to each
other. Not that there had ever been any real dissension or
dispute. In twenty-five years of married life, they had never
been heard to quarrel and at their rare and unavoidable meetings on the stairs, in the corridor of the flat, or at the Canon's
table, they treated each other with extreme politeness. It was
merely that the links between them had broken, and they
had become as much strangers to one another as if they had
never met.

A short while after Loulou's birth, repeated attacks of
migraine had obliged the beautiful Minnie to have a separate
room. No one could tell whether little Count Vladimir had
minded. Then, a few years later, Minnie had had a bathroom
put in. Vlad had kept his own; and their opportunities for
talking things over had been to that extent reduced.

Minnie de Mondez was active and social. Fittings took up
a good deal of her time. Her dressmaker adored her, as a
pastry cook might adore a customer who ordered a set-piece
once a fortnight.

Minnie always represented the family at those functions at
which it was necessary to be seen. She made her uncle's, aunt's
and husband's excuses; and her majestic appearance did
honor to the weeping widow, the girl crowned with orange

blossom, or the new magistrate for whom she was putting herself out. She had an art of walking up the naves of churches and reaching the font or the vestry first which was peculiarly her own.

She looked after the Aubagne farm, where the family, with the exception of Vladimir, went to spend the hottest weeks of summer. She was vice-president of the Slice of Bread Society, and a member of the committee of the Spoonful of Milk Society. She was, moreover, an excellent bridge player, and declared that year in, year out, she made the cost of her fares.

The expense of so much energy was evidence of a certain confidence in life, and accorded ill with the congenital pessimism and weak physique of Count Vladimir.

He had joined up in 1918, but the war had come to an end before he had time to take part in it; nevertheless, he had developed pleurisy while in the army and considered that he had never completely got over it; it had been a lesson to him. In the general victory he had lost his famous Polish estates, and the mistake of having married a wife who was far too tall for him had not improved matters.

The Count de Mondez had come to the conclusion early in life that all we do for other people, in charity, devotion or even simple kindness, is only a sign of a perverse egoism, of a need to be admired, thanked, considered indispensable, or indeed of the yet baser desire to get something back in return. Examples of this virtuous hypocrisy were in evidence all about him. Having no need for other people's esteem in order to preserve his own opinion of himself, the Count de Mondez would not have raised his little finger for anyone and, it must be admitted, it would never have occurred to anyone to expect even the smallest service from him.

Those who live alone think much. The Count de Mondez had meditated on the origins of living things. The principle of life is contained in embryos, seeds and pips. The pip of an apple contains the energy to make the future apple-tree, and the heart of a melon encloses enough to sow a whole field of melons. Furthermore, it is a fact that alcohol preserves cellular matter. And that was why the Count de Mondez gathered stones and pips with so much care at meals. First he dried them on his window-sill and then placed them in bottles of pure alcohol from the chemist so as to retain their "principle." In this way he concocted thoroughly disgusting drinks from which he was able to absorb, by sipping now one, now another, in expert alternation, all the energies of the garden, and with which he was slowly destroying his liver.

When his wife burst into his room that evening, he asked in surprise: "What's the matter, my dear? This isn't the end of the month."

For, indeed, the Count and Countess de Mondez had a monthly meeting to go over their joint accounts. Their incomes were separate. The Mondez had taken this precaution at the time of the marriage because of the Polish estates. Husband and wife each paid their own expenses. Vladimir's income was exceedingly reduced. To save the expense of a housemaid, the Count swept his own room, which was immediately above the Canon's study, and waited every morning for Madame Alexandre to leave the courtyard to throw the dust out of the window.

Minnie, on the other hand, was very extravagant. She left the light burning in her room till a late hour of the night. It seemed that her father, Monsieur d'Oléon-Vaudan, a former judge of the Civil Court, had cut up a good deal better than the Mondez had expected. Unless, of course, Minnie had turned out to be a good business woman, had taken sound advice, and managed to increase her capital herself. In any case, Vladimir had never had anything to do with it.

"What's the matter, Marguerite?" he asked, using for the first time in years his wife's real Christian name, so as to emphasize the fact that her visit was most unusual.

At the very hour at which the Countess was revealing their

son's misconduct to her husband, Loulou himself, having finished taking an important report in shorthand on the price of citrus fruits, was holding forth in the Café Glacier to a group of friends. Here, he felt himself to be king. They called him "de Mondez," they listened to him; he was not even expected always to pay for the drinks. Among these sons of ship-owners, these young princes of oil, these heirs-apparent to soap, he was looked on as a real aristocrat.

Leaning back in his chair, a *noilly-cassis* in front of him, slowly swinging his leg backward and forward, he was talking about women with a knowledge that induced respect. At the moment, so it appeared, he had a Corsican for mistress, a splendid girl, who had settled in Marseilles for love of him. Indeed, such was her passion for him that sometimes at night she began weeping for no reason at all.

"One simply has to realize that their nerves aren't like ours. Besides, she must be aware instinctively that it can't go on forever, that it's the end."

For Loulou was beginning to grow tired of her as he had of so many others. He was thinking seriously of getting married.

"Sooner or later, we have to come to it. Besides, in my sort of family, there's a name to carry on, traditions to bequeath. And, as everyone knows, the best husbands are those who have had the most experience in their youth."

As dinnertime was drawing near, he set off for the Allées, his head held high, strutting a little, and vastly pleased with himself. He met Monsieur de Mondez waiting for him under the plane-trees. His father looked at him with considerable disappointment.

The atmosphere in Mondez House during the next week was most distressing. There was crisis there, present, evident, in their very midst, latent in every word they uttered, fostered by every glance and every sigh. They whispered together in doorways; they exchanged afflicted winks. No one could think of a solution, no one even dared suggest one. There was a child in the maid's womb, but one might have thought there was a dead body in the house and that the undertakers refused to deal with it.

Loulou had made no attempt to deny things; indeed, he could not. He had merely flapped his arms and tried to place the responsibility elsewhere. After all, Térésa was as guilty as he was. Besides, his family gave him no money, and how could he maintain a decent liaison on what he earned at the Chamber of Commerce? And had a similar adventure occurred with a *cocotte*, things would have been even worse, no doubt.

"Why couldn't you have an affair with a married woman, like everyone else?" his mother said.

As for the Count de Mondez, he said that in the old days, Loulou would have been sent to Madagascar or even to the Cameroons. And that would have been good-by!

"What, send the poor boy to the Cameroons!" said Mademoiselle de Mondez indignantly. "Vlad, you're really quite heartless."

"The trouble is I haven't the means to pay his passage, nor the capital to set him up as a planter," Vladimir replied.

Now that she had admitted her misfortune, there was no holding Térésa. She swept the hall in the middle of the afternoon, broke a plate a day and sniffed as she served up burnt dishes.

"What can be the matter with poor Térésa, crying like that all the time?" the Canon asked innocently.

He felt he must pretend to an ignorance that only his sister believed in.

"Just think of a scandal like this in a priest's house!" Mademoiselle de Mondez groaned.

Misfortunes never happen singly. Mademoiselle de Mondez, having received a five thousand franc note from one of her tenants, had folded it "six times over" and kept it in the palm of her hand, so that no one should know that she had received any money. She had gone about with it like this during the whole morning, and then the note had vanished from out of her hand and she was unable to find it. Térésa again, no doubt. It was just like the bracelet, which no one now dared mention.

"The hussy's taking advantage of us; she's got us in the hollow of her hand," said Mademoiselle de Mondez.

Madame Alexandre could not resist rubbing vinegar into the wound.

"You know what these Corsicans are. They're all crazy, always flying to extremes. It would be just like Térésa in the present state she is to go and throw herself out of a window one fine morning!"

"That would be the last straw," said the old lady.

In Marseilles, gossip spreads from courtyard to courtyard, and the district was beginning to get wind of the affair. The Mondez' misfortune was beginning to creep up staircases, insinuate itself into kitchens and was thereby spreading slowly through the neighboring houses.

One thing was certain: Térésa had no wish in any circumstances or at any price to return to her own country. Indeed, there was no question of price; Count Vladimir declared he wouldn't put up a penny, and you could trust him there. Mademoiselle de Mondez said that she would be prepared to resign herself to selling a piece of furniture or a crucifix. But how could anything be removed from the house without the Abbé noticing it? It was, clearly, unthinkable.

"And what about you, Minnie? After all, he's your son!"

Minnie waved her hands about in a vague way. She had talked to Térésa and believed that the girl had no thought of turning the situation to her material advantage.

"I'm not surprised," said Mademoiselle de Mondez, "when you think of what she's stolen! But what does she really want? It's quite frightening, just when poor dear Loulou was beginning to think of getting married, and had found a presentable girl. I've looked into it. The Asnaises are very well off indeed. The whole town will soon know all about it. And how can you expect, in the circumstances . . ."

"Of course, it would be monstrous," said Minnie thoughtfully, though what she meant by the remark remained in doubt.

The Countess de Mondez's sense of fairness worked in unexpected ways.

Since her luncheon in the Allées, Marie-Françoise had been living in a state of exaltation. There was something touching in the way she revealed her enthusiasms. According to her, Mondez House was the last bastion of aristocratic thought, and the Mondezes themselves the most remarkable people she had ever met. The house, which was entirely furnished in the "medieval style," or so she said when she got home, contained a collection worthy of a museum. Loulou de Mondez lived in a real monk's cell. At luncheon, the conversation had been conducted either in Latin or German, as if it was the most natural thing in the world. Count Vladimir was undoubtedly a descendant of the kings of Poland. As for the Canon, who had vouchsafed her the honor of a long literary conversation, he was one of the first writers of France, of the more serious kind, of course; it was really surprising that it was not better known.

It was clear that, during the course of this one meal, Marie-Françoise had learnt more than in a whole nineteen years of middle-class education in the Rue Paradis and the bosom of her family.

"At the Mondezes, the napkins aren't folded like that . . . At the Mondezes, you have coffee in the dining room . . . At the Mondezes . . ."

Monsieur Asnais, her father, was beginning to get fed up with listening to her.

"Well, if everything's so wonderful at Mondez House, go and live there, my child!"

"Well, you see, the fact is . . ."

And Marie-Françoise tried to persuade her mother to invite Loulou. It was only polite. But Marie-Françoise hoped the luncheon would take place in a restaurant.

"Very well, we shall do so; but we mustn't seem to be in a hurry," Madame Asnais replied.

And Miss Nell shook her head in devoted concern.

At the same time, Marie-Françoise's behavior had undergone some alterations. She suddenly felt it necessary to go to Mass on Sunday mornings, a thing she had neglected to do since about the time of her Confirmation. Films no longer interested her; she spent her afternoons in the municipal library, pouring over the quarto volumes of *The Treasures of the Churches of Provence.*

"Are you preparing a thesis, Mademoiselle?" the librarian asked her. "It's not a book I'm often asked for."

And then, when late one morning the telephone rang at the Asnaises and the Countess de Mondez invited Marie-Françoise to have tea with her that very day at Castelmuro, Marie-Françoise began dancing through the flat all on her own. There could be no doubt about it; this was the essential, the decisive interview between future mother-in-law and future daughter-in-law before the official proposal was made.

"This is all very fine, very fine indeed," muttered Monsieur Asnais between his thick lips. "But I shall have to talk seriously to the young man; and, I warn you, I shall look at the marriage contract very closely indeed."

At bottom, he was flattered enough, for his grandfather had spent his life picking olives, that his daughter should be so urgently sought after by people who, if Marie-Françoise was to be believed, had never once bent down to lace their own shoes in six centuries.

Once again, Marie-Françoise borrowed her mother's necklace of small pearls and pinned Miss Nell's hideous ladybird into her small buttonhole. Her face shone with certainty; her cheeks bulged with joy; and she seemed to be breathing enough air for the whole street.

The beautiful Countess de Mondez's entrance into the Castelmuro, wearing a bersagliere hat, always caused the Cadet sisters, who ran that elegant teashop, a certain excitement. The elder Mademoiselle Cadet felt it incumbent on her to leave her cash-desk and take her abundant curves across to her distinguished customer's table.

She made the proper civil speeches, inquired after Monsieur le Comte's health, Monsieur le Chanoine's work, and whether Mademoiselle Aimée's strength was keeping up, and then returned to the cash-desk from which she had been watching the comings and goings of the best Marseilles society for the last twenty years.

Dressed suitably for their professions, the Mesdemoiselles Cadet relieved the black of their dresses with glass beads and brooches which, on them, looked almost like confectionery; they might have been wearing sugared almonds and pralines. And everything about them, their rosy complexions, so little in keeping with their age, the attitudes they struck which were entirely suited to the covers of chocolate boxes, indeed even the way in which they talked, all had a sort of sugary quality.

The County's curiosity, the women's idleness and the children's gluttony, were catered for at five o'clock each day at Castelmuro between the Louis XVI wainscoting and the stucco garlands. Mirrors reflected the coming and going, and enabled people to stare at each other without impertinence. Conversation was private. A tactful staff moved among the tables serving syrupy liquids topped with cream. Every minute or so, some woman would get suddenly to her feet, plate in hand, and go to the cabriole-legged sideboard where the cakes were stacked. She looked like a hen making for its corn. She would cackle for a moment, bow to the assembled company, and return to her seat, laden, clucking, satisfied.

Marie-Françoise went straight to the table where the Countess de Mondez, leaning over an iced coffee with a straw in her mouth, was signaling to her.

"That little Asnais is as fresh as a powder-puff," murmured the elder Cadet.

"Her taking tea here with the Countess can't be just a mere matter of chance," replied the younger. "It wouldn't surprise me if there were some question of a marriage."

"Let's hope we'll get the contract for the wedding-breakfast."

Marie-Françoise made her excuses to Minnie.

"I didn't think I was late."

"You're not at all late, my dear. It's I who am always early."

For a while the conversation turned to the current fashions. The Countess expressed herself in favor of round-toed shoes rather than pointed-toed.

"They're suitable only for housemaids."

Since Marie-Françoise was wearing pointed-toed shoes, she hid her feet under her chair.

As for nails, "for women of a certain rank in society" colorless varnish was alone appropriate. And Marie-Françoise concealed her fingers beneath the edge of her saucer.

Then, suddenly, the Countess launched her attack.

"It has not escaped me, my dear child, that you take a certain interest in my son, and that he, on his side, has shown a very keen interest in you."

Marie-Françoise blushed scarlet. Had they been in a more appropriate place, she would have flung her arms round Madame de Mondez's neck. "Of course, Loulou has asked his mother to tell me what he dared not tell me himself," she thought.

"The only thing is, my dear, that men, as you must know, are men," the Countess went on, emitting a deep sigh. "There are things I feel it my duty to tell you."

Oh, how tactfully the Countess de Mondez did her duty! How delicately she set about opening the innocent young girl's eyes! What heroism is required to reveal to Marie-Françoise the drama that was upsetting the Mondez family, and how she wished the secret of its shame need never sully her lips! What a calvary for a mother to have to mention these things! But could she, in all conscience, keep silent? She had too much esteem for Marie-Françoise; she had, she felt, no right to let her harbor illusions. She did not wish Marie-Françoise to find herself, for lack of proper warning, in a ridiculous, indeed a scandalous situation. She felt a moral obligation. Yes, Loulou was about to have a child. Yes, it was the servant, whom Marie-Françoise had seen waiting at table. It had been only a moment of aberration but, alas, one of those aberrations that can wreck a whole life. Minnie trusted that Marie-Françoise would appreciate the confidence she was showing in her and would keep her lips utterly sealed.

"There it is, my poor child, men are men," she concluded. She had been so busy listening to her own voice, admiring her greatness of soul and her diplomatic talent, that she perceived the results of that talent only at the very moment the little Asnais, who had turned whiter than the cloth, seemed on the point of fainting.

Minnie made her drink a glass of water and said: "Well, really! Were things already as serious as that? In that case, I have acted very wisely! Sooner or later, you would certainly have learned it. It's like an operation, the longer you put it off, the worse it is."

She gazed attentively at the girl once more. "No, indeed," she thought, "I could never have taken her to the Danselmes or elsewhere and said: 'Do you know my daughter-in-law?' "

She had chosen between the misfortune of being a grand-mother and the misfortune of being a mother-in-law and, since the first could not be avoided, at least she could use it to prevent the second. Besides, one could at least manage to conceal an illegitimate child, but not a daughter-in-law; and there are certain moments in a woman's life when rivalry is intolerable.

Marie-Françoise managed to control herself till she reached the door of the teashop, where the Countess de Mondez kissed her almost maternally on both cheeks, because of the anxious glances of the Cadet sisters. But once alone on the pavement, Marie-Françoise felt she could not go home in her present state. She could not bring herself to answer questions and explain what had happened. No one could understand and her family least of all. Her father would have a wonder-ful opportunity of teasing her about her disappointment. Her life was shattered forever. One could never recover from so deep a humiliation, so tragic a disappointment. Instead of going up the Rue Paradis, she went and concealed her dismay among the crowds in the Canebière.

Fate so ordained things that Loulou, who was at this hour leaving the Chamber of Commerce and on his way, as was his custom, to the Café Glacier, should see her. She was walking along somewhat uncertainly, her eyes on the ground and her handkerchief to her nose.

"Hullo, what's the matter, Marie-Françoise?"

"Oh, no, I never want to see you again!" cried Marie-Françoise, putting out her hand. "Your mother has told me everything. It's simply appalling. Your child!"

"You mean to say my mother told you? How dare she interfere?"

"Oh, I won't listen to a word against your mother. She was wonderful. She has such a splendid sense of moral duty! It's you who are a monster!"

There was a look of fury in Loulou's grey eyes and he nervously jerked his hair back from his forehead.

"A sense of moral duty!" he repeated. "I'll make her pay for it, the bitch!"

This word, which was very far removed from the idea she entertained of the language the Mondezes used, and particularly from a son about his mother, somewhat surprised Marie-Françoise. But, after all, one must expect a young man like Loulou to be capable of anything.

Count Vladimir had finished his housework. Leaning at the window over his drying pips, he had been waiting for a quarter of an hour, a dustbin in his hand, for Madame Alexandre to leave the courtyard so that he might throw his sweepings into it.

His son surprised him in this attitude. The Count turned; people were really coming into his room a good deal these days.

Loulou was carrying a large chocolate box; it looked far from new; it had come originally from Castelmuro and was encircled by a pink ribbon that seemed to have been tied and untied very frequently.

"Mama has torpedoed my marriage," he said. "She went and told Mademoiselle Asnais all about it, as a moral duty, it appears. So, as evidence of Mama's morals. I've brought you something that may interest you."

Count Vladimir raised his eyebrows and opened his drooping eyelids a little wider.

"Where did you get that?" he asked.

"In Mama's desk."

"How did you open it?"

"It's an ordinary lock. It was easy enough with a pen-knife."

Vladimir looked at the boy for a moment or two. That flat skull, that mouth with drooping corners, that narrow, un-youthful face, these were his son. Whenever Count Vladimir

looked at Loulou he was always forced to the disagreeable
conclusion that his son resembled him.

"Men must hang together," Loulou said, embarrassed by
his father's gaze.

He put the chocolate box down on the table and went out.

Vladimir thought for a moment, then he undid the pink
ribbon and took off the lid with its faded gilding. Letters
overflowed from the box onto the carpet. Vladimir did not
even have to search for a signature to discover who was
responsible for this correspondence. Monsieur Dudoy de
Saint-Flon had the weakness of being in love with his own
features and the old chocolate box held almost as many
photographs as it did letters: Jacques de Saint-Flon present-
ing a cup at a horse show, opening a race-course, the
handsome Saint-Flon hunting, at the helm of a yacht, judging
a regatta. Saint-Flon attending a tennis-match, or as host
at The Blue Wave Club of which he was president. There
he was, in bathing dress, in white trousers and straw hat, in
a bowler, in riding breeches, with a racket in his hand, with
a smile on his lips, with black hair in the older photographs
and grey hair at the temples in the more recent. It had been
going on for eighteen years.

A glance at the letters soon proved to Count Vladimir that
there was no question here of an unrequited love, of an
unassuaged passion, of one of those hopeless admirations
which, throughout a whole lifetime, may be trammeled by
the stark prohibitions of virtue and of which the woman
who has been their object yet preserves the evidences, so as
to be able, occasionally of an evening, to give free rein to
her nostalgia. Monsieur de Saint-Flon's enterprise had undoubtedly been crowned with rapid success, his embraces
seemed quickly to have become a matter of routine, for his
passionate declarations had early received their meed of
abandon, ardor and even frenzy.

Monsieur de Saint-Flon's epistolary style was not notable

for its restraint. Count Vladimir was therefore able to learn many things he had never suspected concerning the amorous habits of his wife, her audacities, the violence of her appetites and the freedom with which she assuaged them. He had always looked on this large blond creature as sensually some-what cold and reserved. How one deceived oneself, when one was being deceived! He had to admit that Monsieur de Saint-Flon, on the evidence of what he wrote of himself, and without so much as a shadow of modesty, must be quite a chap and something of a champion in this sport as he was in others. For eighteen years, Minnie had clearly been an ideal partner in these private tournaments.

The letters revealed to little Count Vladimir certain aspects of love, and a scale of intensity and frequency, which had never previously occurred to his imagination.

This was the real surprise; as for the basic fact of the affair's existence, and the discovery that as a husband he had been flouted for so long, he felt neither anger nor even astonishment.

In fact, he had always *known*. But he had obstinately shut his eyes to it, thrust suspicion aside, been careful not to ask questions and to avoid all appearance of exercising control over his wife, simply that he might live in the security of ignorance. He had known, but he had not wished to know; certainty without proof was never absolute certainty.

And now his eyes had been wickedly forced open; now Minnie's nightly migraines, which had necessitated first a separate bed and then a separate room, were explained; now all his wife's feigned preoccupations—the hat that must be tried on a dozen times, the committee meetings of the Spoonful of Milk Society, those indispensable visits to the Aubagne farm, those recurrent funerals, those bridge-parties at the Danselmes, which invariably ended later than other people's bridge-parties—all the reasons for these things as well as the use to which they had been put were now clear.

When the Countess went out, she went to the Boulevard du Prado and the big villa, half Norman chalet, half Loire château, standing in its garden of magnolias, in which Monsieur de Saint-Flon lived his elegant bachelor life. And the money Minnie had to spend no doubt had its source there too.

"As a man, I've not been much good," Vladimir thought, "and, what's more, as a husband, I've been deceived. I thought to maintain a certain façade; and that façade, I now know, was shattered by ridicule. But, then, why on earth did she marry me?"

For when the superb Mademoiselle d'Oléan-Vaudan, the daughter of a penniless, minor judge, had thrown herself at his head, shown measureless admiration for him and an inexplicable devotion, Vladimir, surprised as he had been, had thought it must be due to love. But now that he was almost on the eve of old age, he knew better.

"She was marrying a coronet, a title, a house in the Allées, all of which enabled her to enter a certain society. Indeed, had she not been the Countess de Mondez, she would have had little chance of becoming the mistress of the handsome Baron de Saint-Flon. That's what it has done for her! And, what's more, I've no doubt people feel sorry for her being married to a man as ugly as I am! And Saint-Flon's always so polite—the way he crosses the street to shake my hand, constantly invites me to parties, to which I never go, and always sends me New Year's greetings. Well he may, for I've given him a happy life all right!"

Vladimir replaced the love letters in their box, together with the photographs which had given a face, a moustache, shoulders and hands, flesh and blood to his misfortune. He calmly tied the pink ribbon into a bow.

"If only Minnie had begun it three or four years earlier, I should, at least, have the consolation of being able to think that that horrid little Loulou was not my son. Alas!"

He buttoned his cuffs, which were a little soiled by housework, put on his coat and his black felt hat. On the point of going out, he suddenly realized he had forgotten to empty the dustbin and threw its contents casually out of the window. There were cries from below. Madame Alexandre had received them on her head. She was still shouting and swearing at the top of her voice, when Count Vladimir crossed the hall on his way to the front door.

"And to hell with you for a roaring start, Madame Alexandre," he said in his calm little voice as he went by.

She stood there aghast. Never in human memory had the Count been heard to say such a thing before.

When they sat down to luncheon in the Canon's flat, he had not yet come in. He arrived ten minutes late, carrying in one hand a huge green plant, which was much too heavy for him, and the Castelmuro chocolate box in the other.

"What's all this, Vlad? Nobody's got a birthday today," Mademoiselle de Mondez said in surprise.

Vladimir placed the green plant in the very center of the table; the leaves, which were bushy as a shrub, reached up to the bronze chandelier, draped in its tulle.

"This," he said, "will prevent my having to look at my wife, and the sight of her face will not embarrass me at the only times at which I still have occasion to see it."

Then, handing the chocolate box to Loulou, he added: "Give this back to your mother; it belongs to her, I believe."

"Vlad, really! To behave like this in front of the Abbé! You must be mad!" cried Mademoiselle de Mondez, while Minnie collapsed in her chair, apparently on the point of fainting.

The old lady ran for her smelling salts, which she did her best to apply to her brother's nose.

"Attend to your niece, she seems to have more need of it than I!" said the Canon, rising to his feet and throwing his napkin angrily into the middle of the table.

Then he went to shut himself up in his study; he would lunch off a few spoonfuls of honey.

Paying no attention to any of them, Count Vladimir began scraping the pips out of a melon.

A week went by. Things never happened quickly in Mondez House. None of them was on speaking terms. Minnie no longer spoke to Loulou; Vlad no longer spoke to Minnie; Aimée no longer spoke either to Minnie or to Vlad. And the Canon, so as not to get involved, spoke to no one at all.

Only Térésa whimpered to Mademoiselle de Mondez from time to time: "What shall I do, Mademoiselle?"

"Well, really, my girl; in the first place, it's all your own fault."

"But, after all, Mademoiselle, it's I who am pregnant!"

One morning, Vladimir went to the Canon's study to borrow a sheet of writing-paper.

The Canon had reached the last chapter of his work on Phocaean colonization. In spite of family dramas, he had reached the end of the book quicker than he had expected. One might have thought that the troubled atmosphere in the house had stimulated his mind.

"And thus, as we have seen above, the Phocaeans established trading posts along the coasts," he had just written, "but they made no attempt to conquer the neighboring territories nor to impose tyrannical rule over the people with whom they traded. Their Marseillais descendants, who, about the year 1650, founded the Compagnie d'Afrique, an earlier organization than the East India Company, continued to pursue these wise principles. . . ."

"There! That's one in the eye for the English! That's the stuff to give them!" he thought, without reflecting that it was extremely doubtful that any English reader would ever set eyes on his little work.

The borrowing of a sheet of writing-paper was clearly only a pretext, for Vlad stayed in the room. Becoming aware of his lingering presence, the Canon put down his pen. Vlad clearly had something to say to him, but could not bring himself to begin. Several minutes went by. At last, Vlad made up his mind.

"Do you think it would be a mistake for me to divorce at my age, uncle?" he asked.

The Canon took his time so as to weigh his answer carefully.

"Certainly, my dear fellow, most certainly," he said. "And not from the Christian point of view alone, which is the only one that should count with me. If your wife, as I fear and suspect, has been unfaithful to you, it is no reason for you to infringe the law of God and make her sin a scandalous example. I am doing my best to see things from your point of view. Oh, I know that to have forgiven the woman taken in adultery was all very fine, but our Lord was not her husband! But just consider: what good would a divorce be to you? You're over fifty. You've lived your life."

"And lived it ill," Vlad said. "The fact is, I was wrong to marry. But I was the last of the Mondezes and I wanted to have an heir. And look at the result! I've lived unhappily in the shadow of that giantess. . . ."

The Canon began walking up and down the room. His tiny boots, with their slightly turned-up toes, crushed the scattered funeral announcements and he fluttered the skirts of his soutane, which made the few remaining white hairs on the back of his little wrinkled skull quiver.

"It's the same with me, you know, exactly the same with me," he went on. "At bottom, I was wrong to set up house with my sister. Since she's two years older than I am, she still treats me as a small boy even though I'm seventy-one. Besides, she's a bigot. I've always submitted; I've let her have her own way, so as to have a little peace. But she's prevented my living a proper life. In any case, I took orders too young. I ought to have seen something of the world. I know nothing of my neighbors' problems and can be of no use to anyone. For instance, no later than this morning, I went to say Mass at

the Réformés. A woman came up to me and whispered something in my ear. I paid no particular attention and said: 'I'm
not one of the officiating priests of this church, Madame; if
you want to be confessed, go and ask at the sacristy.' She said:
'It's not that, Monsieur l'Abbé, it's not for confession; it's
your sash that's come undone.' You see, it's always other people who do me a service; and what do I do for them?"

He fell silent and, for several minutes, the silence was dis-
turbed only by the rustling of his soutane and by the little
noise Vladimir made scratching at a stain on his trousers.

"Bastards are not rejected in Polish families," Vladimir
said at last.

"Yes, I know," the Canon replied. "But we really can't
marry Loulou to the maid."

"Yet it's all he deserves."

"The sacrament of Marriage must not be inflicted as a
punishment," the Canon said, "and in trying to make the
good triumph, we should add merely to the evil. I've thought
a lot these last days, trying to rise above bourgeois prejudice
and consider only the demands of religion. Oh, of course, if
Loulou loved the poor girl, we should have simply to encourage him to do the right thing! But he gives no sign of doing
so. Nor does she, what's more. I've tried to get them to talk;
without telling your aunt, of course. They seem both to have
yielded to the temptation of an unfortunate promiscuity.
When love is not present to palliate social inequality, what
chance is there for a Christian marriage in such conditions?
Only too often, forced marriages end in divorce, and the child
is abandoned by the father. The Church does not encourage
these forced unions, and one has to ask oneself if an engagement entered into more or less under duress is really valid.
Perhaps I shall write a little book on the subject one of these
days. . . ."

The Canon looked out of the window.

"Ah, it's noon," he said automatically, glancing across the

little courtyards toward the balcony on the Boulevard Dugommier.

"Nevertheless, the child, whether one wants it or not, will be a Mondez and, perhaps, the only one we shall have," Vladimir went on.

"Loulou can acknowledge it without marrying the mother."

"And how will he bring it up? It'll be hidden away in an attic and he'll never see it, and I'll have to pay the expenses. . . . Apart from the expenses, I did think for a moment . . ."

"What did you think?" the Canon asked.

"Unfortunately, it's impossible. I thought of adopting the child myself and bringing it up here. But I've looked into it; if you've already got a child, the law prohibits it."

They both fell silent again. Vladimir was staring at the carpet and biting the end of his moustache.

"Is it impossible, uncle," he went on thoughtfully, "is it impossible for a priest to adopt a child?"

"Yes, alas, my dear Vlad," the Canon said. "I had also thought of that solution, you know. I'd even gone so far as to speak to the bishop."

"Really?"

"Yes. But the rules of the Church, as I suspected, do not permit it. Adoption is looked on, more or less, as a substitution for the natural paternal link, which is incompatible with priesthood. The Italians even say ironically: 'A priest is a man whom everyone calls *Father*, except his own children who call him *uncle*.' "

"In that case, I can see no solution," Vladimir murmured.

And then, suddenly, at the very same moment, a gleam appeared in the eyes of both of them. On the instant, they had both seen the means of taking their revenge, with one blow, for all the hypocrisies, the lies and the conventional morality in which their lives had been bound. Here was a way, and indeed a superlative bombshell to explode in the middle of the family.

They talked for another quarter of an hour, until Térésa came to announce luncheon. They entered the dining room with their heads held high, strong in their alliance and decision.

Vladimir took his place behind his green plant. The Canon unfolded his napkin, coughed to clear his throat, and declared in a voice that admitted of no argument: "Vlad and I have had a long talk and have found that we are entirely in agreement. We have decided that my sister Aimée must adopt Térésa's child.

Nothing that Aimée or Minnie could say had any effect. Vladimir threatened to institute proceedings for divorce and the Canon to leave the house and have the joint tenancy dissolved, if she did not act as they wished.

"But where will the child be brought up?" Minnie asked.

"Here, of course, my dear," Vlad replied. "It'll be your grandson if, as I hope, it turns out to be a boy. Besides, he'll be legally our cousin."

"And what about Aunt Aimée's inheritance then?"

"Naturally, it'll pass Loulou by. And I think the Canon will also make dispositions which will not be much to his advantage."

"I must admit it serves Loulou right," Minnie replied, for she preserved a deep grudge against her son. "And what about Térésa?"

"There can be no question of separating a mother from her child. She'll stay with us as long as she pleases."

To show obstinacy would merely have served to unleash even greater scandals, and Minnie was forced to yield to her husband, as was Aimée to her brother.

"To make me adopt a child of sin at my age!" the old lady groaned.

"This, my dear sister, is the first opportunity you've had in your life of making yourself really useful."

"How ungrateful!"

But the fear of seeing her brother leave the house—"he doesn't realize what it would mean; it'd kill the poor Abbé"—made her give way.

Mademoiselle Asnais's attitude was as surprising as it was admirable. Having been plunged into the abyss of despair, and passed several weeks in a state of prostration which caused her family much anxiety, Marie-Françoise took up her pen one morning and wrote Loulou a letter, which she had to begin all over again three times. It was a masterpiece of self-denial. She regretted her display of anger the last time they had met; she understood, accepted and forgave. The sad event (for it was thus she referred to the maid's pregnancy) was perhaps simply an ordeal sent by God so that she might look with greater clarity into her own heart and discover how strong and unalterable her feelings toward Loulou were. She was prepared to share his life for better or worse; and, since the worse had already occurred, nothing but the better could happen now. In a word, she could see no obstacle to their marriage, and the whole style of the letter proved that Marie-Françoise had been reading the Canon's works.

So nothing was spared the Countess de Mondez; she realized, too late, that the unfortunate initiative she had taken "in the name of morality" of summoning the girl to the Castelmuro had produced the most unexpected results of bringing her liaison with Monsieur de Saint-Flon to light and of precipitating what she had most wished to prevent by making a project actual that had, in fact, been in only a very tentative stage. Marie-Françoise was now behaving as if she were unofficially engaged.

The Canon, when consulted by his niece who, in the circumstances, no longer felt very sure of herself, raised no objection.

"But really, uncle, the daughter of an oil merchant!"

"With that baby in the house, with the knowledge and in the sight of all, do you think your son can expect anything much better? Indeed, it seems to me he's extremely lucky. He showed me a letter from her. The girl writes extremely well."

As for Vladimir, he took no interest in the matter at all.

"Loulou's of age and can do as he wishes. I merely warn him that I shan't give him a penny."

Loulou, completely carried away by events, was now persuaded that he had been in love with Mademoiselle Asnais since that first meeting. He asserted that this marriage was the one thing in the world he wanted.

On her side, Marie-Françoise had pointed out at great length to her family (for the matter of the child had now of course become known) that bastards were a tradition in aristocratic families. Only vulgar people took offense at it. It was well known that Louis XIV had had natural children, as had Charles V and many others.

In the end, after a month or so of argument, Monsieur Asnais gave his consent.

"After all, I've only one daughter, and I don't want her to be unhappy. Anyway, let her be unhappy in her own way," he declared. "All right, become the Countess de Mondez, my child, if that will give you pleasure."

The wedding date was fixed for the end of November, so that at least six weeks should elapse after the child's birth, but Térésa must have made a mistake in her calculations for, though very substantially pregnant, she had not yet been brought to bed by the last days of October. It was feared she might well be tactless enough to give birth on the very morning of the wedding. They were all living in some apprehension. Mademoiselle de Mondez questioned her ten times a day as to whether she felt the first signs of labor.

But God be thanked, the signs appeared a good fortnight before the date fixed for the marriage contract tea. Madame

Belmont, an octogenarian midwife, who had tied the umbilical cords of Louis, killed at the Dardanelles, of Vladimir, and of Loulou himself, was sent for. Not for a moment did it occur to anyone to send Térésa to hospital.

"All the Mondezes are born under their own roof," Vladimir declared, allying, as ever, honorable tradition to avarice.

And in the attic on the third floor, Térésa gave birth to a big, swarthy boy, short of leg, but wide of shoulder, who, from the moment he first uttered a cry, was exactly like his grandfather, the Calvi cobbler.

They searched for a Christian name which had been used by the Mondez family, but not too recently. They lit on Ange, which no one had been called "since the end of the other century" as the Canon said, by which he meant the eighteenth. The last Ange de Mondez had indeed been guillotined during the Revolution.

Térésa had wanted to call her son Napoleon; and it was conceded that he might bear it as a fourth name.

Ange Aimé Vladimir Napoleon de Mondez (the mother having been declared unknown and the formalities of adoption regularized at birth) was baptized in the Canon's study, by his great-uncle, in the presence of the whole family, Madame Alexandre, the Concierge, being co-opted as godmother and Count Vladimir as godfather.

"You know, Monsieur le Comte, in these circumstances the godfather always gives the godmother a present," said Madame Alexandre.

"Oh, yes . . ." said Vladimir.

He tried to think of something that would cost him nothing.

"Very well," he said, "from now on I'll no longer throw my sweepings into the courtyard."

The employees of the Société du Grand Egout Collecteur had been asked to vacate for the day the rooms on the ground floor, where their offices were, so that the Mondez could use them for the marriage contract tea. The cleaners had been in during the morning, and the Cadet sisters had been given the contract for the catering. At least four hundred people were expected.

"We must plan for a lot of people," Mademoiselle de Mondez said. "Owing to the scandal Vlad has made" (for she now considered Vladimir responsible) "everyone will come to stare at us."

While the house was echoing to the noise of the final preparations, while chairs were being taken downstairs and then taken up again because it was discovered that they had a broken leg, while the hired servants were donning their too tight-fitting black dresses in the kitchen and the Cadet sisters were superintending the unpacking of the *petits fours*, the Canon was in his study thinking out the speech he would have to make two days later on the occasion of Loulou's marriage. He disliked being caught unprepared. It was better to consider it at once and even make a note of the principal themes.

He picked up the last funeral announcement he had received—"Dear me, it's my paper-merchant in the Rue de Rome; he was a very nice chap, poor fellow"—and began writing on the back of it.

"(1) 'In my old age I have once again the joy of blessing so suitable a union,' etc. (2) 'You, Mademoiselle,' etc.— eulogy of the girl and her family . . ."

"What on earth can I say about those people?" he wondered. "I might perhaps start with the bridegroom . . ."

That was not so difficult. "You, my dear boy, whom I have watched growing up, and adding year by year to your family's joy in you . . ." Then might follow, in a tone of modesty of course, an account of the family back through the centuries to the Crusades, with a passing mention of the turbulence of noble Polish blood. "That's a really clever idea: an allusion to the *turbulence* of the blood! But what can I say of the girl? They're oil merchants. Ah, the Phocaeans! 'Like the distant Phocaeans in whose tradition he lives, your father has conquered the higher spheres of commerce . . .' But, when you really come to think of it, why on earth is she marrying him?"

He got to his feet and, dreamily swinging his soutane, began composing the speech he would have liked to make, if one could only really say what one thought.

"You, Mademoiselle, you poor little girl, are marrying an address, a façade, a house, a title and an illusion. You believe you're in love with a man, but you're in love with an echo from the past which fascinates you. You're entering a dusty old family, in which we're all slightly mad, you know, behind this appearance of tradition or perhaps even because this very tradition has made us so effete. You have rosy cheeks, bright with plebeian health; and you will soon realize that your husband is not robust, intelligent, or agreeable to live with: in a word, that he was not made for you. For a time, you'll put up with your mistake, and you'll then grow tired of the Allées, and go off to deceive your husband with some Monsieur de Saint-Flon or other in the afternoons. It'll all begin all over again; all that I've seen these last twenty-five years, and about which I've never dared to say a word. . . ."

The Canon stopped pacing to and fro.

"Well, no," he thought. "I really can't say that the day after tomorrow. Let's go back to praising business and good examples from the past. Let me see now, what did I say when I married Vlad and Minnie? On her side, I made an eulogy of the law, because of her father, the magistrate. And it was a very good speech too! It had a great success. I need only to make it again with a few alterations. It was twenty-four years ago, and they'll all have forgotten. And since it's all going to begin again anyway . . ."

He opened the Renaissance cupboard, climbed onto the little library steps, and began searching among the dusty manuscripts of the *Dispersion of the Relics of Saint-Ferréol* and the *Faiences du Marquis de Pigusse.* "I'm sure I put it away here twenty-five years ago." Suddenly his fingers, under a pile of papers, came in contact with a hard, cylindrical object, which was nothing like his pot of honey. He brought it out into the light. It was Minnie's bracelet.

"How the devil did it get here?" the Canon wondered.

And then he remembered. The evening before the unhappy day on which the bracelet's disappearance had brought in its wake such a disastrous sequence of events, Minnie had taken the honey from the cupboard to sweeten her *tisane* in the middle of the night. The bracelet must have slipped from her wrist. And then, the next morning, when he was looking for his pot of honey, he must have hidden the bracelet under the heap of papers he had turned over.

The Canon de Mondez was assailed by the wildest fit of laughter he had known since the far-off days of practical jokes in the seminary. Try as he would, say as he would: "It really isn't funny, it really isn't funny at all!" he couldn't help roaring with laughter all by himself in his study.

He was still laughing when he opened the door to go and tell of his discovery. But his sister came by in a too-short black dress, crying: "Augustin, what are you thinking of, my dear? You ought to be downstairs. Our guests are arriving. Vlad's not there either. I hope you've put on your new soutane."

He at once hid the bracelet behind his back, closed the door, and stood there a moment staring at the ceiling. Then he found an old piece of tissue paper, wrapped the bracelet in it, put an elastic band round it, and placed it in his pocket.

A few minutes later, he went downstairs, as the big drawing-room, which he had not seen in use for many years, was beginning to fill. "My God," the Canon thought nostalgically, "it's just like it was in my mother's day."

A servant was standing at the door and announcing in a splendid Provençal accent: "Monsieur le Comte et Madame la Comtesse de Garousse . . . Madame Cristoforos . . . Monsieur le Chevalier d'Estel de la Palanque . . . Monsieur le Docteur Caroubet . . . Monsieur le Préfet . . ."

Everyone was delicately nibbling the Castelmuro sandwiches. On a long table against the wall, covered with a tablecloth, were displayed the wedding presents with the visiting cards of the donors.

Loulou, throttled by a stiff collar and shaved raw, was busy acknowledging congratulations. Marie-Françoise, all pink from her cheeks to the toes of her satin shoes, was wildly happy and kissing everybody.

The Canon went to her and, in the presence of Aimée and Minnie, who were utterly aghast, gave her the bracelet, saying: "Here is my present, my dear child. It's a family heirloom which we inherited from our grandmother."

At that moment, there was heard a sound of crying from the direction of the front door. Everyone looked round; and there was Count Vladimir de Mondez on his way out, pushing Térésa's child in an old baby carriage he had had brought down from the attics.

As a *mistral* was blowing, Count Vladimir was wearing his overcoat, a most extraordinary garment, which had been in the family for three generations; it was tailored of a black cloth as thick as leather, was frogged, and lined with otter fur. It fell to his ankles, and was all that remained to him of his Polish inheritance.

During an hour by the clock, the Count de Mondez walked up and down the Allées, giving his grandson his first airing under the nose of all the best society of Marseilles. Monsieur de Saint-Flon passed by on the farther pavement. They raised their hats to each other.